ANTHONY CARTWRIGHT was born in Dudley in 1973. In 1993 he left his home town to study English and American Literature at the University of East Anglia. Having worked in Black Country factories, meat-packing plants, pubs and warehouses and as a trainee manager with London Underground, in 1998 he trained as an English teacher and now teaches at the Royal Docks Community School in Newham.

Praise for The Afterglow

'Anthony Cartwright's real achievement is his virtuoso ear for Black Country dialect. His cleverly wrought phonetic dialogue is by turns comic, angry, poignant and poetic and it really gives a powerful sense of place. A promising young novelist'

John Murray

'No doubt about it, Anthony Cartwright can certainly write. This is a painfully honest and accomplished first novel, a realistic account of a working-class Black Country family at home and at work and at play, so utterly faithful to the world it sets out to recreate that one has to admire it. Vivid and dramatic, it penetrates beneath the skin of young and old, and if we are given no more than the remnants of the old working-class world of warmth and solidarity, one that has now had its heart torn out, what afterglow there is comes from the portrait of the mother, Mary; for me she is as strong as she used to be, stumbling with her splitting bags of shopping and looking at her family, "at the little victories of life over death" she has known and remembers'

Philip Callow

'Anthony Cartwright's characters are wholly believable, and he has an instinctive talent for using description to create subtle shades of mood'

Carol Birch

'This is one of those rare novels which give us the real thing, and an excellent read it is from first to last. It is a good story, told with the style and pace of an expert, in spite of it being his first'

Alan Sillitoe

The Afterglow

Anthony Cartwright

TINDAL STREET PRESS

First published in 2004 by
Tindal Street Press Ltd
217 The Custard Factory, Gibb Street, Birmingham, B9 4AA
www.tindalstreet.co.uk

Typesetting: Tindal Street Press Ltd

A CIP catalogue reference for this book is available from the British Library.

ISBN: 0 9541303 6 7

Printed and bound in Great Britain by
Clays Ltd, St Ives PLC

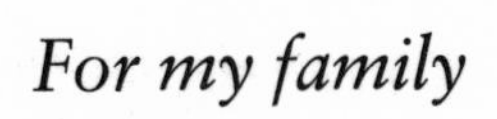
For my family

Acknowledgements

Thanks to Emma and Alan at Tindal Street Press for your support. Also, thanks to Vicky McCarthy and Sporting Hackney FC.

Luke

The bag of flesh and blood was slippery in his gloved hands. Luke took the long plastic sack and held it aloft with his left hand and plunged the knife into it with his right. Half a pig – half frozen, ice crystals glistening in its pink marrow – tumbled onto the bench and splattered his overalls with blood and preservative. He took the side of meat at either end and turned it again and lifted it to the machine. It was like wrestling a giant bar of soap. He got the thing into position and plunged the blades down into the meat. There was a grinding sound and the familiar low thud of the cut flesh dropping out onto the conveyor belt. Down the line a dozen pairs of hands picked up the pork chops and arranged them in plastic cartons before placing them back on the belt. After he'd checked everything was clear of the machine he released the handles and stepped back to begin again.

This couldn't be the stuff you ate with a couple of veg and some gravy; this was something else completely. Flesh, not meat, ripped from bones and splattered with blood. It was fine at this point in the line, the stuff hacked down to a manageable size, but he knew that somewhere back there something much bigger and bloodier was going on. Sometimes he thought he could hear it, under all the other factory noises, impossible though that was at this end of the plant. Or he'd come across a strange and shiny piece of equipment hosed down and hanging from the wall, sharp edges like a rumour of the real reason they were all there.

He understood the process now. At the training sessions on Saturday mornings about six months ago he'd got to visit other areas of the plant. The bosses of each section explained what went on there. Luke's job came right at the end: the cartons that left his line went into packing and then despatch, off to the supermarket in the big chilled lorries that reversed into loading bays out in the yard. People moved back in the chain to earn more money; when he'd started he used to drag pallet trucks of pork chops back and forth from the vacuum packer. One job involved calming the pigs down when they arrived, running and squealing down the aluminium ramp from the back of the lorry. Stressed pigs meant tough meat. Luke had imagined a kind of cabaret act: a bit of juggling maybe, telling a few jokes, watching telly on comfy chairs with them. But what you really had to do was herd them into a low-lit pen and keep taking their temperatures. You got to wear an orange hard hat, though.

There were different coloured hats for different jobs. He looked at the yellow hats bobbing up and down along the conveyor belt, organizing the chops into cartons. His was blue as a machine operator. Other hats in this part of the factory were: white ones for the cleaners; red for the supervisors; green for quality control who came round with clipboards to stick thermometers into the meat every few hours. Perhaps once a day you might see the black hat of one of the bosses.

Luke liked the hat system; he knew where he stood. You couldn't make a mistake and tell a boss you were nipping upstairs for a quick smoke or let a yellow hat from despatch tell you your job. The hard hats looked like the plastic ones that Lego people wore; his sister Kerry had bought some for little Alice. That'd go down a storm at

Christmas, they'd joked: the Lego slaughterhouse, complete with pink pork chop bricks.

There was a tub of bricks at home. His mum had put them on the sideboard in the front room, out of reach, after she'd decided they were too small for Alice, that she might choke on them. Luke and his dad had put together a street of half-built houses and cars that one Sunday afternoon. Every now and then he'd add or take away a few of the colourful bricks. It had become like an ornament that his mum dusted around.

A jet of water hit his machine and splashed up into his face. He wheeled round to see Mario waving his hosepipe in the direction of the line. He looked like something from outer space in his cleaning gear, green overalls and a facemask. Luke put his hand up into the stream of water and it broke into crystals in the electric light.

Wharrum yer doin? he shouted at Mario.

The cleaner winked at him and then flicked the hosepipe so it sent a shower of water into the air. Some of the women on the line screamed as it hit them. Mario put his head down and sprayed the floor around Luke's feet. A few moments later he did it again. One of the older women on Luke's line had seen him.

Oi, yer bloody fool, stop it ull yer? What yer playin at? She glared at Mario and he grinned back at her and blew her a kiss, flashing his gold teeth.

Yer child. I'd have yow for bloody breakfast, mate, I tell yer. She waved a pork chop around as she spoke.

Alf, the supervisor, walked over and scowled. The cleaners were on a different contract to everyone else and worked shifts. People said they earned decent money. Nobody liked them, but Luke thought Mario was a laugh.

There was still an hour to go until the dinner siren and Luke's hands were cold. He was wearing a pair of thick rubber gloves with plastic disposable ones underneath but his fingers were becoming numb. The gloves were one of the best things about operating his machine. The women on the line could only wear disposable ones and their hands were frozen after half an hour, their fingers clawing at the more defrosted bits of meat for warmth. At the end of a shift the women lined up to run their hands under the cold taps for a while to get the feeling back. If they went to the hot taps first, they just got scalded.

All around was the creak, creak, creak of the chain that the empty crates hung on as they went back to the crate-wash. Water was hosed onto the floor and bubbled away down the drains, and there was the sound of talking and shouting and the clatter of pallet trucks delivering sacks of meat. Underneath all this was the radio. It was impossible to listen to it properly, but sometimes at night or at weekends Luke would find he already knew a song he thought he was hearing for the first time.

The aim of his job was to get to the last crate as the people from the freezer wheeled a fresh pallet out, but that never happened.

Ten minutes before the siren, Alf walked over to him with a clipboard. All right, lightnin.

Alf. What yer got here then?

Alf studied the clipboard and then looked at the order form lying on the end of the workbench. He looked down the line with his eyes squinted as if he was scouring the horizon for the enemy.

Ay got much on here today, son. Wharrum gonna do is put the rest o this lot on Banksy's line this after. Yow an im . . . wossisnaeme . . . yer despatch mon?

Inderjit.

Arr, yow an Imbyjit con goo in the marinade room cos tham strugglin in theer.

Luke's face dropped. All the machine operators dreaded the marinade room. For one thing, it meant working something like a cement mixer into which you had to pour barrels of foul-smelling chicken tikka or Cajun barbecue liquid. The smell took days to wash away. If that wasn't bad enough the three women who worked in there just sat talking filth all day and enjoyed nothing better than a good-looking young machine operator coming to join them. It could turn Luke tongue-tied and embarrassed just going in there. Rose, the oldest and most foul-mouthed of the three, used to shout at the top of her voice whenever Luke walked past, Here he is, look, me toyboy. Wheer yer tekkin me tonight, lover?

If he was in a good mood he'd shout, To heaven and back, and all the women would squeal. Then Alf would whisper in his ear something like, To the bloody Darby and Joan more like, the age on her, her's oder than me! Rose and Alf had worked together for years and pretended to hate each other – although she took her teeth out sometimes and threatened to give Alf a blow job to calm him down – but when nobody was around Luke saw them chatting about their grandchildren.

The other two marinade women were younger and quieter, but egged Rose on all the time. Joanne, who had tattoos all up her arms, was Rose's daughter-in-law. Luke would joke with them that he feared for the men in their family and they'd just laugh and say they all knew who was boss.

Tham like the three witches in *Macbeth*, he'd told some of the students working at Paradise Meatpacking for the summer but none of them had laughed because they pretended not to know anything so nobody would pick on them.

And Luke was sure that Alf used the marinade room as punishment if he thought people weren't pulling their weight.

Come on, Alfie, wim doin all right aht here. Wiv done

loads this mornin. I doh wanna goo in theer. Lerrus stop aht. We got three orders left.

But I ay gonna let that tek all afternoon. Any road, they need an operator in there. There's a big barbecue order, cos o the nice weather, like.

Luke frowned and started cleaning off the area around the safety guard with the flat of his hand.

Wha abaht Banksy?

Banksy's got enough work on his line to keep him busy for the wik, I doh know abaht the afternoon. Yow concentrate on yerself.

Looks like thass sorted aht then, doh it.

Alf walked off, looking from his clipboard to a pile of crates to the clipboard again. Luke waited until he'd gone and then kicked an empty crate into the air and against the wall, but then Banksy looked over and so he carried on working, tight-lipped, until the siren went at five to twelve.

They sat with their backs against the factory wall, perched at the top of the steep canal bank, spitting into the water. Legs hunched under their chins to avoid sliding down the bank.

A few people from Luke's estate worked at Paradise, but he preferred to hang around with the lads from Tipton. They were a bit calmer than Wayne Banks and his mates. The four of them ate their sandwiches in silence.

Inderjit looked through a folded copy of the *Mirror* and whistled through his teeth. Mario and Con lit cigarettes. They heard laughter from further along the bank. Con looked down the line of the wall towards the other group, and blew a long stream of smoke in their direction. Levi and Banksy, he said. Nobody replied. Luke watched a blue butterfly flit up and down, back and forth to the water's edge.

Dyer hear abaht that cunt Banksy this mornin? Con asked.

They shook their heads and smiled.

Yer know he's got one o them mobiles. Well he's gorrit dahn on the shap floor wi im, ay he. He's had it stickin aht the top on his overalls, gerrin it aht every five minutes so as to show it off, like. Any road, it day do nuthin all morning, right, then twenny to twelve it started ringin. Saft cunt's onny stopped the whole line so as he could answer it.

Con held his cigarette packet to his ear and mimicked Banksy's voice.

Ullo . . . Ullo? Onny a fuckin wrong number, wor it.

They all started laughing.

He's a beauty im, ay he.

A boster.

Any road, Alf's took it off im, right, but now *he*'s gorrit stickin aht on his overalls. He ay turned it off nor nuthin. Wim gonna ring him safternoon, see what happens, like.

Be panic stations, woh it.

Don't panic, Mr Mainwaring.

Have yer got the number?

Arr.

Who off?

Banksy.

Did he know it?

Iss his phone, ay it.

I know, arr, but he's such a prick I'm surprised he knew it.

When am yer gonna ring him?

Ring im when Peter Thompson's dahn.

Every afternoon the Works Manager, Peter Thompson, would stroll around their part of the plant with Alf, his disinfected boots pulled over a dark blue Marks & Spencer suit. Depending on how things were going he'd pause to ask a question about somebody's work or force a joke with people who caught his eye. Luke tried to stay out of his way but always found himself working harder when he was around, hoping secretly for a glance or nod of approval.

Arr, phone him. Yow con ask him abaht that job thass gooin.

What job?

Yowers.

Ha, ha.

No, there's a job gooin next door, ay there. Iss wi the butchers, but yer know wharris doin?

Wha?

Scraepin aht all the shit an the blood thass left in the pig when they finished wi it.

Fuckin hell. Serious?

Arr.

Lovely.

Nobody ever sticks it, apparently. Iss six pahnd odd an hour, though, cos o wharris doin, like.

Thass decent money though, ay it, tha.

Oh arr, decent money.

Late that afternoon, he stood in a line of people snaking in and out of the shade at the entrance to the market building. A couple of old women tut-tutted at the front of the queue about there being no sign of a 74.

He watched a bald man in green overalls manoeuvre a fork-lift around the stalls in the hangar-like building. An alarm went off whenever the truck reversed; its lights flashed faintly in the sunlight. A few stalls were still being packed away. People walked in and out of the double doors at the far end of the market carrying boxes, rolls of carpet, silhouetted against the bleached concrete of the car park. Sun shone through the girders in the roof, creating a mesh of shadows on the floor.

A familiar face weaved in and out of the bus queues.

Ris, Luke called. Risley. His friend had nearly walked

past him when he looked up, a frown on his face, his head jutting forward. His eyes darted away from Luke's as he looked at him.

Ris. Yow all right, mate? What yow doin dahn here? Luke thought that Risley never left their estate any more, except for darts games.

All right. Yow just finished?

Arr, wheer yow gooin?

Risley shrugged his big frame and wouldn't look at Luke. His right shoulder lifted, higher than his left. He always walked with a stoop, like someone still getting used to their body. Luke was smiling, happy at the coincidence of meeting, generous with the sunshine and the end of the day, not reading the signs. Risley was sweating, his temples shiny and the fringe of his over-long brown hair was wet. They said 1995 was going to be the hottest summer for years, and Risley was still wearing a jumper.

I sometimes come dahn this road. I've gorra pop to me auntie's dahn theer. He nodded down the High Street and looked at the floor, spat on the pavement darkened with market rubbish.

Luke followed his gaze, down the shell-suit bottoms to the black scuffed shoes Risley was wearing. They were caked in mud, orange and brown streaks across the top of his shoes and around the ankles of his trousers. Darker, damper clumps clung to the soles of his shoes.

Wheer yow bin, walkin, Ris?

Oh, I come through the park, he said casually.

Risley's eyes flicked down the street. Luke got the message, or sort of. They stood there in silence for a while. Luke's body mirrored Risley's awkwardness. You wouldn't have guessed they'd known each other for nearly twenty years, more or less all their lives, Luke thought. Risley was like that sometimes. More often lately. He used to be the loudest when they were kids. God knows where he was going, he hadn't got an auntie in Great Bridge as far as Luke knew. All his family lived on Cromwell Green, apart from his dad.

Yer bus is here. Risley's voice brightened.

Arr, it is. All right then. I'll seeya.

The bus queue had turned into a scrum. Luke turned to join it.

Say hello to yer auntie.

Eh? Oh, arr.

Risley looked up at him as he stepped onto the bus. Something close to a smile crossed his face and then he turned away. Luke watched him through the window as he strode off down the High Street in his muddy shoes.

He sat on the sunny side of the bus and felt the warmth drying his hair. He'd stayed in the shower for a long time to wash away the stench of the marinade room. Alf had been doing him a favour, though. Half an hour overtime to get the order finished, when there'd been no overtime in the whole place for months. Alf was a decent bloke, but he'd like to have seen his face when the mobile phone went off while he was talking to Peter Thompson. He was so easy to play up. That was Risley's problem, not working, not talking to other people or having a laugh. Ris had never had a job, just mooched around since they left school five years ago. Things were difficult, but he could've got something. Luke had mentioned about trying to get him a job at Paradise, but he didn't want to know.

The bus juddered up the hill, stopping and starting in the traffic. Luke's eyes kept closing sleepily, then he'd open them with a jolt to look out at the sunshine and the castle on the hill as it veered in and out of view.

He loved this time of day, loved the sense of returning home from work. When he was five or six years old he'd wait by the back step for his dad to rattle through the gate. He'd sit with his dad as he got changed, listen to him talk about the glow of the furnace as he stood there shaving. He was alive with his work, then. He'd tell Luke stories about how the furnace was like a dragon that the men had to keep feeding like zoo-keepers. Or how when they opened it – tapping it they called it – a river of fire came oozing out. And they'd always be going places, like to the football or cricket club if his dad had a game, or walking across to the park. That was before things went wrong, he thought.

A black girl got on the bus at Dudley Port and sat facing back down the bus, opposite Luke. Her lips moved in time to the words of the song she was listening to on her Walkman. She was wearing shorts and a vest top and her skin was a smooth light brown with freckles of darker brown across her nose and bare shoulders. He wanted to talk to her, but couldn't think of anything to say. He thought briefly about Sarah and then about the girl opposite him. Why couldn't he just start chatting to her the way that Jamie would? He was single now, after all. He thought about Sarah again and rubbed the knuckles of his right hand where he could still feel the punch he'd given her boss, if he could call him that, two days ago. If he tried to speak to her, she'd have to take her headphones off; she'd probably think he was the nutter on the bus. He watched her, but then she saw him looking so he closed his eyes and pretended to doze.

He walked up Cromwell Green Road from the bus stop. The houses round where he lived were built in terraces of four, with paths that ran to their front doors through communal gardens. In between the groups of houses were wide alleys that led to paths into the rest of the estate. They were all built in the same 1970s orange-brick style. The other half of the estate, past the shops on the main road, was made up of the original pre-war housing and blocks of flats that looked like temporary accommodation thrown up after some kind of disaster. The old, grey-cladded houses were big inside but falling down. Every now and then, the council put up hoardings advertising the modernization work they were doing and spent ages replacing windows, or fixing pointing, leaving scaffolding up everywhere so people got burgled. Unless you bought your house from the council, of course, then you had to do it yourself. Cromwell Green was surrounded by private housing, but a lot of people on the estate had bought their homes and put on fancy new front doors or had a porch built as a badge of ownership.

At night the estate filled with the shouts of children, half hidden like ghosts down alleyways and dead-ends and in the stairwells of the flats. In the winter, kids would hang around outside the row of shops on Cromwell Green in cheap coats, waiting for things to happen, listening to the screech of cars as they raced around the streets, waiting for their turn, waiting for the helicopter to go up – its beam scattering them back through the streets and alleyways. It'd always been the same, though, Luke thought, but everyone else said things were getting worse. Tham bloody runnin wild, some on em, the older residents would complain.

The last time the council did any work they left miles of cable out in Vanes Road. One night, the police banged on the door of Luke's granny's house and explained that they were worried about the cable being stolen and could they bring it into her yard and leave it safe? While they were in the back yard some kids stole the patrol car and drove it down to the mushroom field to set it on fire.

When he turned the corner Luke could see his dad and Jamie standing in the alley over their old Rover, the bonnet up. Cricket commentary was playing on a radio propped against the kerb.

All right, son. Late, ay yer?

Arr, finished half fower. Half-hour's overtime.

All right for some, ay it?

Fust lot for ages. Was just a one-off, I think. Sonny half-hour.

Doh matter, it all adds up.

Woss up wi this then? Luke nodded at the oily car engine.

Bloody starter motor this time. If it ay that, though, iss summat else. They all looked at the car and shook their heads. Luke watched his dad's face, creased with lines around the eyes and tanned from being out in the sun, his lips pursed in familiar disappointment. Even with his brown, wiry hair grown over his ears and falling onto the collar of his shirt, his face looked lean and thin. Luke touched his own full cheek, as if in comparison.

Woss the scower? He nodded at the radio.

Hundred an odd for seven, his dad said. Hopeless.

Luke couldn't help fix the car and it took the shine off his good mood. He was rubbish at things like that. A lot of the lads on the estate had learned to drive at thirteen or fourteen in stolen bangers on the mushroom field, and clamoured to get on the car maintenance course they'd run at school. Luke still hadn't passed his test now at twenty-one. Jamie drove a delivery van for a living and teased his friend about his ignorance. Luke just called Jamie his chauffeur.

He went through the back door into the kitchen. Some chips were frying on the hob. A bunch of flowers chopped at the stalks, ready for the churchyard, lay on the table. He went to the fridge, took out a bottle of orangeade and walked through to the front room and switched on the television.

He stood and messed with the plastic bricks on the sideboard for a couple of minutes. He took a car from the middle of the street and placed it next to the row of houses, carefully breaking the doors off and laying them out on the floor, then he took three of the little figures and stood them around the broken car, even getting one to scratch his head. They were all still smiling, though. When his mum walked through he pretended to be looking at the photos on the wall and just resting his hands on the Lego street.

Ullo, son. She came through the room with an armful of washing.

The photographs were all old, one of Luke in his school uniform and of his sister, Kerry, with a pink dress on and no front teeth. There was one of his mum and dad in their best clothes and embossed silver writing on the frame: KEN AND MARY: 25 YEARS. In the centre was a picture of his dead brother, Adam, at nursery school. The boy was looking at something off camera. Luke thought it might've been him. He wished they'd get rid of it, or at least get a smaller one, but it had been up there for fifteen years now. Kerry had said something about wanting to take it down once, in the height of an adolescent rant. Mom had slapped her round the face.

He followed her through the kitchen door.

Yow'll atta wait a bit for yer tay, she said, throwing the washing into a basket. I ay even had chance to get up the churchyard wi these yet. She began wrapping the cut flowers in some newspaper. I am late.

Sall right, doh rush. Anythin in theer tonight? Luke nodded at the newspaper, open at the jobs section, lying on the kitchen table.

Luke couldn't remember when his dad last had a proper job, what they called a proper job. He'd worked at Round Oak, the steel works, until he got made redundant in 1980. Since then, he'd been fifteen years in and out of work. It was the same in a lot of families. Round Oak had become Merry Hill, a clean and shiny new shopping centre, but there wasn't a lot of need for men used to meltshops and rolling mills on the checkouts at Sainsbury's. Round Oak had become a kind of code word, signifying how everything used to be better than it was now.

Doh bloody know yet. He's bin messin wi that car all afternoon, ay he.

I sid Sarah today, Luke. His mum's voice was deceptively warm.

He shifted in his chair, not looking at her, but at her fork, pushing a chip around her plate. He thought she was going to say something about him punching Andrew. For a moment he was back on the narrow staircase that led up to the solicitors' and then the bloke was opening his office door and Luke was swinging at him; that pain in his knuckles was still there, reminding him. When Luke hit him he sprawled back across his desk, all arms and legs, sending papers everywhere. Luke hadn't hung around, just bolted back down the stairs again. Things must have been OK, though: no police, no Sarah hammering on the door or phoning every five minutes like she used to when they'd had a row, just silence. It was all over. This business with the affair had been the last straw. He was over forty, for God's sake, two kids and a wife. It was disgusting. He should've punched her, not him. Sometimes his head would just go. He squirmed in his seat, then thought: keep cool.

Oh arr, wheer? he asked.

Up the tahn. Her sid me an all but her day spake. Cleared off sharpish when her sid me lookin.

Oh.

I ay surprised, mind yer. Though I shun't a said nothing. Nothing to do wi me now. I might have asked her when her planned on givin yer that ring back.

Mom, leave it. Sall finished wi now. I'll get that back off her.

Arr. Her looked ever so brown, as her bin away?

How should I know, I ay sid her have I!

Eh. Calm it down. Yer mother's onny asking yer, ay her. His dad spoke sharply into the folded *Express & Star* at the side of his plate.

No, I doh know if her's bin away or wha. Probably. Or her's bin out in the garden. He looked out the kitchen window at the cloudless blue sky.

Yer sister says her went to Gran Canaria. Yow had a lucky escape there, me lad. Yow did. Yome better off without her. Ay that right, love?

His sister seems to know a lot for someone who doh spake to nobody from up here any more, his dad said, talking to the cricket scorecards. He was even more irritated by Kerry's delusions of grandeur – a detached house in Kingswinford and a four-by-four (I'd call it a van, meself, he'd suggested) – than Luke's disastrous relationship. Iss at an end now, he said.

Well it is, apart from him gerrin the money back on that ring.

All right, all right.

The business of the ring was a worry. It crept around the edge of Luke's mind like a thief padding around the edge of a car park, waiting to strike. And it did: leaping into his head when he was bending to pick up a sack of meat at work, or changing a tape in Jamie's van. Punching that Andrew had at least given him something else to worry about. He wished she'd thrown the ring at him when they broke the engagement off, like he'd seen on telly. It would've made things easier. Despite himself, he smiled at the thought of scrabbling around on the canal towpath looking for a glint of gold in the sun.

What yer smiling at now?

Nuthin, it ay funny.

I bloody know that.

As if to underline the end of the conversation his dad took a slice of bread and butter and made a sandwich with his last bit of roe. He leaned back in his chair and looked through the open door into the front room at the television. They continued eating in silence. Luke picked up his plate and walked across to the sink, then filled the kettle.

Anythin in the jobs today, Dad? Even when his dad was in work, Luke had asked the same question every Thursday tea time since he was a kid. Thursday was jobs night. People used to queue at the paper shop for the first delivery, like on Saturday tea times when they'd wait for the *Sports Argus*.

Not in the paeper, no. I phoned after one this morning but it ud already gone.

Oh arr. Wheer was tha?

Down Wednesbury. In a press shap.

Ere yam, son. I'll mek the tay. His mother got up and took the empty plates from the table. Luke took it as a peace sign. I'll mek this, then phone yer sister an have me half-hour at the telly. Goo an sit yerselves down.

He lay for a long time with his hands clasped behind his head, watching the blue walls as shadows moved across them. When he got up to turn the tape over he went to the wardrobe and felt in the pocket of his jeans for his cigarette papers, a half-empty packet of tobacco and a little plastic bag. He sat on the end of the bed and laid out a cigarette paper, spread the tobacco along it and crumbled in the draw from the bag. It wasn't very good quality and seemed to drop in lumps along the spliff. He tore a strip off a postcard from Sarah to use as a roach. Before he lit up he pulled the net curtain back and pushed the window open further. He sat on the end of the bed and looked out.

The setting sun made the spire of Top Church look black against the changing colours behind it, that symmetry of the High Street, with Top and Bottom Churches at either end of the hill, the market in between. The imposing castle sitting there. It was like in a town in a children's story; the castle, the market, the priory, churches. Not that he knew anyone who went to church. His mum used to go, but now she just went to the churchyard.

The lights of the petrol station and the houses opposite glowed as it grew steadily darker. That was another Thursday ritual – as regular as the jobs pages in the paper – fresh flowers for Adam's grave. He'd died just there, three years old, underneath the window when he ran out into the road. Lorries used to take a short cut through Cromwell Green to jump the traffic on Birmingham New Road. They only put speed bumps in years later. A summer's night, the front door was open, and he'd toddled out and down the front path before anyone noticed. Luke, three years older, had been in the back yard playing with him. All he could remember was having to sit with Solomon and Iris next door for hours, not that it had stopped him trying to fill the gap in his memory.

You'd run too, he thought, three years old with the front door astonishingly open in your sticky grasp. You'd run too, with a whole new world to explore, with no adult hand to pull you back or older brother or sister to nag you. You'd run too, over the uneven path, hands swatting at summer bees and flowers swaying in the breeze of the traffic, to the main road that ran like a river outside your house, your little world, to places that you'd only just begun to dream of. Out into the path of a speeding truck packed tight with steel tube, with a driver trying to read his *A–Z*. Oh, yes, you'd run too.

Maybe. Or maybe it wasn't like that at all.

Jamie

There was a pub in Heathtown where you could buy a gun. Kenny had told him about it at work. You could just walk in there, say the right thing at the bar and a bloke with one of those Chelsea smiles cut into his face would show you round to a lockup and let you take your pick. That was what he'd do: get a gun, buy one of those Elvis masks from the fancy dress shop, rob a bank. Then he'd have a proper go at tracking his dad down, shoot that bastard as well. He'd tell Julie he'd won the Lottery and they could go and live in Rio de Janeiro like Ronnie Biggs.

Jamie was daydreaming in the shower. He'd been in there for half an hour, using all the hot water. The new one was great, a plumber he knew had fitted it in return for him getting hold of some videos. Standing outside the stream of the water, lathered all over in white foam, he was singing: Madonna, all the old ones. He'd started with 'Holiday' – he was going to Majorca later in the summer with Julie – but now he was onto 'Like a Virgin', his all-time favourite. When he first heard the song, used to hear Kerry next door playing it through the wall, he hadn't known what virgin meant but he knew from how she sang the word there was some kind of secret, some knowledge and power there, and he'd wanted it. Then Dawn Thomas explained it to him, wriggling around on the coach on a school trip to Blackpool. Afterwards, he'd wanted that power even more.

What he'd wanted that afternoon was some music on while he helped Ken, but Ken had been too busy listening to the cricket. No wonder he was bloody miserable, it was nothing to do with being out of work. It was listening to those posh voices drone on and on for five days at a time. Jamie didn't get it. That was the good thing about his job, driving around with the radio on and not having to stand around in the warehouse lifting boxes and talking about sport, like he gave a fuck. Sometimes he wondered if he'd have been keener if his dad had been around when he was growing up: had he missed out on something? It used to frustrate him when Luke, Risley and Nicky got talking and he'd have to just keep nodding to show he was following their conversation. He didn't do it as much now. Or going to Albion games with them, which bored him apart from the singing, and he'd spend more time looking around the crowd than at the pitch, his mates thinking he was a wannabe hooligan and him just interested in what shirts people were wearing. It had its advantages, though: while they all sat around and talked about football he could talk to the ladies and then everybody would ask him how he managed it. A stupid, irritating question. Just talk, he wanted to say, just talk about something that's not football or fighting or nonsense, take an interest, and maybe put your tongue back in your mouth while you're at it.

He was running late, but it'd be OK. He'd explain about helping Ken with the car. Julie's mum and dad would love that; they loved him anyway. Not that he'd been any help with it. This car needs an undertaker not a doctor, he'd joked to Ken when they first started, but Ken's face had stayed expressionless, just stared down at the engine, so he'd worked doubly hard to try to help get it going. That was the trouble: people wanted things to last for ever. Then Luke turned up and looked at him like he was stealing his dad from him or something. And the way Luke and Ken spoke to each other, just talking about the cricket like it was some sort of secret language – but it was how everyone talked to each other. He did it himself, he knew it. What was it? When you talked about something but meant something else? Metaphor. This car needs an undertaker. It was all metaphor, meaningless.

He took the hair gel from the bathroom cabinet, walked through to his bedroom and looked in the mirror. As he worked his hair, he narrowed his eyes and pouted his lips, always the same routine, even when he was running late. He couldn't understand people not making an effort with their appearance. It was what everyone judged you on. Idiots at work would ask him how they could get a girl like Julie. Well, they never said *like Julie*, they just described someone a bit like her. Talk to them, he'd explain, exasperated, try running an iron over your shirt every now and again. He was glad they never did, though. It gave him some kind of advantage.

His shirts were lined up neatly in the wardrobe. His mum had been doing some ironing when he called back for a cold drink just after dinner on his way to a delivery in Tividale. That was another good thing about this job: nipping home. He pulled two shirts from the wardrobe, chose a blue checked one. The telephone rang downstairs. He guessed it was Julie, but his mum didn't call him. She'd never disturb him while he was getting ready.

Julie phoned while yow was in the shower, Jay. His mum was watching *EastEnders*. Her said to remind yer not to have anythin, cos tham havin a barbecue. I said yow ud have et two tays any road an her just loffed.

I would an all. He grinned. Is that all yome havin?

His mum held a sandwich in one hand. Lettuce poked out from between the slices of white bread and a streak of salad cream shone on her lip. She had her legs pulled under her into the seat. In the space where her legs might have been lay Bella, their Alsatian, breathing heavily, her tongue out and her eyes half closed.

I doh feel like much, his mum said. I'll have summat else later.

I'll fetch yer summat back from the barbecue if I con.

Doh worry. Yer woh have time to walk Bella, now.

I'll do it when I gerrin.

Yow ay stoppin dahn Julie's then?

I doh think so. I'll phone yer if there's any change.

I need yer to have a look at the washing machine an all. Iss still mekkin that funny noise.

I will, Mom, arr, but not tonight. I'll do it over the wikend. Try not to use it so much.

I've gorra do the washin.

He walked towards her and picked up his van keys from the cushion where he'd thrown them.

I ay kissin yer goodbye until yow've wiped that salad cream off yer face, though.

She took a tissue and wiped her mouth. Is that better?

Arr, thass it. It was onny a bit. Jamie kissed her on the cheek.

Yow look nice, she said. Doh be too late, then.

I woh. What yow doin?

Watchin the telly. I might have me a glass of wine after. Might put me shoppin channel on. See if they got any bargains.

Jamie had thought that getting satellite was a good idea, but all it had done was give his mum another excuse to stay in. He wanted her to go out and have a good time. She only ever went out to work or to the shops and because she was a dinner lady she wouldn't be going out at all now it was the holidays. She stayed inside with the curtains closed against the heat. It's such a waste, he thought.

All right, I'll seeya later.

*

He got back late. They had to sit around with Julie's parents and her sister and brother-in-law and the new baby, Kyle. Julie kept leaving him to go and sit with her sister and hold her nephew and go all broody. That left Jamie talking to Neil, her idiot brother-in-law, all proud of himself at having proved his manhood, and Julie's old man, who kept winking at him and saying, Yow two next. He didn't know how much more he could take. They were booked to go to Majorca soon but he thought she might not last that long. She asked him to stay and he said no, as a punishment for a shit night.

Families. All that pretending you all liked each other when really – really it was the same as with everybody else – it was all about who'd got the biggest house or car. He'd only got his mum, so it was easier in lots of ways. That's what he told himself anyway. Still, he felt that pang whenever he went round to Luke's granny's on a Sunday, when they had a house full, that it was something he'd missed out on, that when it was good it was the best feeling in the world.

Bella was standing in the kitchen with her nose pointed at the back door. Jamie didn't feel like walking her but she wasn't going to let him get away with it. He put the plate of food from Julie's down on the kitchen table, popping the cling film and taking out a sausage from the plate. Bella turned and slobbered at his hand. He felt her teeth and tongue as she devoured the meat.

Thass it, good dog, good dog. Yer like that, doh yer? With his spare hand he ruffled her head and scratched her ears.

She was old now, eleven, just over. They'd got her to replace Goldie, his grandad's dog. Goldie had died and they got Bella for him and his grandad to share, but then his grandad got ill. When he died they'd moved here from the old house on Watson's Green Road. There was a picture of the old man with Goldie in a paw-shaped frame on the kitchen windowsill.

Jamie rubbed his hand over Bella's face. One eye was half closed and bloodshot. She couldn't see out of it properly. Someone had shot her with a pellet gun on the mushroom field when she was small – he'd thought it was Wayne Banks and all that lot. They had an air rifle and used to go up to the golf course on Sunday mornings to shoot at the horses as they came down the bridle path. But Banksy had come up and asked him what had happened and offered to help him get whoever did it, so he was never sure. Jamie could still remember the sound Bella made when it happened: the howl and then the whimpering; her eye a mass of blood and tissue. Her heart thumping with pain as he struggled to carry her back home – she was nearly as heavy as him then – his own eyes stinging with tears. They got her to the vet and he patched her up. The vet told him that she was a brave girl and he was a brave boy. Sometimes, when she was lying in her basket, her bad eye would weep uncontrollably.

Jamie rattled the lead from its hook and Bella bolted upright.

Just a quick one then, he said, yawning.

They made their way down the alley at the back of the house and out past Ken's rusting car. He said he left it unlocked to see if someone would pinch it so he could claim the insurance money, but there was still a bar-lock attached to the steering wheel. Jamie looked at his own van, parked deliberately under a streetlight. Kids had tried the lock a few times, but they couldn't get in. There were scratches in the paintwork where somebody had had a go at it with a screwdriver. It didn't matter if they got in anyway because it belonged to work. He wasn't going to worry about it. They'd probably just abandon it on the car park by the bus station in Dudley or else up by the maisonettes.

Jamie yanked Bella on the lead and turned left towards the shops. He glanced up at the houses. His mum was asleep, although she always woke up when he came in, no matter how quiet he was. Further along, Luke's light was on. The window was open and the net curtain flapped outside. Luke had told him once that he couldn't sleep without the light on. He was drunk and had started rambling on about his little brother. You had to watch him when he was drunk, he could go psycho like Banksy. Jamie didn't know what to say to him sometimes. Luke's problem since they were kids was that he was too clever, got all moody and frustrated because of it, and now he'd become lazy and couldn't be bothered doing anything with his life. Jamie hadn't believed him about not sleeping, but ever since then he'd been checking and the light was always on.

They must have had the light off, though, when he stayed at Sarah's. That was a bad situation; that was something to ramble on about when you were drunk. To think that she was seeing her boss all that time. Working late, weekends away, like something from the telly. His name, Hall, was stencilled up in gold lettering on the window of the solicitors' offices in Stone Street. She hadn't just got off with him, they'd been having a proper affair. She could've done that with me, Jamie thought. That Hall must have been forty if he was a day. And he had a couple of kids at private school. He was loaded. That must've been why she went with him, for what she could get. He liked that in Sarah. Luke had punched the bloke. A girl in the office next door had told him when he'd delivered some paper, and he realized that Luke never told him anything any more. It couldn't be a good idea, though, punching a solicitor.

When he got up to the shops he could hear talking and giggling. Two girls were sitting on the low wall next to the post office.

Eh, sexy, one of the girls called to him. Risley's little sister.

All right, Anna. He nodded, suddenly a bit sheepish. Bella sniffed around the shop shutters and squatted to piss. Iss a bit late for yow to be out on yer own, ay it?

Hark at him. I'm sixteen this year, Jay.

Arr, wim nearly legal.

The two girls giggled. Jamie didn't recognize Anna's friend, not that he should have. Her T-shirt showed off a bellybutton ring. Her legs were long and bare and stretched out across the cracked pavement towards him. Anna was dressed in the same way except her ringless belly pushed out over the top of her tight shorts. He pulled at Bella's lead, but she was still sniffing the post office's metal shutter.

Thass a lovely dog, Anna's friend said. She bent down and ruffled the top of Bella's head. Yome lovely, ay yer, yow am. Woss her naeme?

Bella.

Bella, yome beautiful, ay yer. Bella means beautiful, doh it? An yow am ay yer, she said again to the dog.

Jay, this is me mate, Katie.

All right.

All right, Jamie. She looked at him and held his stare. He looked away first.

Katie sat back on the wall. Bella, it means beautiful in Italian. She nodded at Anna. Anna passed a green plastic bottle of cider to her and sighed.

All right Einstein, fuckin hell.

Katie took a drink from the bottle and offered it to Jamie.

No, ta. He grinned. He hoped no one he knew came walking along the road.

Too good for us, look, Anna said. Wheer yow bin all dressed up, any road?

Wheer'd yow get that mouth on yer all on a sudden, Anna? he snapped at her, half seriously. She used to be a plump little girl who lay on the bottom of the stairs, getting in the way at Risley's house. Any road these am me normal clothes an I bin dahn me girlfriend's.

See, look, thinks he's too good for the likes o we.

He turned to her, getting angry, thinking that was something Risley might have said about him. Not that he'd even seen Risley for ages. What yow gooin on abaht?

Wheer's yer girlfriend live? Katie was looking at him again.

Dahn Dudley Wood, I bin theer tonight.

Did yer drive dahn?

Arr.

What sort of car yer got?

A van, a works van. See, Anna, I ay got a Mercedes nor nuthin, yet.

Ask Banksy, he'll get one for yer.

Jamie grinned and shook his head at her joke.

Do yow know Banksy? Katie was still looking at him.

Which one?

Her bloke, she said, nodding at Anna, Jason.

I know him, arr. I was in the saeme class as Wayne, his brother, at school.

I day know he went to school, Anna said.

Well, arr, when he was theer, like.

He went when he was there, Katie said, laughing.

Wim waiting for Jase now, Anna said. He's comin to pick us up. He's gone to drap his mate off.

His mate that yow tried to fix me up with, Katie complained. He was abaht this big, she said holding her hand out in front of her. An he had a moustache an a leather jacket on even in this weather.

Wor he yower sort, then? Jamie teased, holding her stare this time.

Nah, her sort's more the type o bloke who wears nice check shirts an gels his hair an thinks he's too good for everybody else, Anna said, snorting.

Shurrup.

Ah, well, I doh know wheer yow'd find a bloke like tha. Jamie pulled the lead and Bella's paws slipped across the pavement as she strained against his pull.

Woss up with her eye? Katie asked.

He nearly said, Anna's boyfriend's brother shot her, but stopped and said instead, Somebody shot her with a pellet gun over the mushroom field when her was a puppy.

God, serious? Thass terrible. Yow cor believe people do things like tha. Tham the animals, I tell yer.

Katie was stroking Bella again. Jamie bent down and did the same. He let his hand touch hers. Anna looked away down the street.

As Jamie stood up again a breeze blew down the road and he saw goosebumps rise on Katie's arm. The outside of her arm was tanned but when she lifted her hand he could see the inside was pale like a frog's belly.

Yow code? he asked.

Needs somebody to keep her warm, Anna said and took a drink from the bottle and passed it to Katie.

Katie blushed and hid it by taking a big swig, some of it splashing out onto her top. She giggled. Jamie put his hand out and took the bottle. He'd forgotten what cider tasted like. Flat and greasy, like they'd eaten chips and then drunk from it. Probably had.

Anna got up from the wall.

I'm gonna see if he's comin, she said in a light voice. She walked a little way down the street to where the telephone boxes were.

Jamie put the bottle down on the wall. He knew he should go. Did that hurt when yow had it done? He nodded at the blue stone in Katie's bellybutton.

She shook her head, looking at him. He hadn't noticed how drunk she was before; her eyes had that glaze to them, focusing and then refocusing. She nodded and looked down.

Yeah, it fuckin killed, actually. Was wuth it, though, I think.

Iss nice.

I got a tattoo an all, dyer wanna see it?

She stood up from the wall and did an exaggerated stumble, as if she was falling over. Jamie put his arm out. Bella barked and they both jumped and laughed at each other and the dog. Jamie's heart started racing with the noise and he looked up and down the street again. Down at the telephone boxes Anna said something he didn't catch.

Iss nuthin to worry abaht, Bella, he said and stroked the dog's head, dropping the lead to her side, thinking, I've brought my conscience out for a walk with me. Wheer is it then, yer tattoo?

Katie grinned and leaned towards him. It was her turn to look up and down the street. Here look, iss a Chinese symbol. Slowly, she rolled the top of her shorts down and held them out from her body. He looked down and saw the stroke of a Chinese character above the line of her pink knickers. He steadied her with his hand, their faces almost touching. She pushed at the material clumsily, revealing the whole of the tattoo. He noticed a faint bruise and a vein running away under her pale skin.

Oh arr, he said softly. Thass nice.

The noise of a car engine came out of the darkness. They stepped away from each other. The car was racing between speed bumps and as it came around the bend in the road they were caught in the full beam of one headlight. The stereo was on; the throb of the bass filled the street.

Here he is look, Anna shouted down the road.

Shit, Jamie said, as if we hadn't noticed.

The car pulled up a little way past them, a white Fiesta with one blue door on the front passenger's side. Two heads were bobbing up and down in the front. The driver was Jason Banks. Jamie recognized him now – he was bare-chested, nobody in that family ever wore a shirt.

Anna came hurrying after the car. He's brought Dekker with him, look, am yer comin? As she came past them she grabbed Katie's arm and pulled her. She took a few unsteady paces towards the car.

Wharrum yow doin? Katie asked Jamie.

I'm walkin um, purrin her to bed I spose. He nodded at Bella.

All right then, I better goo wi these, I con get a lift back. She looked young and awkward, standing under the street-light.

All right, then. I'll seeya. Anna opened the back door and slid across the seat, leaving the door open for Katie.

Be careful, Jamie said quietly as if to no one in particular.

I ay stupid, she said and turned to the car.

Seeya, Jamie Palmer, Anna shouted loudly and knowingly from the back of the car, enough to wake the whole estate.

Seeya, Anna, he replied. Say hello to David for me. But they were already tearing away from the kerb, the back door swinging open and then slamming shut as the car hit a speed bump.

Jamie walked back quickly, thirsty from the cider. Luke's light was still on when he passed his window. He got the urge to shout up to him but he just went inside; work tomorrow, after all.

Even an hour or so in the warehouse was too much for him. He hated it. All the monkeys coming back and forth on fork-lifts and with pallet trucks making jokes about the

Wolves or singing loudly and tunelessly to the radio. The drivers had called the warehouse boys monkeys for so long that that was what they called themselves now. He'd been a monkey once. All the monkeys wanted to do was become drivers, which was fair enough. The problem was that once you'd been a driver for a while the only step up was to become a chief monkey back in the warehouse.

He paced around the forecourt, strolling in and out of the hot sunlight and then back into the shade again, an order form crumpled in his fist. He was checking his deliveries off as the monkeys arrived with them from the store. The other drivers had already gone, but there'd been hassle over some paper he was meant to deliver to an office in Tipton.

Doh tek much, really, does it? Jamie moaned as a fat, ginger-haired boy not long out of school loped off to find Alan, the supervisor. More of an orang-utan than a monkey, really, he suggested to Kenny.

No, he replied. Cos tham clever, ay they.

It was cruel really. Jamie was going to stop getting caught up in it.

He checked the contents of the van against the printed paper in his hand. A filing cabinet for a place in Stourbridge and a couple of easy deliveries in Kingswinford, paper and pens all bubble-wrapped, ready to be signed for by some sweet-looking receptionist, all the usual Friday jobs, just as he liked it. He had some other business to do as well. He dragged his foot over some weeds growing up through the tarmac, then walked across to the fence impatiently.

He pulled his sunglasses from his jeans pocket and looked across the concrete and the main road to the green slope that led up to the back of Netherton Church. The summer he and Luke left school, they became friendly with some girls who lived up there in the houses backing onto the reservoir. They'd spent a few afternoons sitting on the muddy banks, pretending it was the beach.

Jamie had swum in the reservoir once. The water was so cold he thought his heart had stopped and he couldn't get his breath or feel his limbs for ages after. He remembered lying on the oily grass to dry out, listening to them all talk about him, scared at himself because he really had nearly drowned. His arms and legs had stopped working with the shock of the cold, he'd dipped below the surface with a mouthful of water and come up spluttering and gasping. Everyone had laughed. Except Luke, who'd crouched by the water with his usual concerned expression and, while Jamie lay recovering, dived in off the wooden jetty, swimming strongly in an arc back round to them and jumping out of the water grinning. Luke had always been good at useless things. And he liked to prove it, Jamie thought.

He'd be in Majorca soon, stretched out on a sunbed with hot sand sticking to him and San Miguel making his head throb slowly in the heat. Girls weaving through the crowds giving out flyers, promises. The sea there ready for him to cool off. No monkeys. No worries. That was what Netherton reservoir needed: water warm enough to swim in and maybe a couple of watermelon sellers. It did in this weather, anyway.

Come on, then. Alan came waddling from the warehouse with a ream of paper and an order form under his arm. Yome gonna meet yerself comin back in a minute. They ay payin yer to sit on yer arse all day, yer know.

Technically, Al, they am. I doh drive stondin up.

Bloody smart-arse. Come on, less be havin yer.

There were times when he was driving along and he knew that he didn't want to be anywhere else in the world, when everything seemed to be OK, to fall into place. Like the M6 coming around the top of Birmingham on the bit after Spaghetti, past the cemetery and Villa Park, all the high-rises away to the left, and the sun setting over the Black Country, dance music on the stereo. Or slow afternoons driving through Kingswinford or Wombourne or Himley with an expensive young blonde glancing in through the van window for a moment and smiling or, even better, keeping on that perfect, icy face before opening the door of her Audi. Mornings up the hill at Colley Gate or along Old Hill High Street with half the street in shadow and the pavements wet from being washed and the shops looking like he'd just driven back into the 1950s and Elvis was still number one.

He felt sorry for the monkeys stuck in the dark warehouse and the people cooped up in the works he delivered to; static, their lives just going on in their heads while he was out there driving around, free. That was what he was going to do – work at this job for a few years and then set up on his own, maybe removals, that sort of thing. Standing still was just no life at all. That was where they all went wrong.

He stopped off to collect the videos from Abdul. Abdul lived in a terraced house on Kate's Hill. It was part of a typical row: the houses were all the same but people went mad trying to make them look different, with gaudily painted walls and new windows and front doors.

Abdul motioned for him to go down the entry. Me grandad's in the front, he explained.

They walked past the back door and out into the yard. Abdul was wearing his mosque clothes, a flowing white overshirt over a Liverpool shirt and a purple cap with little mirrors on it like the scarves the Asian girls wore at school. Jamie used to have a thing for a girl called Rukshana in his class, who'd had the longest hair he'd ever seen. He used to imagine her wrapping her body in it. His body in it. Abdul was a year younger than Jamie, at university now, doing a degree in computers, but he made some holiday money by copying videos. Jamie sold them on to a bloke in Langley and picked up cheap blank tapes from one of the drivers at work.

Here yam. Abdul passed Jamie a can of Coke. Wiv gorra be quick cos I've gorra drive me grandad to the mosque. He's doin his nut.

Jamie sat on the low wall and opened the Coke. Abdul pulled open the rickety outhouse door. Electrical equipment was stacked up in a pile, three or four video recorders on top of one another and a workbench with bits of wire and a soldering iron on it. A big old television was teetering on top of the video recorders and a computer terminal was stuck at the other end of the bench. Abdul stooped to pick up the box of videos and then turned and closed the outhouse door behind him with his foot.

Yer wanna get that door sorted aht, mate. People ull be in here nickin yer stuff.

Nah, nobody robs from the Pakis, onny the shops, they think we ay got nuthin in the house. Kate's Hill's a safe area, man, not like Cromwell Green.

Huh, I'll send some on em up here if yer want. What yer got anyway, saeme as what we said?

Course. Action stuff, like yow asked for. There's some Jean-Claude Van Damme ones and then some Kung Fu ones, proper fightin, like yer said he asked for.

There ay any of em filmed in the cinema is there? Folks' heads keep bobbin abaht in the picture? He did his nut over that befower.

No, these am good copies, yer know. Dyer wanna check some?

No, I trust yer. He'll check em when I get dahn theer anyway.

The Van Damme one's got Japanese subtitles on it.

Iss in English, though, ay it?

What dyer think I am?

Course.

Thass all right then. Here yam, thirty. Thass sixty then, yeah?

Jamie pulled the notes from his pocket and passed them to Abdul.

Me rent's gooin up next year at uni. I might put me prices up soon.

Mate, this is already all right for an holiday job. Iss better than stackin shelves dahn the Tesco.

Or workin in me uncle's shop. Abdul grinned. I might be able to chip some games soon, PlayStation like, see if he's interested, will yer?

All right arr, I doh know nuthin abaht tha, though.

They shook hands before Jamie picked up the box and made his way back down the entry. He could hear Abdul's grandad shouting something and then Abdul shouting something back in Urdu.

Instead of driving back through Cromwell Green and calling in to see his mum, like he usually did if he thought he could get away with it, Jamie drove slowly along Oakham Road and daydreamed about the big houses and the people in them.

He drove past the house where Sarah lived with her mum and dad and brother, but there were no cars on the drive or signs of life. Then past the thatched cottage. He was going to buy that house one day and live in it with his beautiful wife and six kids, or maybe get something bigger, one of those on the other side of the road, and convert it so his mum could live there too. That was when he'd got his removals business.

He knew what'd happen, though. He'd start to make a fortune, buy a big house on Oakham Road, and his dad would show up out of the blue, the way that Risley's dad used to. That was the way things worked. He felt sure that his dad always knew what he was doing.

He got an idea in his head once, when his grandad was still alive, to find him, pestered his mum about it. All his grandad would say was that his dad had been a bad man and it was best not to think about him. The way he said it made him not ask any more, but the feeling that he was missing something was always there.

Buy a flash house and his dad was bound to come crawling out of the woodwork. He sighed: he made some extra cash on a few dodgy videos and he was already buying a mock-Tudor detached, bay windows and everything, as well as a new pair of trainers for Majorca. He put his foot down and drove over the hill.

He was late getting back home in the end. Fat Tommy, the bloke in Langley, kept him waiting for ages, sitting in the yard of his scrap metal place with Jamie worrying because people could see the van from the main road, but then he paid him extra, putting him fifty pounds up.

Dyer reckon yer con get hold of summat a bit spicier? Fat Tommy had asked.

Jamie looked at him blankly, then embarrassed when he realized he meant porn. Fat Tommy reckoned it'd pay better, but Jamie wasn't sure about Abdul. He wasn't sure himself, it'd make it worse if they got caught, so he just said he'd see what he could do.

He came down the path whistling, examining his sunglasses in the reflection from the back door. Then he stepped into a couple of inches of water. The dog basket was on the kitchen table and the washing machine was pulled away from the wall. Towels were on the lino, soaking up some of the water, but it had spread in a dark stain through the door and onto the living-room carpet.

Ooh Jay, look. I tode yer there was summat wrong wi the

washin machine. Look woss happened. I was onny upstairs changing the beds an I come down an theer's water everywheer. His mum came charging through the living room with bundles of towels in her arms.

All right, all right. He backed out of the door, took off his trainers and socks and rolled up the bottoms of his jeans. Wheer's Bella?

Her's upstairs in the bedroom, chick. Her's miserable in the heat an her was tryin to drink this water. There's all soap in it, look. I was gonna shout next door to get Ken to help, but he's gone in now. I'm glad yome back.

All right then, less get organized. He padded around in his bare feet. Least iss onny the lino in here. Least the floor ull be clayn. He stifled a laugh. She started to smile despite herself. Keep puttin stuff down to mop it up and I'll have a look at the machine. Less get the telly wire up aht the waeter or we'll all be electrocuted. Thass it, Mom, put them towels down theer an then yow con sweep the rest o this water aht the back door. Thass it.

I tode yer summat was wrong wi it.

I know, Mom, I know. He bent down to look at the seal on the machine door. If we need to get Pete rahnd, yer know, the bloke who fitted the shower, I'll give him a ring after.

I tode yer theer was summat the matter. It was mekkin a funny noise all wik.

All right, I know. Jamie emptied his pockets and dropped the contents onto the work surface, looking wistfully at the notes loose from his wallet. It ull be all right.

His mum went to get the broom. He ended up sitting in the puddle of water to look at the machine. She came back in.

Like this, dyer mean? His mum began sweeping hard at the water, splashing it out of the open back door, laughing, moving one step forwards and then two back.

Jus like that, Mom, arr, jus like tha.

He sighed and looked at the ruined machine and thought about his fifty pounds swimming down the drain with the soapy water. This washin machine needs a bloody undertaker not a doctor, he thought.

Luke

He walked through the clamour of the changing rooms to his locker. Con had fallen over in a heap in the corner putting on his overalls and a crowd was surrounding him, laughing. The women from the marinade room noticed Luke in his shorts and nudged each other. Rose wolf-whistled. He took a crumpled pair of jeans from his locker and pulled them on, unhooked his fresh overalls from the hanger.

Yer sid Houdini over theer? Alf walked over and stood next to him and nodded at Con still rolling around in the corner. If he's right in this world I know wheer theer's an house full, I tell yer.

Huh. I know, arr.

Luke fastened his boots quickly. Most people were beginning to file downstairs to clock in. He followed Mario through the double doors, still adjusting his hairnet, with his hard hat tucked under his arm. His overalls flapped open and fell off one shoulder. The metal staircase rang with the impact of boots. When he got to the bottom the familiar disinfectant and meat smell of the factory and the chill of the refrigeration hit him as he splashed through the footbath. The butchers' chainmail aprons hung on hooks on either side of the narrow corridor. The floor shone wet with soapsuds running away to the drains and the factory roared as it started up. Luke and Mario stood next to a wheelie bin of hollowed out and eyeless pigs' heads and looked at the women from the lines bustling past in a hurry to clock in.

Cor wait to start, some on em. Luke shook his head.

I know, arr. Doh gi em nuthin for free, mate. Doh gi em nuthin, Mario muttered.

Luke felt a tap on his shoulder as he struggled with a plastic sack. His heart stopped: a pig's snout stuck in his face, its mouth twisted in a grimace; Con's eyes flitted back and forth in the space where the pig's eyes had been. It was a perfect fit, he'd give him that.

Fuckin hell, Con. It ay funny. Yow could get the sack for tha.

How dyer know iss me? asked a muffled voice.

Who else ud it be? Doh let Alf see yer. Iss disgusting, mate. Yow'll catch summat.

Con wandered around, pretending to tick things off on a clipboard. Luke could see that Inderjit was pulling the pallet truck too quickly for what he was about to meet. Sure enough, Indy reached the corner with the pallet truck, looked up, and saw a pig standing six foot tall in overalls and a black hat, waiting to check his work. Indy hit the edge of Luke's machine and spilled the contents of the crates across the wet floor.

The women stopped working and began to shout at Luke to hurry up, but then they saw a gaffer's black hat and Inderjit scrambling to pick up the spilled crates. The boss turned around slowly to reveal his pig's face. The women started screaming and shouting. Con hurried to the plastic doors, turned, and raised his arm in a salute before disappearing into refrigeration.

Iss disgusting!

We ay gorra purrup wi things like tha, yer know.

Dirty little bastard.

I'm gonna report him.
He's a disgusting pig.
Laughter.
The cleaners, paper masks over their faces, came to move the mess. Mario stood for ages disinfecting the floor and the area around the machine.
Super Mario, Luke and Inderjit said together.
You had to be pretty bored to do something like that, Luke thought. Con wouldn't last much longer. He really hated the job. Nobody liked work, nobody he knew anyway. His dad used to like it. But for Luke work was just something you had to do. It was all very well proving how shit you thought it was, but when you had none that was when the real problems started.
You just had to fill your time, that was all. Take the line, for example. He'd just sent another pile of pork chops sliding down the conveyor belt. The women were back in their routine. It wasn't as if they were concentrating on laying the meat out in those cartons. It didn't take concentration, you just did it. It became automatic.
Luke looked at Jen, one of the packers, watching her face and trying to work out what she was thinking. Maybe what to do for her little boy's tea. It might have been much more exciting, though: an old boyfriend, bits of a song, chopping up Con into little bits on the machine. You just couldn't tell. She was frowning and kept opening and closing her right hand; it was probably cold. The thoughts that went on inside people's heads: romantic and violent and mundane.
Like Luke that morning. Before he was interrupted by Con he'd been thinking about the news last night: pictures of twisted and bloody bodies beginning to bloat on some dusty Bosnian roadside, with a reporter in a flak jacket giving details. There'd been a close-up of a dead man's face with the kind of expression that painters give Jesus on the

cross. But this man's face had flies crawling on it. The newsreader had said to look away before the report. They always said that, but Luke always looked. There was a little boy lying there at the roadside. It was as if he was just curled up and asleep, but there was something awkward about the position of his arms and legs. You could see where the ground was dark with blood on the other side of the body. Something about it, like he'd seen it before, made him think about Adam.

That had been his morning. Moving on his belly up the road, tasting the dust on his lips, gunfire overhead, firing his rifle over the low wall, crawling over bodies towards smoke rising from burning buildings. He'd seen it in a film once. A girl was trapped under a wall by a bridge. He could see her face. She looked like a girl who worked in one of the offices upstairs or maybe with Sarah at the solicitors'. Shooting. He was going to save her. He got up, made a break for it. Near the bridge a boy huddled, screaming. Luke was going to save him next. Then the boy was lying at the side of the road, his arms and legs in strange positions, a dark stain spreading on the ground next to him.

He pulled the handles of the machine down to cut the meat, heard it hitting the belt. That was how the time went: you just got to thinking and couldn't stop, filling in the gaps, the things you didn't know.

Watchin the bloody clock ay yer, lightnin?

I am Alf, arr. Three o'clock, mate, an thass it. Shutdown.

Doh blaeme yer, son. Doh blaeme yer. Bet yome aht on the razzle tonight, ay yer?

Well, I'm gooin aht, arr.

I bet. Wim off to the caravan.

Alf was leaning against the cage of the machine. Luke was wiping his bench down lazily, waiting for the last of the meat to get pulled out of the stores. The last hour of Friday afternoon and the electric light glowed like the sunshine outside. Three o'clock shutdown and no Saturday morning shift made for a long weekend – the only consolation of losing the overtime.

One of the women had complained to Alf about Con. So Alf had spent the afternoon getting everyone's story. Luke said he hadn't seen anything. Alf didn't seem to mind. He only had to pass it on anyway. Con would be getting a written warning.

Thass the least he deserved though, ay it, really?

It is Alf, iss disgusting. Well, from what everybody said, like. Luke smiled.

He's lucky not to get the push. He's gonna atta be careful. It ay like there ay plenty folks who ud do the job, an wi less fuss than him. He's a decent worker, though, I spose. When he ay actin the goat.

I musn't a sid it, Alf. I thought he was dressed as a pig, not a goat.

Eh? Doh yow start yer saftness. Any road, has yer ode mon had any luck findin summat again? Alf knew his dad from years ago at Round Oak.

Nuthin yet, Alf.

Hopeless, ay it? I doh know. Gi im me best, son.

When he walked through the back door into the kitchen, his mum and Kerry were sitting at the table leaning towards each other. They both jumped as he came in.

Er, sorry. All right?

All right, son.

Hello, Luke.

Wheer's Alice?

Hello, Kerry. How are you? I haven't seen you for two weeks. I ask you, I'm a person as well, you know. His sister grinned.

Her accent irritated him. He thought she put it on. Huh. Sorry. Wheer is Alice? he asked.

I give up. Upstairs asleep. I think the sun's got over her a bit this afternoon. I'll wake her up for her tea in a minute.

Leave her, her'll be all right. Mary stood up, hurriedly pushed something into the pocket of her apron and walked across to the sink.

He guessed that Kerry had slipped her some money. He was glad, but it made him feel guilty about the money he owed for the ring and for having been for a drink, pissing what money he had up the wall. Mind you, Kerry was loaded. Well, her husband Tim was, the tight bastard.

Yow bin boozin already?

We had a couple when we knocked off.

Thought yow was late.

Where did you go, Luke?

The Lagoon, Tipton.

Go to all the best places, you.

Tek after me sister, doh I?

Yome gooin aht tonight, ay yer?

Arr, wi Jay. The usual. I think wim gooin up Caesar's.

Well, yer doh follow yer sister for that.

How's Tim?

All right, thanks.

All right on his own side, eh?

Oi, doh start. Had his bloody saft half-pint, look yer. Mary gave Luke a sharp look, wiped her hands on the front of her apron. She looked at her daughter and rolled her eyes.

Wheer's me dad?

In the front.

I think the sun got over Dad as well.

Goo on in. I better get movin wi yer tay. Soak some o that beer up.

His dad sat in the armchair watching *Jobfinder*. He had

the curtains drawn against the sunlight. Luke sprawled out in the other chair.

Woss this on the text now?

No. I taped it off the telly last night. I set it up wrong, though, so an hour of it's *Prisoner Cell Block H*.

Here look, there's a good un. Vacancies at Burger King.

I know, arr. Waeste o time, it is. Ken stopped the video.

There's summat gooin at our place but iss for the butchers like, really.

No good then, is it?

They turned the video off to watch the news.

I'm waking Alice up. There'll be no chance of any rest tonight if I don't, Kerry announced and went upstairs to coax Alice awake.

That's it, come on, good girl, see Grandad and Uncle Luke. Alice slid a step at a time down the stairs.

Bump, bump, bump, Kerry said.

Bump, bump, bump, Alice repeated.

Alice tottered forward against Ken's legs and into his lap. Her face was red on one side where she'd been lying, tear streaks on her cheek. He picked her up and held her in the air, her face looking into his.

Grandad! Grandad! Grandad! Alice squealed and clapped her hands.

Luke found a bag of plastic zoo animals that Alice had been playing with and emptied them onto the settee. They'd been his. His mum and dad were getting out all the old toys for Alice to play with. He used to show these to Adam and try to teach him the names. Turning the monkeys, tigers, giraffes over in his hand he noticed grains of dirt crusted to them and a sudden wave of memory rose in him, like a feeling of vertigo. He'd done this on the night of the accident: emptied the bag out on the backyard path, made a pretend jungle in the garden border. He'd never thought of that before. Now, he put a lion and a bear onto the Lego street and turned the plastic people away from the car they were fixing so they could run away.

When he first started going out with Sarah an eagle had escaped from the zoo and sat high in the trees on Priory Park. No one would walk their dog for fear of the eagle swooping. For ages afterwards he'd daydreamed about them all breaking out: lions in the market, elephants charging through the bus station. Some time later he'd seen a news report about the animals at the Sarajevo Zoo. They'd all died during the siege. The brown bear was the last – it survived lived so long because it'd eaten the two other bears in its enclosure. Luke wondered why, when things got really bad, someone hadn't just opened the cages and let the animals free. He took one of the Lego people and crumpled them at the side of the road, arms and legs at strange angles, like on the news report, like the boy in his head.

Luke sat perched on the edge of the kitchen table wearing just his trousers and shoes, watching his mum iron a shirt. There was a quick knock on the back door and Jamie walked in.

Ready then, he said, nodding at the ironing board.

Woh be a minute, Jay. Gorra look me best.

Yer know him, Jamie. Late for his own funeral, mate. Yer know what time he starts to get ready? Ten to. Then he comes down here an asks me to iron him a shirt. I doh know.

Yow should mek him iron his own.

I should really, but I doh know what state he ud goo out lookin like.

Oh arr, cos yow iron all yer own shirts, doh yer? Luke looked at Jamie. His diamond stud earring glinted, his shirt was swimming-pool blue. The room smelled of aftershave.

Jamie winked at Luke and lifted four cans of lager from

the plastic bag he was carrying and passed one to him. Jus to gerrus warmed up.

Jamie looked like a peacock, with his blue shirt and his hair shiny with gel. It always looked as if he was wearing makeup – his lips big and pink and full, his eyes dark and narrow. Chink fuckin drag queen, Wayne Banks had cursed one time when Jamie ripped him off over a box of videotapes. Anyone else would have had their legs broken, but Jamie got away with things. He was trying to get Luke to smuggle meat out of the factory so they could flog it on the estate, but Luke was having none of it.

Jamie was unreliable, out for number one, but could be kind-hearted too, like when he'd taken that old cine film of Adam and got a mate of his to convert it to video. They all sat and watched it one Saturday night. Adam in a push-chair at his gran's, splashing at the edge of the sea at Uncle Mick's caravan in Barmouth: Luke's mum and nan and sister crying softly as they watched. It seemed to last for hours. Then they watched it all over again.

Has yer mother had a new washin machine yet, Jay?

Nah, wim gonna get one soon. Her's bin washin every-thin by ond this wik.

I tode her to come an use owern. Tham pricey, ay they.

Tell me abaht it. A bloke I know's gerrin one for us, but we gorra wait on the, erm, supplier, he said, choosing his words carefully.

Ere yam then. Thass ready. His mother passed Luke the shirt. Listen, watch what yome doin tonight an watch what yome havin to drink. I know what yome like. Keep an eye on him, Jamie. Am yer seein Julie tonight?

Nah, her's gone dahn her sister's.

Oh, well definitely watch what yome doin then. Yow con watch wha he's drinkin an he con keep an eye on yow wi the women. I know. Yer think I doh know nuthin.

They left through the back door as she folded up the

ironing board. Luke pushed Jamie up the path, shouting another goodbye after a mouthful of beer. A warm breeze ruffled the leaves of the trees and bushes in the row of gardens. Next door had a sprinkler on, the drops of water catching the sunlight. Luke took a long drink from his can as he pushed back the hydrangea bush that lolled across the path.

Y'know wha our Alice said today?

Wha?

Her was messin abaht in that bush, like, an so Kerry goes over to see what her's doin. Her'd picked up a rock or summat an her'd got all these woodlice crawlin over her onds. Kerry says to her to stop messin wi em, to put em down. Alice says, Sall right Mommy, they'm me friends. Kerry was havin a fit, like.

Funny, kids. I used to ate woodlice when I was a little un, an worms. I jus used to put things in me mouth, see what they tasted like.

Chinese ate em, doh they?

Wha, woodlice?

Well, insects. Ants and bees an tha. In chocolate. Yow can get em in tins.

Fuckin hell. Serious?

Arr.

Thass all right, like. I doh wanna ate em now. Jamie pulled a face. Prefer a bag o scratchins meself.

Fuckin hell, Jimmy Tarbuck.

He told it as if it was funny, but the thing with Alice troubled him.

He was always out in the back garden with Adam, turning stones over to look for woodlice and worms, then making a jungle for the toy animals on the night it had happened.

Not long after Adam died, the houses were infested with

a plague of rats that came from the building site where they were extending the school. His dad used to sit by the kitchen door and kill any that were already groggy with poison with a cricket bat. He'd bury them in the soil at the end of the back garden path. One Sunday morning Luke was with his dad in the garden, messing around with a trowel he'd let him play with. Turning the earth over by the fence he'd uncovered a rat's carcass, swarming with maggots, their white bodies writhing in the shape of the rat's body. Luke, six years old, had screamed, terrified.

Iss OK, iss just one of them nasty rats, his dad said to reassure him, but with that Luke had bolted upstairs to his bedroom, hysterical, rocking on the bed, shouting, Yow said yow went to heaven when yome dead! Yow said yer went to heaven!

His mum came upstairs and held him and stroked his hair. Not yer body, darlin, not yer body, just yer soul, just yerself, inside yer head, not yer body. But as his sobs quietened, her reassurances just echoed around the room.

So yer body just lies in the ground? His mum nodded, staring at the wall of the bedroom.

Rats doh goo to heaven any road, son, his dad said to fill the silence.

Luke stayed in his bedroom for the rest of that day, rocking on the edge of the bed, thinking of the writhing, rotting mass in the ground.

They walked along the main road into town, throwing their empty cans over the wall of Teddy Gray's factory. On Hall Street a car raced past, dance music booming from its open windows, a group of women packed tightly inside.

Ladies, said Jamie and pushed out his chest, walking with a swagger. A bus followed the car, two boys pressed against the upstairs back window giving Luke and Jamie the finger, the bass from the car stereo still pounding in the air. The sun reflected off the bus and glowed against the taller buildings in the town and the flats at Eve Hill.

Woss the plan, then? Luke asked.

Dunno, what dyer reckon? The Sarras? The Cowshed? The Griffin? I ay bothered.

Dyer wanna try gerrin in Caesar's afower eleven?

Dunno, see how iss gooin, like.

Gonna have me a good night tonight, though, I tell yer.

They walked in step along the High Street. Luke finished the last of his second can. The beer tasted sugary and metallic, the heat still left in the day had warmed the tin. Jamie nodded a change of direction and they weaved in between empty market stalls, the light flickering in squares of sunlight and shade as they walked beneath the canopies.

A few lads stood drinking outside the Saracen's Head, young men like Luke and Jamie dressed in pastel shirts and smartly pressed trousers. Jamie nodded a couple of hellos at familiar faces as they entered the pub. The bouncer stepped briefly into their path and then away again.

Warren, Luke said.

All right, lads. Warren King stood leaning against the doorframe. He looked the part, a tall black man with a crooked pink scar under his left eye. Luke and Jamie had been at school with one of his younger brothers, Carl, who was away after trying to rob Cromwell Green post office with a toy gun. Jamie had bought some stuff from him a few times. Nothing big time. It paid to be on Warren's right side.

Yow ay got any tickets for Caesar's tonight, have yer, Warren?

Caesar's? Second division, lads. Yer wanna get yerselves down the Merry Hill. Loads o fanny. Especially in this weather. Or there's a bus to Wolvo from here tonight. Wanna get yerselves on tha. There's fuck all up Caesar's.

All right. Cheers, Warren.

We know there's fuck all up Caesar's, Luke said quietly as they headed for the bar.

How come Caesar's is second division the week he ay got tickets? Iss the fuckin dog's bollocks the rest o the time according to him. Jamie shook his head. Wanna get yerselves down the Merry Hill, lads. Loads o fanny.

Sarah.

Luke, wharrum yow doin here?

What dyer think? Doh start that cos yer know I come up here on a Friday. Luke glanced at Jamie and he walked away to the bar. Anyway wharrum yow doin here, ay yer stoppin?

Wim gooin down the Merry Hill. I met Michelle in here.

No fancy man tonight then? I wudn't a thought the Waterfront was his scene.

No, but Andrew's all right, thank you. His black eye's much better. She smiled.

Yer think iss funny, doh yer?

No, Luke, I think it's pathetic.

No, yer think iss funny, look. Yow love it. Yow love bein able to tell everybody yow've got two blokes fightin over yer. Warren looked over when Luke raised his voice, but then he just turned back to the door.

It was hardly fightin. Yome really lucky, Luke, yow could o really hurt him, or he could o got the police involved.

I know, arr. He ay, though, is he? Luke felt a surge of panic.

No. I told him not to.

An he listens to yower advice. God help him.

She shrugged. I doh expect yer to thank me.

Sarah's friend, Michelle, came out of the toilets and nearly barged straight into them. Sarah motioned her towards the bar with a jerk of her head.

He's left his wife, ay he?

They'm separated, yeah.
Cos o yow.
Don't start this here.
Dyer know what yome doin? Again, quietly. He knew the answer, after all.
No, not really.
She looked as if she was about to cry and shook her head a couple of times. They stood there and said nothing for a while, looking at each other and then at the floor. Luke saw that Jamie was talking to Michelle at the bar.
Dyer miss me, Luke? I miss you.
Sometimes, I spose, arr.
Onny sometimes?
Yome lookin brown, dyer goo away?
You know I did. I went to the Canary Islands wi Michelle. Yome lookin well yerself.
Arr well, this is just rust.
Wiv gorra talk about things properly, Luke.
No we ay. His voice got louder again. We ay gorra talk abaht anythin. Iss finished.
Look, me mom an dad am away wikends at the minute wi the caravan. Ring me if yer wanna come round. She was looking straight at him now.
I got nuthin I wanna see yer abaht, except gerrin that fuckin ring off yer.
Well, there yer go then. She smiled this time, gave him a look like she used to. She squeezed his hand, kissed him on the cheek and walked towards the front doors. Michelle went past him as he walked to the bar and said, All right, Luke, in a cheerful voice.
Jamie tapped a pint of lager going flat on the bar. Luke swore and drank half of it off, pulled a fiver out of his pocket to get a round in.
That was successful, then, Jamie said.
Luke grunted.

That Michelle's all right, yer know. Remember when I shagged her over the park an the parkie catched me?

Fuckin hell, Jay.

A DJ was setting up in the conservatory. They stood at the bar for a while in silence.

Anybody else out tonight? Luke asked, glancing round at the half-empty pub.

Arr, Michelle an Sarah.

Fuckin hell, Jay, am yer jus tryin to wind me up? He took two steps back, two steps forward and smacked his hands on top of the bar. His knuckles hurt. Fuckin honestly, yow doh know how close yer come sometimes.

All right, sorry. Yow cor lerrit ruin yer Friday night, though.

Luke looked across the bar and then down at his shoes. I know. Iss jus that I got me mother carryin on an all. I've still gorra get that fuckin ring off her somehow.

Woss her keepin that for? Iss bin wiks since yer tode her, ay it?

Fuck knows.

Yer wanna get that sorted out, mate. Money ud be handy.

Easier said than done tha, ay it. Tay even my money. If it was, I'd jus sack it, I think. Me mom an dad gid it me just afower he got med redundant again, the last time. Luke shook his head, swallowed the rest of his pint and leaned into the bar to get the round in.

As the pub filled up they wandered through to the long bar next to the main room. It was still early and they paced themselves for money and drink. Luke preferred this room, with its mix of old and young couples talking at the tables. The air was smoky; the music from next door vibrated dully in the walls and exploded into the room when anyone opened the connecting doors. Through the skylight Luke could see an aeroplane glinting as it slid past the clouds.

Have yer sid who's in here? Jamie pointed at the bar.

Huh, Tommy Clancey. He's had a good day an all from the look on him.

A grey-haired figure in an old blue suit jacket stood clinging to the edge of the bar. Staring at the floor half singing, half talking to himself. Every few minutes his tattooed hands would lose their grip and he'd stagger back and forth to correct his balance. As he did this he'd raise his dirty face and stare around the room. His eyes were a cool, light blue and looked as sober as the rest of him looked drunk. People passing him at the bar avoided his stare.

Wonder when he got let aht then?

Doh know. Wonder how he got let in here. I thought he was banned from everywheer. Last time I sid him he was hangin round the market wi the kids drinkin one o them bottles o cider.

Thass a new girl on the bar, ay it? Perhaps her doh know him. I doh know how he would o got past Warren. I shun't like to try throwin him out now, the state he's in.

Perhaps he got in here early. Looks like he's bin on it all day.

He could o climbed through the winder in the bogs.

Arr, could of. What an entrance, eh.

Remember that New Year's Eve when we was sixteen? Jamie said, suddenly excited. He come over to me and held the flat of his hand out in front o me. He'd got a boil right theer on the palm. An inch across it was. He said, Tek a look at tha, kid. I said, Thass a corker ay it, Tommy, or summat like tha. Next thing is he's took a swing at me. Catched me on the side o the head cos I was ducking, like. Me ear was sore for wiks after. Remember? I legged it up to yow lot at the Griffin. Shit meself, I tell yer.

Everyone had a Tommy Clancey story. In his sixties, he'd been in and out of prison for forty years. Always fighting, always up to something, he carried a screwdriver behind the lapel of his jacket, a knife tucked into his sock. Luke heard he'd spent a summer once drinking cider and meths and sleeping on the banks of the river at Stourport.

Tommy's head turned towards their table. They both looked down at their drinks.

Wiv gorra get aht on here, Jamie said.

Arr, otherwise we'll end up like him.

They stood on the pavement with the crowd waiting for the minibus.

Yer wanna come wi us, Luke? Stevo asked.

No, yome all right, mate.

Sure? It'll be a good night.

Nah, I know. Jus doh feel up to it really.

Stevo shifted his weight from foot to foot as he talked, playing with the gold stud in his left ear. As he bent his arm his shirt rode up over his bicep to reveal a dolphin tattoo. He was always fixing up things like this – a minibus to Wolverhampton here, a bag of gear to sell in the pub toilets there. Most of the dozen or so waiting for the minibus had just returned from Ibiza. Luke felt pale and badly dressed in front of them with their tans and white shirts and shiny, expensive trainers. Donna, Stevo's girlfriend, came over. She had a bottle of Corona in one hand and a spliff in the other. Stevo took the spliff from her and passed it to Luke without taking any himself.

Be fuckin asleep if I have any. They'll atta mek a bed up for me in the club.

Donna giggled at her boyfriend.

I was jus tellin him about Ibiza, babes. Fuckin brilliant, it was. I was tellin him about that night out in the caves.

Yeah, they had this club set up in these caves. Promoter we met out there told us about it, day he? It was an all-nighter and they had so many rooms, well, caves y'know.

You just got lost. It'd a bin really scary if we aint bin so mashed.

Tell him abaht the chill-out room.

God, yeah. The chill-out room, cave, right, was this cave with all them stalactites or stalagmites, y'know, and it had this spring running through it. Just this water bubbling up out o the ground. You just drank straight out of it. It was beautiful, ice-cold.

When the sun come up, right, everybody went out on top o this cliff to watch it an they'd put out all these boxes of oranges. So we was there watching the sun come up, eating these oranges. Then back by the pool to recover an get ready for the next night. That was the best bit, though, the caves.

Am yow gonna goo away, Luke?

No, no. Got nothing sorted out, really.

Thass a shame, yow shoulda come with us.

Is Nicky back soon? Nicky was Luke and Jamie's mate from school. He'd gone to university and then taken off travelling.

He's meant to be back this wikend. I spoke to his mom but her ay heard from him for wiks. I doh know. He'll be back when he's ready I suppose, you know what he's like.

Yow ever thought o travellin, Luke? Donna asked.

Nah, I doh know as iss my cup o tay, to be honest. How abaht yow?

Wid love to really, Stevo said. Iss a bit difficult wi work, like, but maybe next year. We need to save up like Nicky did. Yow wanna goo to India, doh yer, babes?

I'd love to, she said. Jus to see summat different. Summat that ay round here.

One of the lads behind them sneered. Iss like fuckin India rahnd here.

Shurrup, yer prick, Donna shouted.

If he says one more fuckin stupid thing I'm gonna ban

him, Stevo said, frowning. He can fuck off up Caesar's wi the rest o the fuckin gypos. Wheer yow off to tonight, Luke, any road?

Eh? Oh, just rahnd the tahn, like.

Someone at the back of the queue was thumping the corrugated-iron cladding of the building. It boomed as it rippled along the tunnel that led to the club entrance. Two bouncers hurried past towards the offending noise, one barged Luke's shoulder and called, Stay in against the wall.

Luke glared at the bouncer's back as it disappeared round the corner and shuffled his weight from foot to foot. *Wanker*, he muttered at his shoes. Jamie nudged him and pointed at a group of four girls in front.

Tekkin their time, ay they? Luke looked towards the brightly lit entrance of the club. There were a dozen people in front of them but nobody was being let in.

Waitin to get it past eleven, ay they. Jamie looked at his watch. Five to, look. Their faces shone green in the neon of the Caesar's sign suspended in ten-foot letters on the wall behind them. Luke flicked his cigarette butt out into the gutter.

The bouncers returned down the line of people. Move back against the wall, ordered the same one who'd barged Luke. Again he stared at the wide back, this time as it marched towards the square of orange light at the entrance. He shook his head and muttered, catching the eye of one of the girls Jamie had pointed out. She smiled at him and then glanced at the passing bouncer. Luke grinned. She was dark, with curly hair falling onto the shoulder straps of her black dress. She was swaying slightly, partly in time to the music, partly with the drink, he thought. When she smiled he noticed a little gap between her front teeth. Her dress had a zip which ran all the way up the front, from the hem to the squared-off neck. There was a cheer as the queue began to move. As they moved forward, Luke noticed the girl looking back and he smiled at her. She turned away but then looked back again, the way it happens.

Luke went to the bar. Jamie bounded towards another group of Cromwell Green boys.

Luke murmured hellos to the group Jamie was standing with on the edge of the dance floor. Luke handed him his pint and nodded vaguely at Wayne Banks, who was holding forth.

So I cudn't fuckin believe it, I tell yer. The bloke's down, right, an I'm fuckin purrin the boot in. An I've gid him a couple in the ribs but jus warmin up, like, an I'm gonna goo dahn for his head. Any road, next thing I know the cunt's grabbed ode o me legs an pulled me over the top on him. He'd already had a palin by then, mind yer, but he was a gaeme bloke, fuckin gaeme bloke for a Paki, I tell yer. He gorra couple in while I was dahn, an all. I was shittin meself, like, cos they carry them knives under their shirts, doh they?

Thass just Sikhs, Banks.

Oh, thass them wi the hats on, ay it? Any road, wim rollin rahnd on the street, ay we, an our Lyndon comes rahnd the corner wi his mate who's back um on leave for the wikend. Fuckin hell. I tell yer wha, they gid him a lampin then. I thought they was gonna kill him. They finished up tryin to throw him through the winder o Boots the chemist.

Thass Boots the chemist as opposed to Boots the fuckin antique dealers, Jamie whispered to Luke. Then, when Banksy stared at him he said, This is last Sunday night, ay it, Banks?

It is arr. All right, Luke. Busy today, wor we, mate? None o these fuckers know what work is, I tell yer. Any road, our Lyndon fuckin lamped me after, an all. He felt his swollen cheek, seemingly with a mixture of pain and fraternal pride. Said I was a disgrace, not bein able to handle a Paki on me own. Oh well, gaeme bloke, credit wheer credit's due, like.

They stood in front of the bar which ran alongside the dance floor.

They am fuckin headcases, mate.

I know arr, really. Jamie kept his eyes on the dance floor and the sofas on the far side of the room as he talked. Animals. The thing is, though, iss best to keep on the right side on em. Banksy's a fuckin nutter. I doh know how yer can work wi him.

I doh spake to him at work. Wim on different lines, ay we? Iss easy.

Jamie drifted over onto the dance floor and disappeared into a group of moving bodies. Pipes sprayed dry ice everywhere and the lights switched from flashing yellow to blue as the lighting rig moved. The DJ said something into his microphone and a group of women in the middle of the floor raised their hands. Luke leaned against a column in front of the bar. He watched the dancers, then glanced round at those just standing talking or watching, like him. He thought he might go upstairs soon where there was a quieter bar with a balcony overlooking the rest of the club. The lights changed to a strobe effect and Luke watched Jamie framed in various unlikely poses, his shirt illuminated. He felt sweat running down his back as the club filled with people, the DJ shouted. All eyes turned to a dancer in the cage to the left of the DJ who was grinding herself against the bars. When she left the cage a bouncer had to escort her through the forest of leering lads surrounding the podium, clapping and cheering. Then a male dancer got in the cage. Women squealed, eager to get their own back on their boyfriends.

Yer not dancin? It was the girl from the queue.

Eh? Oh, no. I ay got me dancin shoes on. Luke smiled and lifted one foot slightly to show her.

They look all right to me.

Doh think I could compete wi John Travolta up theer, any road. Luke nodded at the dancer in the cage. She laughed. A terrible joke and she still laughed.

I think it's yer mate yer should be more worried about.

Woss he doin?

Nothing really, he seems to be enjoying himself, though.

He does the dancin for both of us.

Am yow enjoyin yerself?

Luke shrugged. Sall right. How about you?

Yeah, iss a laugh, I spose. I've never really bin up here, we usually goo to the Merry Hill. Yer from round here, am yer?

Arr, just up the road, like, Cromwell Green. I wudn't travel to come here. Listen, dyer wanna drink?

No, iss all right. I've gorra get em in for me mates. Maybe yer can buy me one in a bit.

All right, then. I might even come an have a dance later.

I'll believe that when I see it. Seeya later.

She moved off to the bar. He followed her with his eyes. She pulled a face at a drunken man in a red blazer who almost spilled his pint on her and then she looked back at Luke and smiled. He watched her check her reflection in the mirrored tiles as she walked towards the dance floor with the bottles of beer. He wondered if Jamie had asked her to come over to talk to him, then decided he didn't care if he had.

Luke sat on a stool on the balcony overlooking the dance floor.

A boy with a tattoo on his neck was sitting on a sofa in what the lettering above the bar said was a cocktail lounge. He was kissing a woman who had bleached hair and was wearing a lacy white top, a leather skirt and lots of gold. She looked about fifty. The boy kept trying to put his hand up her skirt. She was resisting, but not very forcefully. Luke watched, leaning against the balcony rail, drinking a special offer rum and Coke. Some time later, the boy kissing her neck and his hand at its destination, she looked across to the bar and mouthed something at Luke. He was glad he couldn't understand.

I like yer dress, Lisa. Luke's fingers were gently holding the zip at the front of her dress. He pulled it down slowly, to show an inch or so more flesh. She took his hand and pulled it away from the zip.

Not here, she said, and giggled and looked around. The lights were coming on and the club was emptying, the last record fading away into the shouts from the bouncers. Can you start making a move now, please? She lifted her face up to his and they kissed. She tasted of Silk Cut.

You OK? he asked.

Yeah, of course.

They kissed again, still moving back and forth to the fading music. She squeezed him tight.

Jamie was with some girl against the side of Caesar's. Luke was deciding whether to hang about or not. Lisa had gone home with her mates, but he'd got her phone number written in eye pencil on a cigarette packet. He saw Banksy walking down the street with one of those flashing yellow lamps that the council put around holes in the road held high above his head, his shirt open to the waist, and he decided to stay in the shadows. A bloke in a white shirt approached. Hayley? he said. Jamie and the girl surfaced for air.

Come here, yer fucker! White Shirt swung a wild punch at Jamie. He seemed to catch the girl as well and they both went ducking down against the wall. Startled, Luke grabbed the bloke's shoulder and swung him round. White Shirt's head snapped forward and butted him. Luke felt gelled hair hit his chin but nothing else. White Shirt's head went back to try again and Luke saw his pale face and eyes that could hardly focus, then he punched him and heard that deep, almost sucking sound of a good punch and felt that pain in his knuckles again. White Shirt went flying backwards, like someone in a cartoon. Luke felt something within himself that sounded like a whoop of delight. The lad crashed against the wall, propped up by it, half sitting. Luke kicked his legs from under him, kicked him again. The impact made a noise like he was kicking a deflated ball. The girl started screaming.

Someone grabbed Luke from behind and began pulling him off. He threw his elbow and heard a grunt. Once he got going, he could kill somebody. Iss me, yer fucker! It was Banksy, pulling him into the road.

White Shirt had blood on his face, down his front. Luke could see flashing blue lights from the corner of his eye. Banksy pulled him in front of a reversing taxi, then they ran up the slope, the same direction as Jamie and the girl, overtaking them and stopping at the corner. They all started talking and swearing at the same time. Luke thought he was going to be sick, put his hands on his knees.

What the fuck was that all abaht? he asked and then said, Cheers, Wayne, to Banksy.

I shun't a bothered but the pigs am here, mate.

Fuck, am they comin?

Nah, there's a big bost-up on the car parks wi them from the Sledmere, tham watchin tha.

Shit, yow sure?

Cheers, lads, Jamie said in a normal voice.

What the fuck yow playin at? Luke turned to Jamie. Jamie looked like a clown, pink lipstick smeared across his face.

Oh sorry, he said, I am rude. Hayley, these am me mates, Luke an Banksy. She giggled. Jamie was propping her up.

All right, she said, chewing and playing with her gold chains that seemed to have got tangled in her hair.

Who's that, yer boyfriend?

She giggled again. Me ex. He's allus like it.

Oh, right. Luke stood shaking his head. He could see White Shirt up on his feet, standing with a group of mates in the crowd outside the club, looking around. Suddenly, he just wanted to go home. I'm gerrin a taxi.

Am we gooin for that coffee? Jamie turned to Hayley. She was trying to kiss him again. Come on then, he said, and took a few steps up the road. He turned again. Cheers, lads, serious, he said. Thanks, Luke. Yow all right?

Luke shrugged. I'm all right, arr.

Banksy had stopped a cab and was arguing about whether he could take his lamp with him or not. Oh, fuck yer then, he said, and slammed it down on the pavement and jumped in the car's passenger seat.

Here yam, Jamie said, jump in with him. I'm gonna tek her back. He winked and put his hand up for the taxi behind. Goo to Pensnett, mate?

Come on, Luke, Banksy ordered.

The taxi had to wait for the queue for the burger van to move. A group of crop-haired lads stood in the electric glow of its window. A bloke paid for his burger with one hand, while with his other he unzipped his trousers and pissed calmly on the side of the van and all over his shoes. His face looked shiny and pink in the circle of light and heat that the van threw out. The people behind all laughed.

Banksy gave an address on Dixon's Green. When the car pulled up he shouted, Seeya, Luke, then opened the door and went sprinting off up the hill. The taxi driver started shouting but calmed down when Luke took all of his money and slammed it onto the front seat.

To avoid seeing any more people he walked back the Cawney Bank way, and eventually stumbled back home, fumbled with his key in the back door and staggered across the kitchen to slump, drunk and dead tired, into the chair by the door.

He woke with a pain in his side from the arm of the chair sticking into him, his hand swollen from the punch. He could see a dark blue square of sky through the kitchen window. Birds were singing. Wriggling in the chair, he tried to get comfortable. His mouth was parched. Licking his lips didn't help, so he pulled himself up to the sink. The clock on the oven read 5.05. He ran the cold tap and drank from it and stood watching the water. After a while he pushed the fingers of his good hand into his mouth, touched the back of his throat and heaved. Nothing happened, so he did the same again. This time he was sick – a yellow-brown liquid splattering the sink and swirling round in the water. He heaved three more times and then wiped the sides of the sink with his hand and took a long drink of water. He spat a couple of times, stood up straight and walked through the door to the front room and upstairs to bed. The bed covers felt cool on his skin, like lotion after sunburn he imagined, as he drifted off into sleep.

Sarah

Sarah looked at the purple line of Andrew's bruised eye as she turned to kiss him. It had been a couple of weeks: older men took longer to heal. He'd been quite proud of it, never had a black eye before.

You OK? He was always asking that. That was one of the things that had drawn her to him in the first place: he could actually think about other people. She'd come to wonder, though, if he did it out of habit, a kind of reflex.

Yeah, course I am.

He put his arms round her.

Have you thought about what I asked you? He kissed the top of her head between words. He'd been on about her moving in with him now that he had a flat sorted out, now that he'd left Jennifer and the kids. She'd been trying to put him off, didn't know how serious he was.

Course I have.

Well, what do you think?

She talked into his suit lapel. It sounds really nice but –

But what?

Swallowing hard, she didn't know what to say. Well, yer know, I just wonder if I'm ready for all that, yer know –

She was shaking a little bit and wanted him to notice. He'd loosened his grip and she swayed back to look at him as he spoke.

You know I love you.

Sarah had a sensation that she was looking at a complete stranger, this man twice her age that she'd gone to bed with, had wanted to be with. She was panicking now. What had she done? She held her hand over her mouth, like someone remembering a secret.

I can't do this, Andrew. Not now. I'm sorry.

Saying this made her feel stronger, but at the same time she felt this wave pass over her, the inadequacy of words, like she was talking to him across a big black hole into which the words would just fall and disappear.

I just can't. Just can't.

He stood there stiffly as she turned and hurried through the reception area to the stairs. Between the thump of her steps she could hear him saying her name. She burst onto the street, crying, running away.

They were at the Waterfront at Merry Hill but it could've been anywhere, Sarah thought, especially on a summer night like this one, and that was why people loved it so much. It was like a blank slate, and that was what she wanted. It must have been what a lot of people wanted. She swilled the ice around in the bottom of her Bacardi.

She sat with Michelle at one of the tables furthest from the bars, right on the roadside. The air smelled of after-shave and exhaust fumes. A procession of taxis and shiny cars crept past and people squeezed between the packed tables and went in and out of the bars along the water-front. The noises of a Friday night out rose into the air.

A woman in a white dress came out of the Greek restaurant a few doors along and fell over as quick as if a sniper had picked her off. The people she was with walked away towards the car parks, not noticing, then turned around when they saw she wasn't with them.

Nice perm, Michelle said quietly. Her tits have fell out that dress, look.

Sarah shook her head and stifled a laugh. Michelle could always cheer her up. A group of lads on the next table noticed the woman and began shouting over to her. Her boyfriend was walking back to get her.

Just leave me, leave me! The woman slapped her boyfriend in the chest when he arrived. He grabbed her by the wrists, started dragging her away, leaving her shoes by the side of the kerb. The boys on the next table laughed and cheered. The woman started to cry: big uncontrollable drunken sobs.

Arr, woss her blaertin abaht? Michelle snorted into her bottle of beer.

Two or three of the lads on the next table smiled across at them. They'd just got a double round in and looked tanned and happy, back from Magaluf or San Antonio, all drinking bottles of Sol and still in a holiday mood. One of them looked like Luke – well, except that he kept smiling.

Michelle jerked her head towards the other table. The lad that looked like Luke was still staring. Michelle screwed her face up. Sarah laughed again.

Iss bloody packed, ay it?

It is arr. I'm glad wim on the guest list.

Sarah didn't want to go to the club. She was happy enough where she was, looking out across the road and at the lights reflected in the canal. She watched a couple, expensively dressed and happy, walking slowly across the bridge to the Copthorne bar.

Yow all right? Michelle asked. Try not to think abaht it.

No, no, I'm fine. Sarah sipped her drink. The ice was melting, making it watery, and she wanted another. I'm fine. Bit tired, thass all. I need another holiday to recover.

Michelle smiled. I'll get the drinks. Dyer want the saeme?

Hang on a minute. I'll get em. I got paid yesterday an iss my turn. I've sid the shoes I'm gonna get. They've gorrem in Ravel dahn here. I should save me money, I spose, cus

I'm gonna have to hand me notice in. I ay gooin back. Dyer fancy comin dahn here tomorra?

Arr, maybe. Not too early, though.

No, afternoon probably. I might give Rob a lift.

Is he still the clown?

Arr, yow wudn't believe it, ud yer? He loves it.

Has he tode yer mom and dad yet?

No, he says he's workin in Woolworths on the checkout. Yer know what me dad ud be like if he found out. He meks his life a misery as it is, tekkin the piss.

Michelle laughed.

He come back with some makeup still on the other day. I could see me dad lookin at him, scared to ask, like. He never said nuthin. Maybe he thinks he's a transvestite or summat.

Iss funny, though, cos he's so quiet, ay he?

I know. All he does is stay in the house and do his schoolwork. I went in his room the other day and he'd got this jazz on the radio – summat Andrew listens to actually, but still – he's seventeen gooin on seventy, I tell yer.

An then he dresses as a clown all day on a Saturday, giving out balloons to kids in the middle o the Merry Hill.

Arr, well.

Do his mates know he does it? Doh kids tek the piss at school?

I doh know, really. He never says nuthin. His onny mates am all the sort that just do their work an that, really. Mind you, I was like that, wor I? Iss onny after school that I loudened up really, wor it?

Arr, yow used to speak in that posh little voice an all.

No, I day, everyone just said tha.

Iss how come yow con get rich solicitors to tell yer they love yer, honest, I cor spake like it.

I doh know what yome gooin on abaht. Sarah made her accent as broad as she could.

Michelle smiled and then yawned. I want me lie-in an me bacon sandwich in the mornin, I tell yer.

Is yer dad still doin that for yer?

Arr, he loves it. Since Mom's left he's just et fry-ups all the while. Just ates fry-ups and teks his happy pills. He's purron abaht a stone. I keep tellin him he's gonna gi hisself a heart attack. Iss fuckin great, really. Murder for me skin, though. I'm covered in spots. I've got abaht two inches o foundation on.

Doh be stupid, yow've got great skin.

I've got the wust skin of any beautician ever. I jus cor be arsed with it all. It ull happen tonight, I know it. I'll wek up in the morning an me piller ull look like the bloody Sahara desert an I'll a them big panda eyes an there'll be a full bottle o Clarins an a roll o cotton wool on me bedside gatherin dust.

An a load o phone numbers off blokes who wanna goo aht wi yer. Yow shun't put yerself down, yer know. Andrew had taught her that, to be confident.

I doh. I ay bothered. Come on, what dyer want?

She sneaked away early: phoned for a taxi and then let Michelle know what she was doing while she was talking to her friends from work, the ones who'd got them on the guest list. It meant Michelle didn't try too hard to persuade her to stay out. She was only being a friend, though, helping to keep her mind off things. And so she was home at a reasonable time – not ordering pizza on Brierley Hill High Street at three o'clock in the morning – and up to see her parents pulling off the drive at half past six.

You could come with us, you know, her mum had said unconvincingly.

No, I couldn't. Don't be silly. I'll be fine.

Her dad came and kissed her and gave her a hug. They were only taking the caravan to Devon for a few days.

There's money in the tin if yer need anythin desperate, love.

Standing on the drive in her pink slippers as they pulled away, Sarah realized that her mum hadn't kissed her goodbye and that made her angry and upset again, then angry about being angry. She put the kettle on and went back to bed with a cup of tea and watched Saturday morning cartoons with the sound turned down.

They'd been OK, her mum and dad, but not brilliant.

You just go in, love, her mum said the other night when they got back from doing the shopping and Sandra from next door started waving them over. She knew she'd become an embarrassment. It used to be, Sarah's dealing with this at the solicitors' or Sarah's doing this course, in between bragging about the caravan. Now it was, You just go inside, love, like her mum didn't want to be seen with her.

It had always been the same. Her mum and dad liked to fit in, would always check that they were doing things right for this area and then sneer at people who didn't. Like when they changed from having the *Mirror* to the *Mail*, or when her mum began to drink gin and tonic. Their faces gave them away, checking everyone else, scared that some unnamed authority was going to come along and take it all from them – the good job with the council, their detached four-bedroom home – and deposit them back where they'd come from on Cromwell Green, where they still belonged. That was one of the reasons she'd been attracted to Andrew in the first place. He didn't have to worry about things like that. Perhaps he'd made her think this way about her parents. They were her mum and dad, after all. She was just taking things out on them.

That Saturday the traffic around the Merry Hill was terrible as usual. The car was hot and Sarah could feel Rob becoming more and more tense as it got close to his start time. Her back was stuck to the leather seat. She turned the radio on and began to sing along. Rob pulled a face.

Doh try an be all superior, Rob, not while yome dressed like that, anyway.

At least he'd been able to get changed at the house today. He was wearing baggy blue trousers and a bright orange waistcoat over his T-shirt. A big pair of clown shoes and a curly red wig sat on his lap. He couldn't put the shoes on and fit in the Mini. Sarah stood laughing at him on the drive as he tried to get in. He'd remained completely straight-faced.

I thought yow was meant to be a clown. Crack yer face, will yer?

I ay meant to be the one laughing, yow am, so I must be doin summat right.

Sarah stalled the car at the island and car horns sounded behind her. Rob sighed and tapped his fingers against his giant shoes.

Yow coulda got the bus if yer wanted, yer know.

All right, sorry, I was just worried about being late, thass all.

What yer doin tomorra, Rob?

Nuthin much, I've got some physics to do.

Oh right, yow ay gooin aht then?

No, why? Dyer want me to?

To be honest, iss just that I saw Luke last week an he said he might come round one o the Sundays.

I day think yow was seein each other.

Well, we've got a lot to talk about.

Oh, right. So you want the house to yerselves. For a talk.

Thass right, yeah. I doh want yer to say nuthin to Mom and Dad, though, all right. Like I doh say nuthin about yer clown job.

Oh right, yeah. I'll goo out then if yer want.

Yer doh have to. I doh know if it'll be tomorrow, just one o the Sundays. You could just stay in yer room an do yer work.

She knew he'd be OK about Luke. When they'd first started going out Luke would kick a football about with Rob in the garden while he waited for Sarah to get ready. It saved him from having to sit and talk to her dad. That was before Rob went into his shell and became more interested in physics than impressing his sister's boyfriend. She'd talked about it with Luke once. He reckoned all his mates had gone into reverse, they were all bright at primary school and then lost interest later on. Risley had been really clever apparently. Even Banksy used to do his work, Luke said. It was hard to understand what happened to people. Rob was the opposite and it was best to be his way round. That was what Luke said, anyway.

She dropped Rob off at the entrance and went to find a parking space. It was humid and beginning to cloud over. By the time she got in the centre Rob was already performing, made up with a white face and a red plastic nose. She watched for a while, out of sight behind a pillar so as not to put him off, as he stood on tiptoe and pretended to struggle with the balloons he was selling, like they were dragging him skywards. A little girl stood in front of him, laughing. Slowly, he pulled down a Winnie the Pooh balloon for her. Her mum came and paid him, said something and smiled. He smiled back at her, a proper smile, not his usual grimace. Then he jumped into his blue plastic car and pedalled across to a little boy lying on the floor kicking his legs out violently in a temper tantrum, sounding the horn of the car as he went.

It was then that Sarah saw her and ducked back behind the pillar. Jennifer. The eldest girl, Tamsin, was with her. They were holding hands and Tamsin was carrying her riding hat. That's where she'd been going on the Saturday morning that Sarah had first gone over to Andrew's house. Jennifer had been away on business, a career woman. She wasn't wearing any makeup and she kept looking at Tamsin and smiling and nodding, not at all the monster that Andrew described, but then Sarah already knew that. She looked good for her age, her face much softer than in the photo that used to be on Andrew's desk. For her birthday, Andrew had bought Jennifer forty red roses and taken her to Bath for the weekend. Sarah had moped around, miserable with Luke.

They walked past. Sarah was still hiding behind the pillar. This was becoming a habit, avoiding people who terrified her while she was out. A couple of weeks ago, the day after he thumped Andrew, she'd seen Luke's mother in the market and had to turn and hurry away, expecting an earful or a slap round the face. She'd have given some back, though. This was worse. She wouldn't have thought Jennifer was the sort of woman to be shopping at the Merry Hill on a Saturday afternoon. Perhaps Tamsin wanted something. Perhaps they were just doing things to keep their mind off a daddy who'd run away for a 21-year-old girl who didn't even want him.

A woman whose life she'd ruined walked past holding her daughter's hand. For the millionth time since it had happened Sarah wondered how things had ended up the way they had. She wished she could go back and change everything; it wasn't meant to be like this. She kept going over things. If only this or that had been different.

Andrew had told her that the marriage was dead, that they barely spoke to each other. What did yer think he was gonna say, that he loved his wife an was very happy? her mum had screamed. He'd said other things as well, kinder and not so obvious, and the irony was that his marriage *was* over now. He was the one who'd done it. It was him. She never asked him, didn't want it.

And here she was now: a marriage-wrecker, a bitch who had taken a father away, a selfish whore who just went out and got what she wanted and couldn't care less about anyone else's feelings. That was how Luke had put it and who was she to argue?

Jennifer and Tamsin walked into Marks & Spencer. She might have guessed. She hurried away in the opposite direction, taking big gulps to get her breath back, her legs feeling funny as if she was walking through glue. All the people strolling past, getting on with their own lives, seemed alien to her. She didn't want a new pair of shoes now. She was meant to be saving, anyway. All she was doing now was walking around in circles; she'd be better off going home.

Some of it had been great, of course. The creeping around, the not getting caught. The way she could look at the other women in that office, especially the solicitors. She could look at them how they'd looked at her, with contempt. Contempt because she was just the receptionist, the girl who made the tea; jealous, too, because they could never look as young or as good as her in a tight scallop-necked top or in a short skirt with no tights on a summer's day. They needed tights to hold themselves in, the old battleaxes, in their tired suits. Contempt. Or being in his office and taking just too long at the filing cabinet and knowing that he was looking and them knowing that he was looking. Or leaning forward at the front desk. It was corny and exciting. Sexy, even. Yes, some of it had been brilliant.

Andrew had made her feel great and Luke couldn't make anyone feel great, least of all himself. But that didn't mean it was Andrew and not Luke, not for her. It would have to be someone else now. A long time in the future, at least she knew that now. Engaged at seventeen, rushing into work, too quick to grow up; too keen, that was all. It wasn't the worst crime in the world, but it was a crime – Andrew had shown her that: talked to her about all the things she could do with her life, all the possibilities. When she pictured him now, though, close-up in the suit she thought was so smart at work, smelling of whisky or red wine, his grey hair and skin that was so *old*, she shrivelled up inside. She wanted the whole thing to go away.

What was he like, yer know? Michelle had asked her almost in a whisper. Sarah just shook her head and said nothing.

She was back to her brother doing his comic turn with his balloons. Or had he moved? Everything looked the same in here. He was juggling now. Badly, but pretending he was good and doing it on purpose. Really, he couldn't juggle at all, so Sarah supposed that made it extra funny. All the children and old people laughed as the balls went bouncing away from him and he went, all arms and legs and poker-faced, after them. Of all the strange things in the world: her brother the comic genius.

Andrew was sitting in his car, parked on the bend in the road, when she got back. Just sitting there.

She went through it all again that night.

You're too young to be thinking about getting married, he'd said, laughing, when she'd told him she was engaged. It's ridiculous, you've got too much potential, you shouldn't be sitting there as a receptionist all your life. What does Luke do? That was the other thing, he asked about her life, like he was really interested, asked about Luke.

He works in a meat-packing factory making pork chops. Jesus, how bad did that sound? She nearly made something else up. Andrew didn't judge, though. He even said, Isn't he selling himself a bit short as well? He really cared.

That was almost a year ago; one thing led to another. She

knew it was going to happen ages before it did. She was asked to work as his personal secretary; they talked; he lent her some books, told her about the evening access course that might help her go to university; started to give her a lift home every now and then, jazz playing in his car, different to any music she knew.

She'd even told Luke, trying to make him jealous, she supposed, but something else less devious, too, showing him what life could be like. They'd met up at the Christmas do: Andrew and Luke standing at the bar, getting along. Luke having a proper conversation instead of grunting at his mates.

He's all right, yower boss, intelligent, like, Luke said later.

He's definitely selling himself short, Andrew had said to her in bed the day after.

She wanted Luke to find out. Wanted something to shake him out of his apathy, his inertia. He didn't care. She thought he never really cared at all. Not deep down. Even with that macho bit when he went up to the office and punched Andrew, he even did that half heartedly. If he'd really hit him he could have put him through the window. No, it showed her what she knew, that he didn't care about her at all. Nothing would ever get him going.

God knows, she'd spent long enough trying. They'd got engaged at seventeen – but there'd been no real proposal. She thought now that they'd done it as something to fill the time, a reason for a party in the upstairs room at the Saracen's. There was more to it than that, though. When she'd first seen him, she couldn't keep her eyes off him. The way he'd do everything as if he was holding something back, like he could be great at everything if he wanted – even on the edge of the dance floor when he'd do this little dance as if he was warming up for something really good and then just wander back to the bar and not dance at all – it drove her wild, then. She was so happy when they got engaged, kept thinking he'd open up to her, that she'd be the one. But she came to think there was nothing there: he was empty, just interested in looking hard. They were all like it, though, those boys from Cromwell Green. Fighting and posturing was all they were bothered about, like their world was the only one. All the men she knew were like it, until she started talking to Andrew.

Her and Luke had finished weeks before he even found out about Andrew. They both said they'd had enough. She wrote him a letter confessing it in the end. It sums it up, she wrote, that we were engaged for three years and managed to split up without you noticing that I'd been sleeping with my boss for six months! She wasn't even sure if he'd read it. It'd taken him two weeks to go and punch Andrew, and half the town knew about it by then.

When Andrew told her he loved her, she'd felt so bad. She didn't want that. She was twenty-one years old, for God's sake, her whole life in front of her, as he'd been telling her for months. She could do anything. She wasn't going to give up her freedom, even to the person who helped set her free. How had it all gone wrong? It wasn't meant to end with Andrew as the loser, the one with the broken heart. She never asked for it. She never asked for any of that power. Well, maybe over Luke.

She's the one who's an affair with that solicitor, went conversations behind her as she walked down the street. He's got two children an all, left his wife an everythin, left wi nuthin now.

It was like everything around here, she thought. Things you said or did, multiplied by ten, took on a life of their own, never forgiven or forgotten. You couldn't just walk away; even the air felt heavy.

How had this happened? She couldn't have made it happen on her own, could she? It wasn't all her fault. It wasn't her.

*

She and Rob stayed in that night. Michelle had gone to Bingo with her auntie. It was nice and quiet in the house, cool after a storm. She'd got caught in the bad weather, couldn't see a thing in the rain and had ploughed through a huge puddle in the road at the bottom of Lodge Farm. The Mini had struggled to get up and over the hill in the gloom.

Come on, little Mini, she'd coaxed. A boy without a coat had stuck two fingers up at her as she drove past the reservoir wall. Then it began to hail. She recognized Andrew's Mercedes from a long way down the road, and she drove as close to the front door as she could, then made a dash for it, pretending she was running from the hail.

She put a couple of frozen pizzas in the oven for her and Rob and ate some grapes while she watched the Lottery draw. There was some wine in the kitchen somewhere, or she might drink some of her mother's gin if they hadn't taken it in the caravan. She took a pizza up to Rob's room for him, poured a glass of Coke as well.

Here yer go, Coco. I did a Hawaiian, thass yer favourite, ay it?

Used to be, I don't mind now. He sat at his desk with the curtains closed and the reading lamp on.

What yer got the curtains closed for? Iss gone lovely again now. She pulled a curtain back; Andrew's car had gone.

It helps me concentrate.

He kept staring at the thick book in front of him. It had the tiniest writing Sarah had ever seen.

Got yer jazz on again, as well.

Yeah.

She put the plate and the glass down on the desk next to the book. You OK?

Yes. He sounded irritated. She wanted to say something about his clown's act that afternoon but didn't know what.

Onny asked. She backed out of the door and began to move downstairs.

Thanks, he said, for me pizza and tha.

After she'd eaten she found the wine and poured herself a glass. She went to her room and pulled out a folder. She'd taken it from work, had stolen some stationery when Jamie delivered a big order to the office and there'd only been her there. She'd given a lot of it to Rob. She took out her pay-slips and her building society book. She wrote down what money she'd got. She could sell the ring – if he thought he was getting that back he'd got another think coming. Her dad might let her sell the car. Or she might need it. She took the university guide from the folder and began flipping through, trying to decide. Andrew had been to Nottingham. They'd been there together once, pretending to be at a meeting, and walked around the shops. He showed her the university, where he lived when he was there. Maybe she wouldn't look there, then. She studied the map inside the front cover. Aberdeen would be a good one, Belfast perhaps. Somewhere far away, she thought. Andrew, Luke, they could ruin their lives as they saw fit but not her. It wasn't her.

Luke

David Risley stood on the garden path, the sun directly behind him. Luke could only see him in silhouette, his six-foot frame, his hair stuck up in a tuft at the back. Ris was wearing his usual outfit – jumper, jeans and shoes – despite the heat. At least he'd got rid of those shell-suit bottoms. His arms rested at his sides, his fists half clenched.

Yow'll atta sit down, Ris. I cor see yer in the sun.

Risley replied slowly, Yer hat ay working, then? He laughed and walked towards the kitchen door. Luke was wearing a sun visor with a green plastic shade with palm-tree designs and BLACKPOOL printed across the headband. He'd found it in the back of his wardrobe while looking for more old toys to add to Alice's pile downstairs.

Piss off, this is me poker hat. Iss a quality item, this, mate. Yer know when I buyed this?

When?

When we went to Blackpool wi the school. Dyer remember? On the coach, when we was at Cromwell Green in Miss Mitchell's class? Yow rid that donkey into the sea cos yow'd kicked its sides an it took off wi the bloke chasing yer. Thought yer was Zorro or summat. Fuckin funny.

Huh, I remember, arr.

Yow kicked Michael Haynes an Banksy off the back seat so we could sit wi Sally an Donna on the way back. It was brilliant, man.

An the cans o pop.

Oh, fuckin hell, yeah, remember? How much trouble was there abaht shekkin up the cans o pop? Our mum had to goo up the school an see ode Jacko. Onny time her ever had to, mind yer. I knew better after, I got a right good hiding. Funny, though. Remember? Michael Haynes had that stain on his shirt even after the holidays. Scruffy bastard. We used to tek the piss out on him, day we?

Arr. How is it? Risley nodded at Luke's bandaged hand. He'd had it wrapped up for a week, spent four hours at Russell's Hall casualty the afternoon after the fight at Caesar's. At least it'd stopped him going round to Sarah's, he thought.

All right. I've gorra have an x-ray again this wik to see if they gorra break em again. Fuckin painful, I tell yer.

He'd broken two fingers, right by the knuckles. Nobody at the hospital was that sympathetic. He'd tried a story about having fallen over, but the doctor cut him short and said, No you didn't, you punched something or someone, in the kind of authoritative voice that Luke hated.

Risley tutted and sat down on the plastic chair next to him. Luke was reclining in a striped deckchair next to the back door; a radio, a bottle of lemonade and an ashtray on the floor by his bare feet. A plastic bag full of empty beer cans was outside the back door. He'd stayed in the night before, afraid of hurting his hand again. Beneath the visor his eyes were red and puffy, his hair stuck out at angles above the headband. He was wearing baggy blue shorts and an old yellow and green Albion shirt that was too small for him.

Dun yer want some o this? Luke passed Risley the lemonade.

There was a noise from the kitchen. Mary came out to the back step. Ooh, he picked up his bed and walked. She stared at Luke and shook her head.

Ullo, David, yow all right?

All right, arr, thanks. Risley nodded and followed her gaze to Luke in the deckchair.

Look at the state on him. Yome wuss when yer stop in. I cor believe yer drunk all that last night. I thought yow'd onny had a couple. I cor tell yer what yer dad said to me this morning, he's ever so angry wi yer, Luke. Yow left the back door wide open. Anybody could a bin in here. Yow think yow'd learn. I ask yer. An if yome gonna drink that pop out here then put it in a glass. Anybody ud think we day have no cups in the house, swiggin it aht the bottle on the back step.

She went inside and returned with three glasses. Yow con pour me one an all, iss bin too hot this mornin, runnin rahnd.

Wheer yer bin, Kerry's?

Arr, I looked after Alice so as her could goo an do a bit o shopping in peace.

Wheer's Tim?

He's got some work in Manchester this wikend. Comes back tomorra night.

Oh, has he?

I know, arr. I doh know wass gonna happen theer, son, I doh. How's yer mother, David?

All right, thanks.

Tell her I said hello. Yow two gooin out?

Depends whether yow con ode a snooker cue. Risley nodded at Luke's hand.

I con ode one, I doh know abaht usin it right.

Watch what yome doin, for God's sake. I should rest it. His mum looked down at his hand and shook her head.

The garden gate rattled open. Ken walked down the path, his hands and face oily from working on the car.

All right, Dave. How am yer, son?

All right thanks, yeah.

Thass good. Ay it hot? He turned his attention to Luke before crossing the kitchen step, shaking his head.

Well, yow look bloody well in that outfit, yer saft devil.

When everyone had gone, Luke sat dozing in his chair, pretending he was somewhere or somebody else. He wondered how hot it could be in Spain, how much hotter it could feel than this.

Yer mother might a chosen to believe yer story abaht fallin over, but I ay. We wor born yesterday, Luke, his dad had said during the week while they took it in turns pushing Alice on a swing in the park. Luke was off work because of his hand. Iss obvious what yer bin doin. I ay bailin yer out when yer get yerself into trouble. Is there anythin yow need to talk to me abaht?

No, Luke said, I doh know what yome on abaht. I fell over, I tode yer.

Yer wanna pull yerself together.

And Luke hadn't made things any better when he tried joking with his dad on Friday morning. Iss all right, this not havin to goo into work, yer know. Iss like bein on holiday all the while.

Ken answered quietly, didn't even look at him. Iss all right when yer gorra work to goo back to, arr.

It had been a good week, though, sitting out in the sun, playing with Alice when Kerry brought her round, having a beer in the daytime. He rebuilt the Lego street again to show Alice, lined all the people up in little families outside their houses. Then they stampeded the zoo animals down the street: carnage. Alice rolled around giggling, then demanded, Again! Again!

In the garden, going through the names of the animals with her, he'd that same feeling again of being outside of himself, far above everything. Turning the animals over in his hand, saying their names and encouraging Alice to repeat them: he'd done the same thing with Adam. It had been that night. After the accident, the animals were left scattered around the garden for ages like they'd been flung from their cages. He saw himself from above, a six-year-old boy sitting on the back step with his little brother, passing him toy creatures from the bag one at a time. He'd never remembered details like that before. Usually his memory skipped from an image of him in the garden with Adam to, the next thing, sitting in Solomon and Iris's kitchen drinking a milkshake, knowing that something terrible had happened.

Last night he'd just sat out by the back door drinking can after can of lager, just tipping drink into some sort of hole that he'd never fill. He felt as if he'd never get drunk. He must've been, though.

Late on, his head had started working like it did sometimes, filling the gap between this new memory – playing with the animals – and sitting in Solomon and Iris's house, the plastic chair sticking to his legs, pink froth from the milkshake on his lips and nose.

He'd got up and sneaked through the kitchen and living room to the front door. He put it on the latch, tried to claw the door open with his fingertips. It wasn't even the same door. He felt a sudden surge of nausea, disgust, and blundered upstairs to bed, curling up with his clothes still on, trying to shut everything out. That was how he'd left the back door wide open.

Jamie's van pulled up against the fence. Luke thought of going in before Jamie noticed him. He'd seen him twice with the bandage on his hand and hadn't said anything about the fight up at Caesar's, about Luke saving him. Then, on the Saturday afternoon, when Luke had said he thought he might need it x-rayed, Jamie offered to drive him down to the hospital but still hadn't asked him how he was. When it came to it, though, Jamie was at Julie's on

Sunday morning, so Luke got the bus. Since then, not a word from him, the ungrateful bastard.

Luke could hear Jamie and Abdul arguing about how best to unload the washing machine from the van. As the pair of them waddled awkwardly through the gate carrying the machine, Luke saw a look flash across Jamie's face before it split into a grin.

All right, Luke. Yer know Abdul, doh yer? Any chance o some help wi this?

Luke just raised his bandaged hand.

Oh arr, shit. Sorry, mate.

Once they'd got it set up in Jamie's mum's kitchen, Luke thought they might come out to have a chat, but they didn't.

Late that afternoon the weather broke. The wind rose and clouds came over and thunder boomed like houses falling down in the distance. The first big spots of rain splashed through the open windows and his mum rushed around the house banging them all shut. The smell of wet ground drifted through the back door. Do us a bit o good, this ull, cool everythin dahn a bit, Ken said, sitting at the kitchen table.

The sound of car alarms replaced the boom of thunder and the rain was bouncing off the concrete, torrents running along the gutters and down the garden path. Cars crept by on the main road, their headlights cutting through the gloom. Then the hail came and carpeted the front lawn and the road in white and, as the ice glistened and melted, the clouds turned yellow. Frogs and locusts next, Mary said, pulling back the net curtains. Luke watched steam rising off the garden fences, his hangover clearing.

Do us the world o good this ull, Ken muttered, his lined face reflected in the kitchen window. The world o good.

*

Luke was trying to concentrate on the nine o'clock news but the sound was too low and all he could hear was his mum on the telephone, talking to his sister about the price of something at Tesco. On the screen, United Nations soldiers in blue helmets stood around doing not much. He couldn't understand why they wore those helmets, surely it made them easier to identify? Then there were shots of battered old coaches rumbling down a dusty road with thin, hollow faces pushed up against the windows. They discussed the report in the studio. Nobody seemed that bothered. His dad changed the channel. Luke didn't say anything.

At least they hadn't shown anything too bad tonight, although sometimes it was easier to handle when they did. If they just hinted at what was happening, like with those faces pressed up against the windows, it left a gap in his knowledge which his head started working to fill in.

The red ball rattled in the jaws of the pocket and came back out. The cue ball kissed the blue as it rolled back up the table. Luke lowered his head, sighed and then lifted his face and smiled at Risley. Ris had booked a good table. Its smooth green baize glowed in the overhead light. The club was quiet, less than half full. The occasional murmur of *shot* and the click of the balls and spark of cigarette lighters were all that disturbed the musty air. Risley's fat fingers wrapped around the cue butt, Indian ink pin-pricks obvious on the white skin of his knuckles. *Thththsssmack* as he potted the red Luke had missed and the white spun back.

Shot, Ris, Luke murmured and took a sip from his pint of mild.

Risley was a good player and was winning easily, though it was usually closer. They played for twenty pence a frame and Risley was on for a five-frame whitewash. Risley looked at home around the table, always seemed to be thinking a couple of shots ahead, his upper body bent flat against the cloth. He could have really done something with it, Luke thought. Risley left him with a shot from right against the top cushion. Luke stood up, looked at the position of the balls and blew his cheeks out.

Fuckin hell, Ris, yome playin well tonight, mate.

Not too bad, not bad.

On the front step of the snooker club, Luke ceremoniously handed Risley his pound and then lit a cigarette. The club sign and the streetlights reflected red and green and orange in the puddles in the road. They stood leaning against the door for a moment; a swastika and GORNAL WOLVES KICK TO KILL was carved into the scarred, splintered wood.

Fancy some chips afower we walk back?

Arr, goo on then.

We con beat the rush afower the pubs turn aht, unless yer want another pint, like.

Nah, I'm hungry.

Am jus tryin to spend yer winnings for yer, mate.

Huh, arr.

Luke looked at his face in the shiny mirror at Bayliss's fish and chip shop. The mirror of truth Jamie called it; the bright electric light bouncing off the white tiles and the metallic hot cabinets gave sharp lines and definition to every reflection. His face looked grey and tired, and he turned away.

Salt and vinegar, lover?

Arr, plenty please.

Sall in the wrist, look yer. The dark-skinned girl who was serving gave Risley a crooked smile. She wore hooped earrings and sovereign rings, maintaining her stare as she drowned the bag of chips in vinegar. Luke watched the shape of her body underneath her green overall. It was better than looking at himself in the mirror.

Bin out tonight?

Eh? Oh arr, jus for a gaeme o snooker.

Thass another thing needs good wrist action. Dyer win?

Arr.

Thass good. Talkative, ay yer. Here yam. Best chips in the town, yow see.

Arr, thanks. Risley took his chips, turned and shuffled towards the door.

Seeya, then.

Ta-ra.

Seeya, Luke called as he left the shop, but the girl's eyes followed Risley.

They walked along the road eating their chips, towards the empty market stalls where they could sit down.

Fuckin hell, Ris. What yer playin at? Her was gaggin for it, mate. Should o kept her talkin. Yow was in theer.

Risley shrugged and tore his chip bag open wider. A car's headlights moved across them and the striped canopies of the stalls. From away down the High Street came the sound of breaking glass, then laughing and echoing footsteps; then it was quiet again.

I doh know. I cor mek yer out, Ris, seriously, I cor.

The telephone felt hot in his sticky hand and he shifted position on the stairs again. Through the frosted glass of the front door he could see his dad's shape bend and rise as he attended to the roses along the path. He could smell Sunday-morning bacon cooking in the kitchen and hear his mum singing along to Radio 2. He took the cigarette packet with Lisa's number on it out of his pocket, smudged and starting to fade – he still hadn't phoned it. Turning it over in his hands, he dialled Sarah's number. Better the devil you know, he thought.

*

Luke lay on the steep bank at the school end of the mushroom field. The grass was spiky on his bare legs. He watched the football, killing time before he went to Sarah's, groups of Albion, Villa and Wolves shirts swarming around the ball. He put his good hand behind his head and gazed up at the sky.

There were shouts from the pitch as the ball got stuck in the fence of one of the houses that backed onto the field and the players piled in. Wood splintered as kids' bodies crashed against the fence and suddenly the ball was out and halfway across the field again.

Little Lee Banks kept trying to push the ball through everyone's legs. He was a good player – on the books at Walsall – but was as mad as the rest of his family.

Oh yes, it's number six, Lee announced in a gravelly voice that didn't match his age or size. The Banks of England, he shouted. And, a few feet from the pile of shirts and sports bag that made the empty goal, he launched the ball fifty yards into the bushes and stinging nettles at the far end of the field to a volley of abuse from both sides.

What yer done that fower, stupid cunt?

Yow con fetch that nah.

Big-headed little bastard.

Lee blew kisses into the air and kept on running to the fence, scrambled over and disappeared from view. After a lot of grumbling, the players trooped down to the end of the field with sticks to find the ball.

It would be the season again, soon enough. It felt strange, lying there in the sunshine, imagining the muddy, icy Sunday mornings of winter, feeling his skin reddening in the heat as he pictured the steam rising off players and hot tea in the November-damp, freezing wooden shack that served as a dressing room.

All right, Luke, a voice called from the shadows under

the trees. A figure dressed in white trainers, shorts and a tennis shirt stepped from under the hanging branches. The white clothes dazzled in the sunlight.

Nicky! All right, mate. When did yer get back?

Nicky folded his long tanned limbs to sit next to Luke on the bank. His sun-bleached hair flopped onto his face and he pushed it away with one hand, extending the other for a handshake, grinning.

Couple o days ago. I bin catchin up wi me mom an dad an tha. How am yer?

Good, yeah, all right. Saeme as usual really. How was it then? Bet yer got loads o stories.

The last time Luke had seen Nicky had been a leaving party at the Saracen's, before he flew off to Bangkok and six months' travelling in Asia.

I suppose, arr. It's fuckin mad aht theer, though, I tell yer. Great, though. I had a great time. I wanna goo back already like, Australia an tha.

Fuckin hell, back two days an yome off again.

Nah, it ay tha, iss just that yer get used to it, the travellin rahnd.

What was it like on yer own, did yer meet people?

Arr loads, like. All the backpackers goo to the saeme places an yow see the saeme people all the time, like. I teamed up wi this Scottish couple an then an Aussie bloke. Thass how I might end up gooin back aht. Well, to Australia, like. Sydney.

Was there much fanny? Luke wished he could think of a more interesting question.

Fuckin hell, mate, arr. Not so much the locals an tha. A lot of iss a bit dodgy, ladyboys – yer know, blokes med aht to be women, like – but the travellers, arr.

Great stuff.

Woss happenin wi yow then? Yow an Sarah split up, day yer?

Arr, right fuckin headache, really. Still, I'm a free man, I spose. How dyer know tha, any road?

I spoke to Stevo yesterday an he gid me all the gossip.

Was gonna say. It was big news, like, but I day think it ud reached Thailand.

An what yer done theer? He nodded at Luke's hand.

Fell over pissed. They both laughed.

Luke looked at Nicky lying back on the grass. There was a line of white skin where his shorts had pulled up above his tan-line. They'd been best mates for years, through primary school and the first part of secondary school; now they were struggling to find things to say. The two of them and Jamie and Risley had seemed to stand apart a bit from other boys on the estate, not obviously, but automatically, with nods of the head and a cagey, defensive way of talking to those outside the group. Luke remembered his first day back at school after Adam died – telling the other three what had happened in a corner of the playground away from the climbing frame, the tarmac wet after rain. Nicky shared his bottle of pop with him, put his arm around him to push in front in the dinner queue.

An old Sierra drove in through the narrow gate at the bottom end of the field, house music booming from its open windows. The wing mirror on the driver's side hit the gatepost as the car kangarooed onto the grass and the glass shattered. There was laughter from inside and the wheels spun and raised a cloud of dust.

The car turned and began a lap of the pitch. As it neared Luke and Nicky, a shirtless Jason Banks became recognizable, spliff hanging from the corner of his mouth. His brother Lee sat next to him, with two other lads bobbing around on the back seat. Lee's thin arms reached up to unhook the sunroof and he hauled himself up and struggled to get his head and shoulders through the gap. There was a scabbed-over mess of blue tattoo ink under his right shoulder. The music pounded. Luke moved his hand to wave at them – looking at Jason's hooded eyes – but then glanced at Nicky, who was watching the car and shaking his head. As the Sierra continued its lap Lee wriggled his way out to perch on the roof. Suddenly the car veered across the pitch and sent the remaining footballers scurrying. Lee extended his arms in a gesture of triumph. The car jolted along in rhythm to what must have been Jason's spasms of laughter. The footballers cursed, but not too noticeably, in the direction of the car and the whoops of delight coming from it.

People come from halfway around the world to have a look at this, yer know, Luke joked.

Nicky was staring straight ahead, his body chequered now by the shadows from the trees, shaking his head vaguely with a faraway look in his eyes.

Afternoon sunshine poured through the net curtains, patterning the walls. Their skin was stuck together and Luke unpeeled his leg from hers to cool down. She nestled her head in the crook of his arm and turned her face to kiss him on the mouth. For a moment he thought she was moving her whole body back into his but she rested her head on the pillow and took his hand and pressed his fingers against her lips. The yellow light moved slowly across the bedroom wall accompanied by the sounds of children playing in the garden next door.

Sarah's hair smelled of oranges from the cream she got from Michelle and the memories of this sent Luke drifting back through all the other afternoons they'd spent lying here when the house was empty.

He thought about how things happened, just happened, without much thought. Like him and Sarah. They'd got engaged in the week before her eighteenth birthday – it was romantic, he thought, in a way. They threw a big party at the pub, which was what people expected. They agreed on two years of saving before the big day and then kept getting nervous and putting it back. She talked about curtains and microwaves with his sister and came to his gran's house every Sunday night. It was never really roses and candlelight but life never was, was it? You just got together with someone and got on with things the best you could. People's expectations were too high sometimes. They'd been too young, that was all. The thing with the solicitor, it was a blessing in disguise really, although he could never say that, he had to act jealous.

She moved under his arm. You OK?

Yeah, fine. You?

Yeah, I'm glad yer come round.

Good. He squeezed her.

Dyer want anythin?

Wudn't mind a cup o tay. He nuzzled the back of her neck. She giggled.

I'll goo an mek one. Wiv got time, I think.

She pulled herself up and swung her leg across him so she sat astride his chest. The bed cover slipped off her shoulders. Her dark hair hung in her face. Her tight body was brown apart from three pale triangles of bikini skin. He reached up to her breast – they'd unwrapped his bandage and she'd kissed his swollen hand gently – and she sighed and bent down to kiss him, then rolled off and smiled.

I'll mek the tea, then, she said and pulled her dressing gown off the hook on the back of the door.

He heard her walk down the stairs and pad across the lino in the kitchen. The kettle switched on and the radio burst into life. Perfect. Luke pulled himself up from the bed and crept across the pile of clothes scattered on the floor to the set of drawers pushed against the wall. He pulled open the top drawer and scooped a pile of underwear to one side. For a moment he thought it was missing, and his heart skipped, but then his hand rapped against it. He pulled the small jewellery box out from the back of the drawer. He noticed a couple of condoms and tried to remember if he'd left them there. He pulled the box open and there, next to assorted earrings and the watch her grandad had been given for twenty-five years' service at the Revo works, was the ring: a slender gold band with a solitaire diamond. He took it out and pushed the box into the drawer, shovelling the underwear back into place and pushing it shut. Standing up, he paused for a second, seeing his naked body in the mirror on the wardrobe, then grabbed his jeans and pushed the ring down deep into one of the pockets. He got back into bed and pulled the cover right up to his chin.

When she came back upstairs he had his eyes closed, pretending to sleep. She came in carrying a tray with two mugs of tea and some biscuits laid out on a plate.

Here we go, look. She passed him the tray, undid the dressing gown and got back into bed. Wim easy on for time. We got another hour or so before me mom an dad am due back.

Oh arr. He grinned and she lowered her eyes.

Oh, I doh know, Luke, this afternoon's bin so nice. I was disappointed when yer couldn't come last week. I doh know why we jus doh . . .

I know, he said and took a sip of tea. I know.

It was getting dark and the clouds glowed pink and orange beyond the blackening outlines of the houses of the estate. A group of kids were hanging around outside the squat. Two bare-legged, mini-skirted girls sat on the rubble that had once been the front garden wall. One of them looked like Risley's sister. Two older boys stood in front of them, mountain bikes splayed between their legs. The group passed a cigarette between them. The arc it traced caught

Luke's eye as he walked past them on the opposite pavement and tried to look straight ahead. Dim shapes moved behind the broken glass of the bay window of the house. He heard a murmured Who's tha? from the group. Then, He's all right, he's gooin up theer. A few yards on a shout of All right, sexy came from an upstairs window. He didn't turn around.

He entered his granny's house by the back gate. Walking down the path he could hear voices and laughter coming from the kitchen. The summer-night smell of back-garden bonfires and petrol was everywhere. He pushed the door open wide and grinned his hellos.

Iss ower Luke, look yer.

Ooh, iss ower Luke.

He looked around the throng of faces in the kitchen. Only his nan and granny lived there now, but the house was always full on Sunday nights. Sitting down around the foldout table that held plates of sandwiches, cups of tea and a couple of bottles of Mackeson Stout were his nan and Auntie Irene. His mother and Auntie Maureen stood at the sink washing up. His Uncle Ted was sitting on a stool just inside the kitchen door dressed in a three-piece suit, his silver hair slicked all the way back with Brylcreem. In the middle of the room, perched in her NHS easy chair was Granny, his great-grandmother. She was ninety-eight years old and had been receiving Sunday-night visitors for sandwiches and a few drops of beer for seventy years. He bent down to kiss her.

All right, Granny, iss Luke.

I know, there ay no need to shout.

His lips touched her cheek. Her skin felt like crumpled paper, folded around the iron rod of her cheekbone. He thought of newspaper whipped and blown by the wind, caught on the railings of a sea wall or park fence. Wisps of white hair curled across her liver-spotted skull. She was tiny, buried inside the blue cardigan and cream blouse that was her Sunday-best outfit, but her eyes were shiny and you could see in the broad backs and strong faces of her daughter and granddaughter, and hear in her unlikely, deep voice, the woman she'd been. Her father had been a prize-fighter, ended up battered and senseless by the time she grew up, and was buried a few yards away from Adam in St John's churchyard. Her mother had been a farm girl from Worcester who walked it to the Black Country on the promise of running water and streets lit up at night by gaslight and the glow of the furnaces. He'd heard that story about a hundred times.

Luke kissed his nan and picked up a sandwich from the table. He could hear Kerry and Alice and the low voices of his dad and Uncle Mick in the next room. His mum glared at him.

Yome a bit late, ay yer. What yer bin doin?

I was over the field sortin out abaht football for the new season. Nicky was back from Thailand, so I was talkin.

Football season starts bloody earlier and earlier, doh it? his Auntie Irene tutted.

Nicky? Thass Eileen Bell's son, ay it?

Thass right arr, from up the maisonettes. Mind yer, they live in a big house on the Birmingham Road now. Done all right for herself. Mary seemed to aim her words out of the window.

Have yerself a plate for that sandwich will yer, yome drappin crumbs everywheer.

Has he bin away, then?

Arr, Thailand for six months.

What do yer do theer?

I doh know really. Just have a look around an tha, I think.

Ooh.

Iss amazin though, really ay it, these days.

Iss a shaeme yome so late, Luke. Yow missed Bernie an the twins and ower Becky an I think all the salmon's gone.

Sorry. I day notice the time to be honest.

Yow've interrupted the story now an all – goo on, Ted, carry on.

His mum touched his arm. Yer Uncle Ted was tellin us about Charlie Clancey comin in the pub the other day. Luke rolled his eyes and smiled. Charlie was the local rag and bone man.

Yow know who Charlie Clancey is, doh yer? Uncle Ted nodded at him.

Yeah. I sid Tommy in the pub last wik. He's aht again. He wished he hadn't said that.

Doh goo near him.

Yow stop aht on his road, nasty piece o work, him.

Arr, course he does.

Any road, I was in the Shakespeare the other dinnertime an he walks in with a bag under one arm, an leadin his hoss by the reins wi the other.

He took the hoss in the pub?

Arr, iss the truth. The women were beginning to squeal with laughter. Luke was wide-eyed and grinning. Uncle Ted paused, waiting until he got their attention again.

So he's stondin at the bar with the hoss stondin next to him an Keith – who's the landlord – comes from aht the back. Yow should o sin his faece, I tell yer. He says, Yow cor bring that in here, Charlie, I ay servin yer wi that. An Charlie Clancey says . . . hang on a minute. His Uncle Ted stopped to wipe his eyes and clear his throat. Any road, he says I ay servin yer wi that. An Charlie Clancey says, Wha, it ay stolen, I fun it at an house clearance this mornin, an he opens the bloody bag he's got wi him an there's a bloody shotgun in it!

The laughter had brought his dad from the next room to stand in the doorframe.

Wha happened then? Luke asked.

Well, this gun was pointin right at him so Keith says, All right then, what dun yer want? So Charlie says, Two pints o mild. Keith powers em an puts em on the bar an says, Two eighteen please, Charlie. An Charlie says, I ay payin, iss his bloody round, an points at the hoss.

This time the laughter filled the house. Luke doubled over with his hands on his knees and then looked around at the laughing faces. He heard his granny's throat rattling as she joined in the commotion.

As the uproar died down, his mother said in a concerned voice, Mind yer, it ay really funny, is it?

Police had to come in the end, Uncle Ted said from behind his handkerchief. Armed response unit.

It went quiet. Luke nodded a hello to his dad and motioned that he would go through to the living room when he got the chance. Mary spoke again.

Right, I'm gonna mek this cup o tay then wim gonna head off. Is everybody havin one?

Not for us, Mary, wim off dahn the road. Ted and Irene got up at the same time, stiffly, carefully. Irene touched the string of costume pearls at her throat. Ted adjusted his tie.

I'll get yer coat off the back o the cheer, Auntie Irene.

Well, goodnight one and all, Ted announced.

Night, Uncle Ted.

Ta-ra, Auntie Irene.

Irene Goodnight . . . Luke's nan started singing.

Irene Goodnight . . . Everyone else joined in.

Goodnight Irene, goodnight Irene,

I'll see you in my dreams.

More laughter and the back door swung open, letting in the cool air of the summer night. Luke smelled bonfires again.

He loved Sunday nights here. When he was a kid he used to dream of entering through the back door, having been away months or years, overseas somewhere, fighting a war or making his fortune. He used to imagine the crowd of glowing faces surrounding him in this kitchen, wanting to get a look at him, asking him how it had been, what it was like, wanting to touch the magic he'd brought in with him. All hail the conquering hero. I'm wasting my life, he thought abruptly.

He sat in the front room and ate another sandwich while they drank their tea. Alice had gone to sleep curled up in Kerry's lap. I'll have to get moving in a minute, she sighed. His dad and Uncle Mick sat talking on the settee. Luke leaned back in the chair, looking at the ornaments, the china figures and brass shapes, that surrounded the fireplace and then at the gallery of photos of grandchildren and great-grandchildren on the sideboard. Kerry wearing braces, him with spiky, gelled hair, that same angelic picture of Adam glowing down from the wall – next to it a hand-stitched prayer that he tried not to look at. He felt more comfortable with the picture of Adam here, though. The curtain between life and death always seemed thinner in this house, his granny sitting there in her chair, sometimes talking to her husband or even her old sweetheart, killed on the Somme, or her own dad, as if they were in the room with her, glass of beer in hand, rather than dead for forty years or more.

Yow'll atta get a new picture of Alice in theer, Kerry, he said listlessly.

I know, I've given Nan some we took when we went to Worcester the other wik. They come out lovely, actually, down by the river with the swans.

They all nodded their approval.

There was the usual debate about lifts home and who was doing what in the week. The hanging around made Luke think of work the next day – he had to turn up and see Alf and Peter Thompson about doing light duties while his hand healed. Kerry tucked Alice into the child-seat of her car, and Mick and Maureen clambered into their work van. Luke and his parents were walking back. He thought he might smoke the last of his gear out the bedroom window, calm himself down ready for work, and he checked his pocket and felt the hard circle of the ring underneath his keys. They waved their goodbyes to the cars from the pavement and watched his nan walk down the path and in through the back door.

Check her's locked it, his mother said, then they heard the bolt drawn across and saw the shape of his nan waving through the glass. Come on, then.

A spatter of wings came out of the trees behind the house and something small and dark flew above their heads. A bat, I think, his dad said. His mother pulled a face and shuddered. Music pumped from the upstairs rooms of the squat.

Bloody disgrace that is, Ken muttered. Fancy living next to it, he added, shaking his head.

They walked slowly along Cromwell Green Road. His parents walked arm-in-arm, which he liked. He walked balancing on the kerbstones and then caught himself doing it and felt childish. He almost told them about the ring, but then thought better of it. A dog barked and a car stereo boomed somewhere in the distance. As they came over the rise in the road they looked up at the castle. It had been lit from below with a honey-coloured light and glowed above the tops of the trees. A big half-moon hung, silvery, in the starry sky above it. It was beautiful, in a way.

Ken

Ken sat at the kitchen table staring at the shiny strip of paper in front of him. He held the pen ready but pulled his hand back and pursed his lips. He traced the outline of a cigarette burn on the table's laminated surface with his hand. Outside, he could hear children playing and Mary talking across the fence. The air in the kitchen was hot and thick. He looked at the paper again and considered the alchemy that could transform the exotic names – Green Gully, South Yarrowville, Sydney Croatia – into holidays and washing machines, houses and cars, and not having to worry about anything very much at all. He began to mark the paper. X marks the spot, he thought. When he'd finished he sat looking at the pools coupon some more. Outside there were children playing. He heard Mary's voice calling across the fence.

That afternoon, he stood at the fence and made careful sweeps with the paintbrush, checked his work and bent to the pot of creosote. The smell hit the back of his throat, a summer smell, he thought, glancing across at the rickety shed and deciding he should see to that as well, while he was at it. He made wide strokes with the brush and stood back to look at his work, then reached for the mug of tea resting on the fence post, took a drink and flicked it across the grass. He couldn't stand the taste of these new tea bags.

Extra value. Earlier, he'd made a cup using two bags, but it still tasted weak. He supposed he'd get used to it.

There'd been times when this job would've taken about five minutes – time snatched while the light was good after work, or on a weekend morning before going off to football or cricket. Now he tried to make it last all day, standing back every few minutes to check his progress.

Doin a grand job, Kenneth. Solomon walked stiffly up the path in the next garden. He was wearing a straw hat that threw half his face into shadow and a white shirt that hurt Ken's eyes when he looked at it.

Doh know abaht that, Sol.

Yes, yes. A grand job. You can practise on mine as well if you wish. He laughed his deep Barbadian laugh. Ken looked at the beads of sweat glistening in his greying side-burns.

If yer want. I'll do it tomorra. Woh be any trouble.

No, no. Solomon's eyes went wide. I was only joking.

Nah, seriously. I might as well. There's plenty in this pot an it ull be nice if they all look the saeme. I got nuthin else to do, he thought.

Well, Solomon thought about it, then nodded his head. Very good, if you want to it would be greatly appreciated. I think I've got some tonic left, so perhaps you'll enjoy a drop when it's done.

Solomon's tonic was a supply of white rum he got sent over from Barbados. It was 80 per cent proof. He often brought some round on Christmas Eve or on summer nights and he and Ken would sit at the kitchen table, breathing steam clouds with its strength, talking.

Solomon leaned across the fence conspiratorially. In Barbados, you know, we'd call that tonic the ladies' an babies' rum. That stuff just to warm you up before you get onto the real man's stuff. He laughed again and touched Ken on the shoulder. Knock on the door tomorrow when you're starting. His voice trailed off over the magnolia bush in the corner of the garden.

Solomon and Iris were good neighbours; good friends as well. They sat with Luke on the night of Adam's death and helped a lot in the weeks after it. They had no children of their own and always bought Kerry and Luke nice presents for Christmas and birthdays. It was strange, Ken thought, that it was Solomon he'd talked to most about Adam – if he'd talked to anyone at all – during those irregular drinking sessions, not sessions even really, just a couple of fingers of the tonic was enough to loosen the head and tongue. There was something in the way he listened, in the way he held himself, that made it easy to talk. Perhaps it was the feeling that he wouldn't judge. The non-judgement of Solomon: Ken smiled to himself. He felt awkward about their friendship, felt it was too one-sided, that Solomon and Iris had given more than he and Mary could give back, so he was happy painting the fence. He liked doing jobs. He liked working. More's the pity, he thought.

Later in the afternoon, two thirds of the way along the fence, Kerry brought Alice through the back gate.

Grandad's painting, look.

Painting, Grandad!

Thass right, darlin. Doh come too near it. Yer doh wanna gerrit on yer nice dress. Iss sticky, look.

Sticky?

Yer mommy woh be very pleased if yer gerrit on yer dress. He smiled at Kerry.

I won't, Alice, will I? I'll say, Naughty Grandad. Kerry picked Alice up and whirled her away from the strip of cut grass and onto the path. Ken held the pot of creosote.

I'll stop while her's here, if yer want.

No, you're all right. Carry on, Dad.

Yer mom ay in.

I know. I've just seen her at Granny's. She's waiting for the nurse to go round. Her'll be back in a minute. Nanny'll be here in a minute, Alice. I said I'd give her a lift but her wanted to wait.

Ken sighed. Her'll be waitin theer all afternoon again, he grumbled.

I'll make a cup of tea, Dad.

Kerry sat in the deckchair just outside the back door. She'd rolled up the legs of her tracksuit bottoms and held out her arms to the sun. Alice played at turning stones over in the shade of the fence opposite Ken, looking for woodlice. Kerry took some suntan cream from her bag and called Alice to her. Have you got any of this on, Dad?

Ken shook his head.

Come an get some on in a bit. You'll be burning up. What time you bin out here since?

I'm all right.

After a while Kerry announced, This tea's horrible.

Ken took a sip of his and looked at it. It seemed darker than before, perhaps he'd dripped the paintbrush into it. Sall right. Woss the matter wi it?

It tastes all grey an weak. I left it steepin for ages as well.

Ken started to say something, then changed his mind. He took another sip. Theer's nuthin up wi it, he said. Yome too fussy, thass all. It woh hurt yer.

That evening he sat on the back step cleaning the paintbrush. Every now and then he stopped to massage his knees. The fence looked good. Kids had set up a ramp in the alleyway with some wood. He could hear them pedalling down the slope on their bikes and the rattle of the wood as the wheels hit the ramp. Through the gaps in the fence he could see the blur of riders as they rode back to jump again. Eventually, one of the bigger boys split the wood and the game was over.

There was an argument, some pushing and swearing – Yow cudn't control a fuckin tricycle, yer spastic – but nothing else happened. It was terrible, the language they used now. Mind you, what they said wasn't the worst of it. Ken couldn't understand it. He used to give Kerry and Luke a whack if he heard them using language like that. Ken thought the bigger boy was Stan Lewis's grandson from Hinchingbrooke Lane. Stan who'd lost a finger, pulled off by a piece of steel cable hooking his wedding ring when he'd worked at GKN.

The boys began throwing bits of wood around. A pale boy with a shaved head whacked a piece against the fence. Ken thought about getting up to tell them off, then decided against it. People never said anything these days. The children drifted off in twos and threes with their bikes. Tim had been on about getting a little bike for Alice a few Sundays ago. Just before the accident Ken had bought Adam a tricycle. It sat rusting in the shed for years.

Ken sat in his armchair in the living room.

Luke came running downstairs and into the room. He'd had the afternoon off to get another X-ray. Ken had wanted to offer to drive him, but didn't trust the car to make it that far. It was a relief that his fingers were OK, didn't have to be reset. Ken thought Luke was secretly disappointed; he was enjoying light duties, odd jobs in the offices. Ken hoped it made him think about what he could be doing instead of spending eight hours a day at a machine making pork chops.

Luke stood awkwardly between Ken and the television set. The window was directly behind him, so Ken had to squint to look up at him. The chair seemed very low.

Yow all right?

I'm fine, arr, Luke muttered. Then he said, I got summat for yer, Dad. He pulled a folded envelope from his jeans and dropped it onto the arm of the chair. Twenty pound notes poked out of the torn edge. Iss the money for the engagement ring. I got it back off Sarah. It ay the full amount but iss what I could get. Two hundred an twenty.

Ken looked at the envelope without touching it.

Thass great, son, really.

I wen up the Jewellery Quarter after the hospital, thought I'd gerra better price for it. I tried the place we gorrit from but I ay got the receipt, an they onny wanted to gi me one eighty.

Thass what tham like, son. Ken looked up at Luke. The money was a surprise and a godsend. They'd said a hundred at the garage and Ken was worried that this time the car would have to go. Suddenly he resented Luke for standing over him and tried to raise himself from the chair, but the broken springs and his aching knees didn't allow it.

Thass great. Thank you. Ken pictured himself pulling the notes from his trousers at the garage. He thought of a box of proper tea bags and smiled. Does yer mother know?

No, I thought I'd give it yow fust.

Thass great, mate, really. Her'll be ever so pleased. I am.

I'm, err, sorry it took so long. Luke's voice was quiet.

All right, Luke. I know, son, I know. It wor all yower fault, was it?

Luke moved his head. Ken couldn't work out whether he was nodding or shaking it.

I spose, no. Luke moved from the sunlight and went to walk past the chair and into the kitchen.

Ken, still stuck down in the chair, grabbed his good hand. He nearly asked him to give him a hand up.

Iss all right, Luke. Yow've done the right thing. He wasn't sure what he meant. In the few seconds that he held Luke's hand, he was surprised at how rough and hard the skin felt.

Luke went into the kitchen. Ken finally hauled himself up

from the armchair and crossed to the window. His throat felt tight. Bloody cheer, he muttered. He pulled the net curtain back and looked at the railings that the council had put up after Adam's death to stop other children running out into the road. Further along was the gutter where, on bad days, Ken imagined he could still see the stain from a puddle of blood. Blood took ages to wash away, he knew that. Tonight, though, he just stood and took some deep breaths and looked at the traffic, what little there was now with the speed bumps.

Maybe Luke was getting his act together; he needed to, that was for sure. The business with Sarah must've hit him hard, the way he'd been moping around, drinking. Ken tried not to show how angry he got with him but Luke knew, wasting all his abilities, opportunities, when he had a brother who'd never had any chance in life. It was selfish.

Ken unscrewed the hinges of the old wardrobe. A tape measure and his saw lay on the bed. The wardrobe looked as if it might collapse, stuffed with the debris of twenty-odd years of family life: incomplete jigsaw puzzles; a deflated football; an electronic football game with its wires hanging loose. The wardrobe wobbled and three boxes slid from the top shelf and banged against his chest as their contents spilled across the floor. Mary turned the radio down and shouted upstairs but he didn't answer.

He sat on the edge of the bed and sifted through the boxes – folders stuffed with old photographs.

There'd been years when he just couldn't have looked at them. He remembered making a bonfire from some on a raw Sunday afternoon when nobody else was around, one of those November days when it never seemed to get light. It must have been the first autumn after the accident.

Tentatively, he took a few packs of photographs, held them by the edges, and opened them at random.

All of them outside Mick's caravan at Barmouth, Kerry doing a cartwheel across the springy grass.

Him and Mary at the flat in Wolverhampton Street, the orange bars of the electric fire glowing.

Mick at Granny's house cuddling Maia, the whippet he used to race. She went blind, her shrivelled eyes weeping constantly, just like Jamie's Bella.

Luke in an Albion shirt.

Adam wearing a cowboy hat, the nursery school fancy dress parade.

Adam's gravestone, the flowers bright against the washed marble.

Adam.

Luke.

Kerry.

Adam.

Adam.

He sat on the edge of the bed and rubbed his face; he needed a shave. You had to try not to think about it all. They were always there but you tried to shut them out, keep them to the edges. Then something would happen, somebody would say something or a date would come by or a load of old photos would hit you on the head as if they'd fallen from the sky and you just had to look and then the work of pushing things back to the edges began again.

He put the photos back into the folders, not looking again, and held the wardrobe door, ready to take it outside to saw the pieces of the board he needed to put under the armchair's sagging cushion, not thinking, trying not to think.

Kerry was cryin again today. Mary looked over at him from the settee and laid her magazine to one side.

Again? Woss the matter? I day think yow'd sin her today.

I day, I was on the phone to her this afternoon. Yer might know what the matter was. He wudn't let her have any money to get Alice some new dresses for when playschool starts again.

Well, her's got enough clothes, ay her?

Arr, course her has but that ay the point, is it?

No, yome right I suppose, it ay. Has her said anythin else to yer?

No, except her's unhappy an her doh know why her's with him. The usual, yer know.

Her's with him cos her thought he was gonna be her meal ticket, pay the way for her, buy her the things we cudn't.

He was angry with Kerry as well as with Luke. He couldn't work out what they'd done to have her turn out the way she had, not that anything was that bad, just that he'd always expected more.

Doh, Ken, it ay fair.

I know it ay, but it's the truth. I ay sayin I blaeme her neither. Not really.

Her's a good girl, though, love. Her does love Alice an her looks after her well. Her's ever so good wi Granny. Her helps me.

They sat in silence for a while. Ken looked at Mary, the light from the television flickering on her face, her hair tied back. There were streaks of grey in it but her skin was clear, her eyes shone darkly. He thought briefly about the first time he'd seen her, in the foyer at the old Plaza, standing slightly apart from her friends, broad and straight-backed, serious, severe even, her eyes eating everything up. He wanted to make her smile. He almost mentioned that moment, but started talking about Kerry again instead.

Well, if her has to come back here then her has to come. We'll find some way round it. Might be the best thing, to tell yer the truth.

Mary looked at him and shrugged. She went to speak

and then lowered her eyes and looked away. It felt unusual to have the house to themselves.

What?

Nothing, she said. Iss a tidy mess, thass all.

Dyer wanna drink?

Arr, why not. Come on, less cheer up, eh?

Ken walked through to the kitchen. He took some whisky that Luke had bought a while ago from the cupboard. He poured his straight, took a mouthful from it and then added another finger to the glass, then poured one for Mary and mixed it with water from the tap.

When he returned to the living room Mary had turned the television off. She was standing by the old record player, flipping through a handful of LPs she'd pulled from the pile. There was a hiss and the sound of the needle finding the groove and then Aretha Franklin's voice. Mary turned to him and he handed her the whisky. They moved closer to each other, holding their glasses, then embraced. Clumsily at first, bumping feet and the backs of their legs against the settee, they danced slowly around the twilit room.

It was early, half past six, and he left the house quietly. As he left, he'd heard Luke getting up and closing the bathroom door. Ken slipped out of the front door, sandwiches wrapped in foil tucked under his arm, walking quickly, the road wet from a shower of rain. The last summer like this had been the 1970s, the children had been small. Adam wasn't even born. Working the six till two turn, spending the afternoons sitting in the garden and watching the Olympics on television. He'd knocked a fifty in a works game; Mary, Kerry and Luke sitting on the steps of the pavilion. The house was new then. They'd still been working on the rest of the estate, pulling down the old maisonettes on Fairfax Road, boarding up the butcher's shop. He caught himself whistling through his teeth, stopped, thought what the hell, and carried on.

Mick sat waiting in his van outside the community centre at the bottom of the mushroom field. He passed Ken a copy of the *Mirror* as he jumped into the passenger seat.

Mornin.

All right, Ken. All set?

Arr, course I am, mate.

The van swung out onto the main road. Both men looked up and down to check for people watching but it was more a reflex than a fear of being caught. Every so often Mick would help Ken and Mary out with the offer of a day's work. You had to be careful, but they were sensible. That was the reason for the pick-up away from the house. Ken didn't do enough to raise any suspicion and most of the neighbours would only turn a blind eye anyway. You could never tell, but it was hard to picture Solomon on the phone to the Social. Mick talked about the job as the van slid down the dual carriageway, away from town.

Jus strippin these fireplaces really. Iss a lovely house, I tell yer. Ode girl who had it kept it lovely. They'd lived in India, the husband was in the army, like. There was loads o good stuff at the clearance. The couple tharruv bought it wanna replace the fireplaces, saft sods, more money than sense some folks, to be honest. Anway, thass wheer we come in. Yow'll be workin pretty much on yer own. I've tode my blokes that yow know what yome doin. Trev the chippy ull be theer if there's any problems. I'm off to get another job lined up this mornin – then I'll be back this afternoon to have a look at some wirin.

Whereabouts is it again? Martley?

Close. More this side really. Tay as big as Martley, the village, like. Coupla houses, a shop an a pub.

Thass all yer need, ay it?

As they drove Ken decided that he'd take Mary out for a

spin in the countryside when the car came back from the garage. He couldn't remember the last time they'd done that.

The place was a timber-framed cottage with an orchard behind it. Ken worked all morning in an upstairs bedroom. There was a huge, leaded bay window and whitewashed walls – except around the fireplace, where he chipped plaster onto a dust sheet and looked at the pencil markings left there by Mick for the wiring. The radio played in a downstairs room, broken only by the sound of drilling or hammering or shouts from one of the men working around the house.

At eleven he stopped to eat one of the ham sandwiches Mary had cut for him last night. It reminded him of the first time he'd helped open the furnace when he'd started at Round Oak, no more than a kid, ladling the metal off to get it onto a cast, worried it would go wrong, chewing his sandwich in the break afterwards, his throat too dry to swallow, taking one of the older bloke's cold tea to wash it down with.

Twenty-one years he'd worked there, on the furnaces and in the meltshop. The glow of the fires used to creep into his dreams. People got the wrong idea, thought the work was heavy and dirty – which it was, took it for granted when it was there – but a furnace can be beautiful too. Steelmaking was all about transformation, alchemy, a kind of purification. It wasn't something that could just happen by accident, it took all those men and machines, effort, industry, so that when you did your bit – tapping out the molten metal, for example – there was this sense of belonging to something, of being part of something bigger than yourself. That's what it was about, he would always tell Luke.

Iss a crime, he thought to himself, what happened was a crime. Yow tek these thousands o blokes, working, mekkin summat, for God's sake, livin theer lives, and the families they had, and the communities arahnd em. Not just the Round Oak, loads o plaeces. An yer just crush it. Just like tha. An yow expect everythin to goo on as normal afterwards. Well, things doh work like tha.

It was a shopping centre now. Merry Hill, even the name had to change. Like someone had pulled everything apart and just as quickly built this plastic town to cover the traces, like you could do with those Lego bricks he'd got out for Alice.

Kerry loved it, though. Merry Hill formed her in the way that Round Oak formed him. She was more interested in what she'd got, not who she was, but that was the problem with people these days.

I was a babby when I went to work theer, he thought. Fifteen years old, happy to be free of school and his old man. There was only the two of them. His mother had died when he was eight – he remembered a frail, kind woman. She hadn't deserved her husband, Ken thought. His dad was a cruel, silent man, his slight deafness adding to that; taut mouth and sunken eyes.

As Ken scrubbed the wood around the fireplace he could have been back that day scrubbing the stones in their kitchen. It was Saturday and he was meant to be at the district football game. There was a Wolves scout there. They always said that, even nowadays when he'd go and see Luke play. He had to finish the kitchen floor before he could go, rub a shine into the stones: that was the deal, some kind of punishment. His dad stood over him and told him that it wasn't good enough. He missed the match. His old man hated football. He hated everything and everybody, never relented, died that way. Ken never understood why he behaved how he did; perhaps it was grief or guilt. He knew enough about that now to think it was possible.

I started as a babby an left theer as a mon. It forged me,

he thought. An then we was drawn off as slag. An nuthin was ever right afterwards.

Adam died a few months after the closure. They were running these programmes for the redundant men, retraining sessions in Portakabins where you were forced to imagine non-existent jobs into life. That day had exhausted him so much he'd fallen asleep in front of the Midlands news. He never used to sleep in front of the telly when he was in work but the retraining stuff was wearing him down, so he closed his eyes to shut it all out. He'd left the door on the latch. It was Thursday, the night they collected the pools. The boys had been playing out the back. Kerry was in her room, sulking; she'd asked for a pair of shoes they couldn't afford. He'd heard the brakes and the sound of the impact through the open door. There was quiet, then screaming. Everybody out into the street. Somebody was screaming. It might've been him.

Bloody hell, yow've done loads. One of the young lads from downstairs stood in the doorway. Wim all knockin off for a bit downstairs – Mick's back. He's fetchin stuff from the pub up the road, I doh know woss got into him. Yer comin dahn?

Arr. Ken rose slowly from his crouching position. His knees cracked as he stood up. I'll follow yer, he said.

In the garden, Mick wandered in and out of the gate with trays of cheese cobs and pints of cider. One of the young lads complained about the cider.

Bloody cider country dahn here, ay it, near enough. Bloody philistine, Mick grumbled.

Yer bloody gaffer buys yer a drink an yome still moanin.

They sat in the shade with their backs resting against the wall of the house. Ken felt the sharp taste of the cheese and cider burn the back of his throat. He chewed slowly and rubbed his knees.

Mick eased down next to him. Iss a lovely afternoon, Ken.

Oh arr, mate. Lovely. Listen, Mick, Ken said quietly. Thanks for today, like. We really appreciate it.

All right, mate. Yome helping me aht. Doh mention it. Mick patted him on the arm as he spoke.

Ken liked his brother-in-law but always thought he was one for the grand gesture – like getting the drinks in just now; he needed to be the man in charge. He looked across the spiky green carpet of the lawn, eating and drinking slowly, enjoying the sunshine and the company.

That night, the sound of a lorry rattling along the road outside woke him suddenly. It must have hit a speed bump, can't have known they were there. The yellow streetlight outside the window glowed softly through the thin curtain, but it was still dark. Quiet again. He felt Mary breathing deeply next to him. He listened to his own shallow breaths and closed his eyes, then opened them. His heart quickened. He tried to turn but he couldn't move. His heart jumped. Invisible hands pinned him back, into the pillow and the mattress. He knew this feeling, couldn't move. Some force pressed him down; pains in his chest, his arms, his throat. He pushed air through his teeth and hoped it'd wake Mary, willing himself to relax.

He sees himself walking across the yard outside the shed at Round Oak. Nineteen; a thin film of ice cracking beneath his safety boots and then the ice disappearing as he entered the shed. Suddenly, he's playing football. One of the bank holiday games against Ravenscraig, Glasgow. He heads the ball as it drops through a steel-grey sky and a horizon of buildings to the green and black hills. *Well up, Ken.* He's clattered by their number nine. Someone says he had a game for Rangers reserves one time. Ken gives him four, five inches but wins every header that day. He finishes with a black eye, three loose teeth and free drinks all night. Now he's running, through the fields behind his house. The chicken coop, the goat tied up. He's standing in the kitchen there, in front of his mother, his knees grazed and bleeding from the fall, his face hot with tears, the smell of bacon and polish all around.

He tried to relax but memories kept jumping in, jolting him awake. Thinking, not thinking. Not thinking was the way to do it.

Later, he sat alone in the kitchen, swilling the last of his tea around the bottom of the cup. He dragged a hand across his stubbly face, gritty-eyed. Outside birds were singing. He followed one call, clear and shrill as it repeated from one of the trees high above the blue and black roofs. He sat alone as the light of the electric clock on the oven blinked on and off. There was movement upstairs and he stood up, feeling sick with the tea and lack of proper sleep. He moved slowly upstairs and back to bed, creeping through the creaking house.

Gonna have me a walk later, he said.

Watch what yome doin, yow look shattered.

I'm all right.

Mary was off to check on her mother and granny and call to the post office for them. She moved with the urgency of someone with a job to do.

Dyer want anythin doin?

Yow con wash them few things in the sink up if yer want.

Great stuff, he replied in a deadpan voice.

He walked through the streets of the estate. Somewhere in the distance was the sound of a lawnmower and the murmur of traffic. As he passed the row of shops on Cromwell Green he looked for Mary in the queue that snaked out the post office door. No sign of her. A fat woman stood at the entrance to the launderette, apparently gasping for air. A shirtless boy left the newsagent's with an ice-pole hanging from his mouth, a scabby fresh tattoo on his upper arm, and barged through the middle of the queue. Commentary from the morning dogs drifted through the open door of the bookies. Further up the road, outside the flats, was a Montego with all its windows smashed and two wheels missing. Light played on the shattered glass like water splashing from a fountain.

He walked downhill, past the allotments and out onto the Birmingham Road. Lorries and buses juddered past and he told himself he was all right now. He squinted up the hill towards the castle, the gradient pulling at his legs as he began to climb.

It was strange how whole areas had changed name, like the ones he walked past now, sometimes they'd have two names at the same time, used by different people. That was how Round Oak had become Merry Hill. The area where the big Tesco was now had been Ewart's, the brass stampings place, and beyond that Sankeys and Thomas Dudley and the Babcock. The other way, the way he was walking, next to Ewart's had been Gillotts factory and after that the County Ground, where he'd queued to watch Tom Graveney and Basil d'Oliveira. But the County Ground had fallen into the old limestone workings, neglected and dangerous now, disappeared into a hole in the ground. This impermanence of places that had seemed so secure. Ken had seen in the paper that Pailthorpes, the old sausage place with a football pitch so green and perfect that it'd been like playing on carpet, was now called the Quayside and had a huddle of orange starter homes built on it. He didn't know who they thought they were kidding. It seemed to work, though.

His mood lightened as the hill got steeper. What was left of the industrial traffic went rattling down Tipton Road.

He passed the old Hippodrome, the Plaza and the Odeon, and walked alongside the castle walls and listened to the clunk clunk of the empty chairlift climbing up to the castle itself. He looked over the walls and into the zoo. Two llamas, half bald, leaned into the side of the hill and paused to chew at the thick grass around their ankles. Through the turnstiles he could see the flamingos standing around the pool. He thought he should bring Alice to the zoo, wondered briefly if Kerry would approve, remembering her scrawling MEAT IS MURDER across her schoolbooks when she became a vegetarian for about three weeks aged thirteen.

The usual faces strolled up and down the marketplace. He nodded to a couple of people he knew from the estate, killed some time looking in the window display at Cash Converter, examining the mountain bikes and Gameboys that had long since been swapped for ready cash, no doubt long since spent. There were other men like him, wandering around on their own, their hair growing down onto their collars, hands in pockets, going nowhere in particular.

He did a couple of laps and then went home.

On the nights after Adam's death Ken went walking around the estate for hours. Through the empty streets, sobbing and raging. He staggered around until a ribbon of blue appeared over the roofs and the streetlights began to fizzle out. Then he'd lurch in through the back door, have a glass of whisky, a cup of tea, and sleep for a while in the kitchen chair. He should've been with Mary, he knew, but he just couldn't stand it. Those phrases: out of your mind, beside yourself – people used them without understanding what they meant.

On those nights, sounds kept coming from inside his chest, like an animal, from deep down, every few steps. He shuffled past familiar houses, past the shops on Cromwell

Green, along Hinchingbrooke Lane, back round Whitelocke Road, the odd light on in places, life going on. He ran his hand along the rough garden walls and fat garden hedges.

He stood for a while at the end of Vanes Road talking to a sapling: *Yow knew Adam, day yer? I got some bad news, son. He woh be comin to nursery any more. He's had an accident.* Stripping the bark from the thin trunk, leaving it lying there on the pavement like leaves, like autumn come early, the trunk pale and luminous in the early light.

He fell over a few times, came back with grazed hands and knees, from running across the mushroom field, shouting.

Mick drove up alongside him, red-eyed and in his pyjamas. Ken, get in the van, mate.

No.

Come on, get back to Mary. This ay right.

No, no, no.

He cut down the alleyway where the van couldn't follow.

Back to the daytime, to a short sleep in the chair and waking up to realize it all again. Back to a silent, different grief; muscles working to keep his face together, arranging things for the other two to do, endless days, the undertakers, the inquest, keeping it together.

It was his fault. Later, they argued about it. Neither of them saying what they wanted to say, wanting to blame, wanting to absolve. Ten years of silence. Years of not talking at all, to the children, yes, obviously, to her mother, to Granny, to Mick, Maureen, Solomon, Iris. Not to her. Getting on with things.

Silence.

Just cutting the flowers together to lay on the grave, him cleaning, her arranging. He didn't even do that now. Things were easier now, better. Time passed.

We had another son, you know.

Oh, what happened?
He died.
Oh, I'm sorry. People's sad eyes.

Alice squealed with delight as Ken pushed the swing higher. The park was quiet. Later in the day it filled up with teenagers, sitting on the roundabout eating bags of chips or doing tricks on their bikes up the seesaw. Ken had to unwind the swing Alice was sitting on from the crossbar. It was one of those safety swings with a seat and a bar.

Alice squealed again and flapped her arms around above her head.

Higher, again! Ken announced in a big voice. Not really, though. He knew he was already swinging her much higher than Kerry would have been happy with, safety seat or not.

Ken brought Luke and Adam here on Saturday mornings in the year of the accident. Kerry used to stay in to watch Saturday-morning television, already too grown up apparently. That was before the council had done the place up and there'd only been a few swings, a roundabout and a rusty climbing frame. Cinders on the ground. Luke had fallen one morning and taken all the skin off his nose. Mary had gone mad. Now, the floor was spongy, Astro-turf; somebody had tried to rip it up in one corner and it was pockmarked with chewing gum and cigarette butts. If you stood at the fence you could look across to the zoo and the castle. He used to stand there with Luke and Adam, looking down at the trains shunting steel tube to the freight depot, or pretending they could see the lions and tigers at the zoo.

He caught the bar of the swing and pointed for Alice. There's the zoo, look, Alice. Thass wheer wim gooin soon. Do yer know what animals we'll see?

The zoo, Alice repeated.

Thass right, darlin. We'll see lions. Ken roared as he pushed Alice back and forth again.

And bears. He roared, like a lion again. What sound did bears make?

And elephants. He stopped the swing again and put his arm in front of his his face as if it was a trunk. Alice looked a bit scared.

Lots of animals.

Luke had put the toy animals out on the Lego street in the front room. Ken had started building a couple of zoo cages from the spare bricks to put the animals in. He'd shown them Alice that morning.

Few more minutes, darlin, an we'll goo back an see Nanny. She was cheering now on every rise.

He never got phone calls so when the voice asked for him he thought it was somebody from the Social or the job centre, changing his appointment time again.

It is yes – hang on – which one? I'm Ken Wilkinson.

Yes, that's right, Ken. The voice on the other end of the phone was young and enthusiastic. This is Adrian Dobson from Maxtight Site Management. You applied for a job with us a few weeks ago as a security operative.

Yes, thass right. A job.

Well, there's a position come up at one of our new sites, Fairview Glades in Cradley. It would be for eighteen months but we have other permanent sites that we might then want to move you to after that. It's shift work. Earlies, lates and a week of nights every six weeks with three rest days following. Are you still interested in a position with Maxtight?

I am, yes.

Ken wondered if Adrian was reading from a script. He continued talking about pay – which was ridiculous considering it was shift work, but – and conditions and a uniform. Ken tried to take in as much as he could. He fumbled around the drawer for a pen and paper but couldn't find anything and then nearly dropped the phone.

If you could make it to the site tomorrow, say for ten o'clock. I'll meet you there and we can sort out getting you started by the end of the week really.

So, is this an interview tomorrow?

Well, of sorts. But to be honest, Ken, you seem just what we're looking for. We've taken to getting more mature people for these security jobs – people with a bit of responsibility. There's a couple of training sessions you need to go on, but they should be straightforward enough. Your references all look fine. So long as you're happy with things tomorrow and we get things straight with the job centre and get your induction done, we'll want you to start as soon as possible.

Adrian gave Ken the address. Ken wasn't sure where it was, which surprised him. He had to remember it and then run and write it down in the kitchen after the phone call. He tried to take in what Adrian had said. It all seemed very easy. Just turn up, we'll get you started. Like a job from the old days. He was shaking when he came off the phone. He'd forgotten what it was like, this feeling. If he was honest with himself he had all but given up hope this time, a year out of work, in his mid-fifties. Security. It was hardly ideal but, well, it was something. At least I'm joining a growth industry for a change, he thought. He wanted to tell Mary, had to ring her at her mother's. The doctor was going in to see Granny. He misdialled, then it was engaged. He walked into the front room and paced up and down a couple of times.

How many times was this? Five or six, now, since Round Oak, depending if he counted Hacketts Galvanizing, where he worked for two weeks before being stopped and messing all his benefits up.

A security guard? Mary said incredulously. I'm really happy yow've got summat, but is it safe? Yow ay gorra chase any robbers have yer?

He didn't know. Be satisfied, please. It might be all right. He'd see what it was like.

Well done, love. I am really pleased.

An yer gorra have a dog? Luke was laughing.

What?

A dog. They allus have dogs, yer know. Yow've gorra have a uniform an tha, did they say whether yow've gorra have a dog an all?

I bloody hope not.

Later, he sat in the chair with a cup of tea and the cricket on low, having doubts. I never told him I wor very good at locking doors, he thought darkly.

It turned out that Fairview Glades was by Corngreaves Golf Course. It was, in fact, in Cradley Heath and not Cradley. He'd known where it was all along; should've guessed they'd changed the name. Perhaps it improved the price of the land. The site had been levelled and was going to have a few industrial units and houses built on it. It looked out over the back of the golf course and the brook. You could hear the water from where they were standing.

Adrian was as enthusiastic in the flesh as he'd been on the phone. He talked excitedly about the foundations for the homes that were being laid out. There was some kind of old works building still to be pulled down on the far side of the site. Plants had grown in its guttering, making it look like it had a grass roof. A rain cloud closed in on Clent. It was a fair view – more than a fair view, they were doing themselves down.

The job itself was very straightforward. Signing people into a site book on early turns and signing them out on lates. There were different contractors doing different jobs and Maxtight wanted it all done properly. On nights Ken would have to set the alarms, check the perimeter every now and then and record all this in the logbook.

Ken then drove with Adrian back to the Maxtight offices in Birmingham to collect his uniform and sign a few more forms. Ken worried about the car standing up to the drive. There was an induction day on Friday. Then that was it.

That night he paraded up and down the front room wearing his uniform – black trousers, safety shoes and a white shirt with epaulettes – while Mary, Kerry and Luke rolled around on the settee laughing.

Glad I'm the source of all the amusement, he grumbled. He didn't mind, though.

A little boy had drowned in the West Park pond in Wolverhampton. He'd been in the park with his mother and other members of his family but wandered off and was found face-down in a couple of feet of water about ten minutes afterwards. He was five years old. It was in the *Star* and now it was on the Midlands news. Mary stopped as she came through the door to look at the television. Ken sat in his armchair. They were showing a picture of the park and of the flowers left by the side of the pool. Ken got the urge to ask, What did the mother think her was doing? Then he stopped himself. Mary tutted.

Iss terrible for em, ay it? She was biting her lip.

A photo came up on the screen of the little boy. He was grinning at the camera, his hair a bit wild. He wore a blue jumper. Ken imagined that picture on the wall of someone's front room ten, fifteen, twenty years on. The same grin and wild hair. The mother had been sedated, the reporter said.

I bet her has.

There was nothing to prepare you.

The body in the gutter. The way that from that angle it

looked like he was curled up and asleep at the side of the road, then as you got nearer you saw his leg twisted so strangely and the pavement darkening underneath him where the cracked bumper had cut him open. The lorry's front wheel next to his head. His poor boy. There must have been a second, a split-second, when he saw the lorry coming towards him, when he knew there was nobody, no Daddy, there to save him. The terror of it. Or maybe not. Maybe he didn't know. Maybe in that way and with that suddenness and him so young it was all right. The waste, the grief, the guilt. Is Adam coming back from the hospital? Luke had asked a few weeks afterwards. No, darlin, he woh be comin back. He was never coming back. He was always there. He'd left the door on the latch. Not thinking, that was the only way.

The job was reasonable. In fact, it was good apart from the money. It wasn't proper work with other people, other men. The blokes who signed in and out of the site book looked through him as if he was invisible. Maybe it was better on the early shift, when they signed in they wouldn't be in such a hurry to start work as they were to leave, human nature, he supposed. The other security guards were all right. You had a cup of tea together when you changed shifts. George was about to arrive to take him off. It was an easy job, not even really working. Sign in, sign out and a few lines in the logbook, a couple of laps of the site, a jangle of the keys and a check of the padlocks. He had the radio on most of the day. Hardly quantum physics, as George had said.

He was at the end of his first week of lates, doing his last walk around the site. It was good to be back in a routine, at least, and it was a nice spot. The houses were coming on. Quite how it was going to take eighteen months he didn't know. Perhaps they expected an earthquake or something. He checked the padlocks on the equipment stores and looked over the fence across the golf course. Dark clumps of trees lined the fairway and a little bit of mist was settling on the brook. He'd talked to a couple of greenkeepers when they'd been tending that part of the course. Golf wasn't his game at all, but he didn't mind it. There was an old eight-iron in the shed somewhere. Maybe he could get it out, have a bit of a whack about when the night was quiet. The greenkeepers wouldn't mind, he was sure.

There was a sound in the air. He looked up at a flock of geese flying low overhead in a strict V-formation, calling to each other. He'd seen them a few times, or maybe this was a different flock. They flew against the darkening sky. He wondered where they were going, the reservoir perhaps, or Haden Hill Park, or much further south for the winter for all he knew.

Luke

Light duties had been all right but now it was back to this crap. It was chaos. A big order was due out and Luke's machine had broken. Alf was pulling like a maniac at the blades. He was going to slice his fingers off, Luke could see it.

Does this attach direct to the belt? Alf asked.

Look, I doh know how it fuckin works, do I?

All right, watch yer language, I onny asked.

Swearing at Alf was like swearing at his dad; it made him feel terrible immediately. Shit, sorry Alf. I doh know.

Everyone crowded round, looking, then Peter Thompson walked over and began telling them all to get on Banksy's line and that they'd put the whole order through there. They couldn't do anything else, Luke thought, but everyone still started moaning.

Jesus, they want blood here, doh they?

We're staying here until it's done, by the way, Thompson said calmly as people glared at him.

At least there'd be some overtime, Luke thought. Peter Thompson was all right. He'd got a season ticket at the Albion, reckoned they'd got a chance next season. Luke had talked to him a bit while he was on light duties. He'd done some filing for him, stuff from America about how to get the meat through the factory quickly. Surprisingly, it was pretty interesting; he'd sat leaning against a filing cabinet reading about these big meat plants on the High Plains, sipping a cup of tea the secretaries had made for him.

While Alf, Luke and Peter Thompson stood looking at the blades, Con walked over. He patted Luke on the arm and held his hand out to shake. What now? Luke thought.

Can you get back to the other line, please? Thompson asked. Con grabbed Luke's hand and shook it.

Luke, I'm off, mate, had enough, I cor stond any more o this.

What?

I'm off, mate. They con stick this fuckin job up their arses. He snarled at Alf and Thompson then walked off and kicked the fire exit door open. An alarm started ringing and Luke could suddenly see outside from the factory floor: the brightness, the reflection of the long, grey building in the canal. Con went striding off down the towpath towards the bridge, still wearing his boots and overalls. He threw his hard hat into the water, then the door swung shut.

Everyone on Banksy's line had stopped to see what the fuss was about. Pork chops slid past them on the conveyor. Indy was at the end of the line trying to catch them all in a plastic crate.

This is my life, Luke thought.

Alice didn't want to go in. She loved playing jungles with the animals in the flowers so much that she wanted to stay there all night. Luke wanted to go inside.

Come on, darlin, he said as gently as he could, pulling at her arm, less goo an see Mommy. She ignored him. Come on, Alice. He put his hand out to her, touched her arm.

No! she said and swung her arm out at him, catching one of his bad fingers.

No you don't, he said and grabbed her roughly by the

shoulders, picking her up and swinging her round. He knew he was hurting her, wanted to, then let her go when she started crying.

All right, Alice. *Shshsh*, come on, less just go in. She was bawling and the sound brought Kerry to the back door. Luke rolled his eyes at her and mouthed an apology. Alice ran to Kerry.

Sorry, angel, Luke said to Alice, onny we had to come in. Mommy wanted to see yer, look.

Alice looked scared. You've gone a bit overtired, haven't you? Kerry said to her.

He remembered one afternoon at Granny's before Adam was killed, it must've been the winter before. The bars glowing on the fire, and he was playing cars on the rug in front of it. Adam kept getting in the way. Luke grabbed his hand, pushed it against the fire's metal grille. The little boy screamed. Luke kept hold of his wrist and yanked his arm away from the orange glow as everyone came running into the room.

He was touchin the fire! Luke shouted, dragging his screaming brother across the room. His mum, auntie, nan all shouting. Granny was walking then and came hobbling in behind them with her stick, her legs bandaged like a mummy's. His mum bundled Adam into her arms. His nan took Luke.

Yow am a good boy. Well done for grabbin him. Ooh, he is lucky. Yow've saved him from a nasty burn. Yow am a good brother to him.

Luke joined in the crying. Everyone ruffled his hair and made a fuss. Adam had a blister down the side of his hand but it was OK. Next day, his dad bought him a *Star Wars* Han Solo figure as a reward.

This time he rang the number on the cigarette packet. He wondered if he'd left it too long.

Hello, is that Lisa? Lisa iss, erm, Luke. I met yer at Caesar's a few wiks agoo. I wondered if yer fancied maybe gooin aht for a drink or summat this wik?

She said she'd like to, thought he wasn't going to phone.

Oh, I ay bin gooin aht. I broke me fingers an I bin stoppin in. Yeah, I fell on em playin football, tham much better now, arr.

Back at work that week and the sound of the meat hitting the conveyor belt was driving him mad. It sounded like a body hitting the floor, making him think about the little boy he'd seen on the news. The shape of his body kept bringing him back to Adam.

There'd always been that blank when he thought about what had happened. One minute they'd been playing in the garden, the next he was sitting in next-door's kitchen drinking a milkshake. Then there were bits and pieces from the time afterwards, asking Kerry about the funeral, going to the zoo with Uncle Mick, eating Iris's chicken and rice, no one talking to him about it.

But lately, he kept remembering scenes. Like the toy animals: they'd been playing with them, he was sure of it. He'd been showing the animals to Adam, trying to get him to say their names, but Adam was having none of it, kept snatching them out of his hand. He'd become angry with him for spoiling the game, wanted him to just go away if he couldn't play properly.

He always worried that he couldn't remember for a reason – because it was too horrible, because he'd done something wrong. Was that why nobody ever said anything about it? The shape of that boy on the TV had made him think he'd seen Adam like that, at the side of the road. From behind all peaceful, like he was curled up asleep, but something weird about the way his arms and legs lay, and that dark stain appearing around him.

*

Jamie tapped the glass of the back door. Luke thought about not answering, but pulled it open all the same.

All right, Luke.

Luke shrugged. All right, arr. He didn't move out of the way to let Jamie in. Talking to me now then, am yer?

Woss that meant to mean?

I'll tell yer wharris meant to mean. I bost two fingers for yow the other wik, coulda got arrested. I bin off work, an this is the fust time yow've banged on the door since then. I'll tek yer dahn the hospital, Luke, yow said. Bollocks. Yow day even thank me for helpin yer aht.

What dyer mean, I day thank yer? I did. I said thanks on the night. Jamie took a couple of steps back up the path. Yow like fightin, any road.

No I doh, Luke said. He hated it that people thought that about him. Yow day thank me anyway. Yow asked me if I could carry the fuckin washin machine when I had me ond wrapped up.

I was havin a loff.

Yeah, well. Everything's allus a loff to yow, ay it. Fuckin selfish bastard.

Look, I ay stondin listenin to this. I onny come rahnd to see if yer wanted a pint.

Julie packed yer in, then?

Jamie shrugged and looked at the floor.

Oh shit, her has, ay her?

Jamie nodded. One of her mates sid us up at Caesar's. Sid me gerrin in the taxi wi that wench, Hayley. Her was a right slapper, an all.

Shit, sorry.

Was bound to happen wor it, the way I carry on. Thass bin on me mind, like. I'm sorry abaht yer ond. Yome right, yow shoulda let that bloke lamp me. I wudn't a bin dumped then. He smiled. I'd a got all the sympathy.

I wudn't have got a taxi wi Banksy either, Luke said. He did a runner, yer know.
Nuthin changes, does it?
Never.
Jamie pulled a tape from his pocket. Can yer give this to Kerry? I said I'd tape it for her.
An since when am yow an Kerry so friendly?
Calm down. Fuckin hell. Iss onny a tape for her to play in the car. Jesus.
Jamie held it out. Luke took it from him, shaking his head. Jamie started walking back up the path.
Wheer yow gooin? Luke asked.
Jamie shrugged.
Hang on, I'll goo an get me shoes.

His sister used to tell him that he'd killed Adam. She went through a phase of it. It must've been a couple of years after, one of those summers when they were all stuck in the house together, his mum and dad not speaking and Kerry shouting and screaming at their dad about not wanting to wear Dunlop trainers.
It was yow, yer killed him, she'd tell him. Yer pushed him in front of the lorry. It was all yower fault. Doh pretend yer cor remember. Murderer! She'd hiss and he'd start to cry, then she'd say she was only joking, hushing him before their mum came in.

Lisa suggested they went for a walk, it was a change from sitting in a pub, down the bridle path to the farm.
Luke thought it was great, having a proper conversation with someone. He just hoped she wasn't bored. They stood at the fence watching the horses in the field. Lisa looked different from when he'd seen her at Caesar's, less hair-spray, more relaxed. So goo on then, what would you like to do with yer life? she asked.

I doh know really.

Well, you've just said yerself, yer don't fancy making pork chops for ever.

No, I spose not.

What then?

I wudn't mind gooin abroad.

What, to live, like?

No, not really, more just to goo on holiday.

Yer ambition is to go on holiday? She smiled at him. He felt a bit stupid.

I, er, wudn't say me ambition, but yeah, yer know I'd like to go away on holiday. I never really get round to it.

Thass nice then. She blew out a long stream of smoke. Cos you can easily meet yer ambition.

Woss yowers any road?

I doh know. I'm much cleverer when I talk about other people. I'd like to be a horse, running round the fields, eating sugar lumps, no other worries.

Yer wudn't want to be an horse up here. All the kids come dahn from the estate an terrorize em. Really, what dyer wanna do?

I doh know, she said, and looked down the hill over the trees. Lights were coming on in the houses on the main road. To be a better person, I suppose. Yeah, to be better.

She took a drag on her cigarette and let it slip out her fingers; it went down the hill with a gust of wind. I'm givin up, she said. Luke smiled. Seriously, thass me last one. I'm gonna be a better person, a good person.

But what if he'd killed Adam? How could he be a good person then?

Was that why he couldn't remember – because he'd blocked it out? Was that why nobody ever talked about it? He didn't know why he hadn't thought of it before. Maybe you didn't have to run or pull the front door open, Adam.

What if you'd just slipped your hand into your older brother's and wandered happily down to the road. Your older brother, who was sick of you messing up his games. Down to the road, trusting the hands at your back.

It made sense now, that thudding sound that felt like a memory, the shape of that little boy's body, like he was sleeping but with his arms and legs all strange and the spreading stain on the ground. He'd killed him, he was sure. The meat thumped onto the conveyor belt; the sound of a falling body, over and over again.

Risley

Risley woke and lifted his head from the pillow. It was still early; he could tell from the light. The alarm clock on the bedside table had stopped weeks before and he hadn't replaced the batteries. Things had slipped. Ordinarily, he would've been straight to the shop to buy replacements and get everything back to normal like the rest of his room: pairs of shoes lined up carefully against the skirting board; the wardrobe with his clothes hung up neatly; the change sorted into little piles next to the redundant alarm clock; clean surfaces. Lately, though, it'd become an effort to do anything at all.

He stepped out of bed, padded past the pile of football magazines and took a pair of shorts from the drawer. He could hear the television on, so he went downstairs. The living room was a shambles. The clock on the video said 5.45 and there was an Open University programme on – about car production in Germany – showing to an audience of three overflowing ashtrays; chip wrappers scattered across the floor; damp washing laid over the backs of chairs; a pizza box with his sister's half-smoked spliff stubbed out in it; a few empty lager cans; and his mother, sprawled across the settee, an uncapped bottle of vodka with about a glassful left in it lying on the floor by her side.

He walked over, touched her shoulder.

Mom? Mom? Her face was grey and her mouth slightly

open. She was lying on her back and there was that second, as he rocked her by the shoulder, when her head flopped backwards, that he thought that was it, it was all over. On other mornings he'd almost taken the cushion from behind her head and held it over her open mouth and just let her go. How long could it take? he'd ask himself. She was barely breathing anyway.

William? William? Her eyes flashed as she came to for a moment. He had no idea who William was.

No, Mom, iss David. Yome at um on the settee. Come on, yow've bin here all night. Iss nearly six o'clock, Mom. Dyer wanna goo to bed?

Leave me, she managed to say.

Come on. Less put yer to bed. He pulled her slowly up to a sitting position.

No! she moaned, resisting, but then her head flopped to one side again and he pulled her to her feet.

Come on, Mom. Just upstairs an yow con rest. Come on. He propped her left arm around his shoulders and scooped his right arm around her back to lift and push her towards the stairs. He felt a damp patch of sweat through the scratchy material of her blouse against his neck, could smell the alcohol. Slowly they staggered towards the stairs.

Halfway up, her body shifted and she became a dead weight. Her legs thumped against the stairs and he thought she might slip all the way down. He hauled her up by her shoulders and pulled her to the top, her feet banging off each stair. More bruises she wouldn't be able to explain.

His sister opened her bedroom door and looked out at them. Stupid bitch, she said and shut the door.

Ris pushed his mother's bedroom door open with his foot. She retched and splattered the landing floor with lumpy sick. He put her on the bed. Quickly, disgustedly, he undid her blouse and pulled it off. He wiped her mouth with it, rolled her eyelid open but could only see the white.

Throwing the cover over her, he left to clean up the sick, to shower and go downstairs for a cup of tea and watch the day beginning through the front-room window.

He ironed the same shirt three times before leaving – ironing creases into the arms, not out of them. Then he had to go back to check he'd turned the iron off. He always had to do that when he left the house. There was no point either, because when he got in his mother or Anna would have left the television or radio playing, lights on like it was Blackpool, but no sign of them anywhere. This time he'd got as far as the end of Cromwell Green Road and then turned back, looking for an excuse really. When he got back in he nearly put some toast on, but forced himself back out of the house.

It was stupid, he thought, he had to pass three chip shops on the way to Bayliss's and the chips would be cold before he got back, or he'd have to eat them as he walked. He probably wouldn't be able to eat the chips anyway, the way he felt.

The sign above the steps of the Bingo Hall had just flickered into life. A small crowd of people was outside, waiting for it to open. Mostly women, all smelling of perfume and cigarettes, but he saw a man who sometimes used the bookies on Cromwell Green, standing with his wife. They nodded hello. The man was chewing and smoking at the same time, his hair slicked back and pushed up into a quiff. Just after he passed a little cheer went up as the doors opened. He decided it was a good omen.

Risley could see the shop now; as his stomach flipped over, he thought he might walk straight past. Maybe it was enough just to glance in the window and see her. Slowing, he saw his reflection in the barber's window, then he read the display cards in the travel agents. As if he was going anywhere. He didn't know many of the places on the cards, which was strange, because he was good at things like that – capital cities, longest rivers. But holiday places weren't like real places. In the corner of his eye the fruit machine in the chip shop blinked, the gold lights nagging at him as he stared at the holiday destinations.

He walked into the hot, vinegary smell of the shop. The reflection in the big mirror behind the counter made him duck. My hair's uneven, he thought. The floor was covered with torn sachets of ketchup, a few wooden forks and bits of wrapper. An older woman was serving. He felt relieved and disappointed at the same time.

Bag o chips, please.

Hers just bringin some fresh, darlin. Yome in luck.

Then the girl walked through the plastic curtain that shielded the kitchen. Coming through backwards and turning to empty the chips into the chrome unit, the muscles in her small arm tensed. Her skin was very brown and half a dozen bracelets clinked on her wrists. That was what he saw before he looked at the floor again. He slid his money across the counter.

Open or wrapped?

Wrapped, please.

Salt and vinegar?

Plenty, please.

She looked up at him. He thought for a moment she wasn't going to say anything, but he stared at her as she doled out a portion of chips for the other woman to wrap.

Oh, all right? In again.

All right am yer? His throat had gone dry. He'd ask for a can of Coke.

Be better when I can goo um. She smiled at him.

Arr. He looked at the dispenser for the wooden forks. It was yellow and blue with a drawing of a mermaid on it. He took the bag of chips and his change.

Working all night, am yer? His voice got quieter. He could

feel the vinegar seeping through the chip wrapper into his hand.

No, thank God. I finish at eight, Mondays.

Silence, just the feeling of the vinegar on his hand and the coins from his change in the other.

Right then, I'll seeya.

Ta-ra. One of her rings clunked on the counter as she turned back towards the plastic curtain.

Ta-ra, petal, the older woman joined in.

He shuffled out and glanced quickly back through the window as he walked away, but she'd gone. People were still filing into the Bingo Hall when he passed, three or four taxis parked outside with their doors open. When he got home, he put the cold chips in the bin and made some cheese on toast.

Tuesday tea times he always went round to Luke's.

Iss good news abaht me dad's job, ay it, Ris?

Risley paused, looked at his forkful of bacon and egg white and then at the faces around the table. Luke wiped a piece of bread through the brown sauce on his plate. Mary nodded her head vigorously at Luke's question. Ken sat, still wearing his uniform, with his shirt unbuttoned and gaping open.

Iss great news, arr. Bit of a relief, eh?

Yow con say that again, son. Yome proud o that uniform, ay yer, mate? Mary smiled across the table at Ken.

Arr, iss all right, arr, Ken said and pushed his empty plate towards the middle of the table. Lovely that was.

I should think yow bloody am. Yow look like Tom Jones wi them buttons undone.

What yer on abaht?

It's not unusual . . . she started to sing.

Bloody hell.

I'll be throwin me knickers at yer next.

Risley giggled.

God, Mom, gi it a rest, ull yer? Luke moaned, smiling.

Mary laughed. Embarrassed the pair on yer, look. Yow am bashful.

Wiv gorra guest.

Well, yow've heered wuss, David, I'm sure.

Tell her, Ris, yome a sensitive soul.

Risley loved this time. He'd always loved it, been going round every Tuesday since they'd been at primary school. In those days he'd just turn up at the back door.

Her's turned me aht again, Ken, he'd announce about his mother to the concern of the Wilkinson family.

Mary would lay him a place at the table between Kerry and Luke. Iss a good job yome here, love, she'd tell him. Yow con split them two up from fighting.

And that would be that. Even that young, he realized how grateful he was to them, especially Mary, always making room for him no matter what.

Mary and his mother had gone to school together, the same as him and Luke. Mary always asked about her, though God knows when they last saw each other, and she'd tell him some story about when they used to hang around together, sometimes show him photos. His mother with long hair and clear skin standing next to Mary in the back yard at Luke's granny's house. The girls dressed to go out, short skirts and boots on; the allotments, chimneys, the glow of the fires behind them – the photo like an artefact from a lost world. He always wished he knew more, that he could somehow go back to how it was before, to how things were then. One day, he'd think, he'd have the courage to ask it all. These days, though, it was all he could do to build up the courage to get out of bed.

Yow all right, Ris?

Arr, sahnd.

He loved Tuesday nights while he was there but afterwards he felt bad. It was great, the way the Wilkinsons were with one another and with him, but it made him feel uneasy. Who did he have to go back to? Who did he have to sit around the kitchen table with? Things hadn't been easy for them either, with a dead son and brother and Ken in and out of work.

They used to talk at the table about the future, the kind of jobs him and Luke would have, but all that was a long time ago. For a while Ken and Mary had made suggestions, told him about places he might look for work. Once, there'd even been mention of a job going at Luke's place. Now the subject was just avoided.

He was an embarrassment. No job, no girlfriend. Never any chance of one. He felt bad. He never changed, even though he kept willing himself to.

Later, sitting outside the back door drinking cans of beer, Luke asked about the girl in the chip shop.

Have yer bin back theer yet?

No.

Ris had refused to go in there with Luke since he'd first spoken to her. Luke kept nagging him. Never having a girlfriend was another thing he tried to avoid talking about. Every now and again Luke would start up about it, just trying to be his mate, he supposed.

I doh know, Ris, woss up wi yer?

Nuthin, I jus doh feel like it, all right.

But yow never feel like it. I cor mek yer aht.

Just leave it, ull yer?

Risley looked down at the ground between his feet – there was a plastic giraffe half hidden in the soil of the border, Luke had put them there for Alice to find – and then looked back up at his mate, at the dark marks under his eyes. He never looked well lately, all that stuff with Sarah must've taken it out of him. Risley wished he was better at talking about things.

After a while Luke opened another can and said, Woss the wust thing yow've ever done, Ris?

I doh know.

I mean the wust thing, yer know, that yer wished had never, ever happened.

What dyer mean?

Well, everyone does bad things, right? I wondered what the wust thing yow reckoned yow'd ever done.

I doh know, mate.

Luke looked exasperated. Risley wished Ken would come out and join them so they could talk about the Albion.

Deliberately rattling his keys and kicking the bit of the door that always stuck on the back step, Risley came home to find Anna sitting on the settee with Jason Banks. The room was thick with smoke, the ashtray overflowing on the low table next to a bottle of Thunderbird. Empty lager cans lay on the floor round their feet; Jason had his arm around Anna. A video played: buildings exploding and a man running away from them. Subtitles flashed across the screen in Japanese or Chinese or some Oriental language, for some reason. Perhaps they were broadening their horizons. Risley flopped down in the armchair.

All right?

All right, arr.

Where's Mom? he asked.

Gone to bed pissed. Anna breathed out a long stream of smoke. I cor gi a fuck to be honest.

I could, Risley thought.

Her wor too bad tonight, Ris. Banksy offered him a can of beer.

Cheers. Risley took it and lay back in the chair.

There was a corner of sky still pink above the houses outside. The room was lit by the explosions on the screen. Jason giggled at a couple of the really big ones.

After a while Anna and Jason started kissing. He heard their teeth knock together. She sighed as he began to kiss her neck, already bruised with a couple of love bites. She turned her body towards him. Ris could see what was coming.

Cor yow two goo upstairs?

She tore her face away from Jason's and glared at her brother. I ay gorra video in me room, have I?

Arr, cos yome watchin this, ay yer.

Gi it a rest, Ris, ull yer? Just drink yer beer an tek it easy. We ay doin nuthin. As he said this, Jason's hand slipped down Anna's back, squeezed her arse. Anna laughed and kissed him.

Risley got up and moved towards the stairs, stopping to pick up another can of beer. Fuck yer, then, he muttered under his breath, and walked upstairs.

Jealous bastard, he heard Anna say.

The fence had a series of metal plaques bolted to it – ANTI-CLIMB PAINT – and a spiralling length of barbed wire at the top. Further down the towpath, behind the hedgerow of nettles and condoms and empty aerosol cans, there was a fence panel missing. He struggled on. The towpath was covered with weeds and algae. The canal here was only a couple of feet wide, and Risley wondered what a stretch of water this narrow could be for. On the opposite bank was another fence and the ground rose steeply to the Birmingham Road twenty yards away and above him. Traffic went by unseen.

The gap was narrower than he remembered it, but he squeezed through easily enough, snagging his trouser leg on barbed wire as he went. Beyond was another world. It was hundreds of yards to the far fence, even more across ways. The space was empty except for three enormous strips of concrete running parallel through the middle of the site – like huge cricket pitches or airport runways. The first time he'd come here Risley couldn't make out what they were and then it had dawned on him: floors. All that was left of the factory that used to stand there – the buildings long since demolished, the machinery broken down and sold off for scrap. Just a few rusty girders here and there.

He walked across the middle floor, shapes of machines indented in the concrete. Weeds carpeted the tarmac around the concrete strips, but the strips themselves were almost bare. Over by the opposite fence he saw a fox padding along, stop, put its nose in the air, then dodge into the bushes.

This was one of the easier places to get into. There was nothing left to steal and nothing to break. He loved the peaceful expanse of it, the sun glinting, and the castle above the trees in the distance. When he reached the end of his strip of concrete and felt the crumbling tarmac beneath his feet he stopped. In front of him railway tracks ran in an arc towards the fence, going nowhere in particular.

He stood by the tracks and threw a few stones down the concrete strips, bowled one properly and wrenched his shoulder. Then, feeling self-conscious, he sat down and looked at the view. You could spend ages in places like this, just mooching around; it was calming, like sitting in church or something. He didn't know what he was doing. Just killing time, he supposed.

Good darts, he heard somebody behind him shout.

He'd hit the seventeen, leaving double sixteen. A bit of a recovery, he thought to himself. Even so, the other bloke still had three shots at double top. Clouds of smoke hung in the air, illuminated by a TV showing Sky Sports with the sound down. This was a summer cup match, in a big pub in Smethwick. The windows in this half of the pub were all blacked out and the door to the Gents had been pulled off its hinges and was propped against a flashing quiz machine. When they'd pulled into the car park Bill, their captain, had said he hoped there was no food on so they could make a quick getaway. Risley lifted his head from staring at the yellow and brown floor tiles and looked at the table heavy with sandwiches and crisps on the far side of the room. No chance of that, then. At least his team were losing.

He watched his opponent throw. A tall man, stooping over the line to throw. He seemed to write something in the air with the top of the dart before he released. Not one for the purists, Risley thought.

Ooh, he's hit the twenty, said the anonymous voice that had praised Risley. The tall bloke shifted, looked down at the floor and then back at the board. He was wearing blue works overalls and safety boots and squinted through a pair of thick-rimmed glasses, taped together in one corner. The next dart hit the wire of the ten and dropped out. Still in with a chance with a double sixteen, Risley thought. But the next dart thumped firmly into the double ten. Game. He shook hands with his opponent.

Good darts, mate. Played, he said. The skin of his hand felt rough, grated. He smelled of Swarfega.

Swarfega always made him think of his old man; it was how he used to smell when Risley was really young, before he went away. For a couple of years after he left he'd turn up on Saturday afternoons and drag Risley along with him on a crawl of the town's pubs. Anna was a product of those Saturday nights after fish and chips in the kitchen, when his dad hadn't gone back out again but sat watching telly with them and then climbed noisily to bed after *Match of the Day*.

Risley remembered the view as they walked down Cromwell Green Road towards the town, his hands gripping his dad's tight curly hair, his dad whistling and pointing things out. The view: over the playground and past the castle, over factory chimneys and motorways to green behind them. So high, the pavement rolling beneath him as his dad walked.

Once, his dad took him to the Lion. The pub had three rooms, but children weren't allowed in any of them so he was sat on the back step with a bottle of Vimto, was patted on the head and told to be a good lad. There were usually other children around but it was a cold day and nobody else came out into the yard. He remembered the bottle crates strewn around and the taste of the paper straw stuck in the Vimto bottle. He sat and waited for his dad to collect him. Looking back, he thought it could have been all afternoon – four or five hours – but really it was probably an hour or so. He remembered the light changing, the yellow lights in the pub coming on. Frost glistened on the overturned crates and on the smooth cobbles of the yard. Eventually, hungry and cold but still scared of being in trouble for disturbing his dad, he screwed up the courage to go inside.

Has me dad bin in? he'd said to the man collecting glasses. He remembered the blank look and the realization: Iss John Risley's boy!

The commotion that followed: he'd sat in the pub kitchen right up against the bars of the electric heater, the sound of the football scores coming from the television set in the snug. Finally, his dad staggered into the room and took him in his arms. He held Risley to his wet, agonized face. He smelled of beer and his chin was scratchy with stubble.

I wudn't forget yer, son, his dad said over and over. I wudn't forget yer.

He took him up in a crane once, told him he'd got a job as a crane driver. Risley loved cranes. It was when they were building the Merry Hill. They met a man with a load of keys who sloshed through the orange mud and puddles with them.

Up in the cab, his dad showed him the controls. They sat together in the driver's seat. It was amazing. The tiny houses and cars below them; the land green and brown; everything around the base of the crane broken up. It felt like the crane was swaying with the wind, splashes of rain hitting the pane of glass a few inches from his face. His dad was talking quietly, explaining things, pointing things out. Risley didn't understand, but it was OK. The sky was moving above them. They were part of the sky. His dad was holding him. They stayed there for a long time, the sky grey and moving, the land green and brown below and everything broken. When they came down he'd wet himself. His dad went away after that.

Goo on the two dog, goo on!

The dog got bunched on the last corner and, in a scramble of limbs, got boxed out. Number four romped home. There was a close-up of it baring its teeth and going after the hare. Risley screwed up his betting slip and pushed it across the bench.

Hare's running at Monmore Green.

The bell went and the picture on the screen changed. It was early and there was only him in the shop and an old man wearing a pair of slippers and sipping tea from a styrofoam cup.

He leafed through the *Racing Post*. The first part of his day's accumulator had already blown up and it wasn't even twelve o'clock. Trying to concentrate, he studied the three fifteen at Doncaster: Addie Bundren, five-to-two, a banker apparently. He wrote out a slip and got up to take it to the counter. Thirty pence to win. Five-to-two. Big time.

*

When he was younger, it'd been different. He was happy then. He'd been good at school, at least for a while. At Cromwell Green School he never had a care in the world. He hung around with Luke, Jamie and Nicky. They'd play together after school with all the other boys, football and cricket against the playground wall, goals and wickets painted on. Or they'd be round at each other's houses. For a while they had a spell of making little sports magazines with reports about their own matches in them. Risley used to love that. He was going to be a sports reporter. Even when they went to secondary school everything was all right for a while.

He remembered one dinnertime, climbing up the drainpipe and onto the roof to fetch a football that had been kicked up there. He'd always been good at climbing. Everybody watched him as he moved upwards, past the art-room windows where kids were working, two floors high, and hauled himself over the guttering, full of stinking weeds, and onto the narrow ledge at the front of the sloping tiles. The tiles were shiny, slippery, but he walked along the ledge. Kids shouted and cheered below him. One of the teachers started blowing a whistle. Someone yelled at him to come down. He got the ball, but didn't throw it back straight away. He did a little dance with it, waving his arms around and sticking his arse out over the ledge. It was great. Then he threw the ball back, but before the game started up again the crowd watched him as he clambered back down. They clapped when he jumped the last six feet or so to the ground. One of Luke's sister's mates kissed him on the cheek. The headmaster was there to meet him, too; sent him home and said he couldn't come back until his mother came in for a meeting about his behaviour but his mother couldn't be bothered and in the end the headmaster had to give in.

But then he'd had to stop the others coming round to his

house because he got too embarrassed about the mess. They'd stopped coming round so much anyway.

He wasn't sure when he started climbing up buildings for no real reason, without people watching him. One summer holidays, when his mother first got really bad, he'd climbed onto the roof of the maisonettes every morning after making his sister's breakfast, just to get away from everything. The roof was always wet, sticky in the sunshine or slick and puddled in the rain. He didn't mind. He got some peace up there.

Gradually he stopped answering questions in class, stopped doing his schoolwork. He used to make sure his sister got ready and went to school, he'd walk her there himself. Sometimes he'd make sure his mother was up, but it got too hard. He only really talked to Luke and Jamie, then just Luke. He stopped saying anything to anybody, just stared out of the window. Nobody seemed to mind. They moved him into lower groups. He had to sit next to Wayne Banks. Nobody was that bothered.

The train slid beneath the motorway bridge, away from the back of the houses, alongside the canal, past a row of disused factory buildings. The sun made the raindrops on the window sparkle. There was a beauty in these buildings, he thought, the corpses of outlandish beasts decomposing, rotting into the black ground; a beauty in the stillness of their hulks, holding shadowy light in their bellies; a beauty in their spent energy. The train rattled past them, its shape reflected in the water of the canal. Risley stared at the ruins, at a security guard skirting an outhouse, at brown chain dangling from rusty haulage gear, at a group of estate children huddling, then scattering, in the shell of a hangar, bare patches of ground showing where machinery had stood.

He stood, bore witness. The train curved away from the

buildings and crossed beneath the motorway again, the traffic flashing by above it. Someone had put up a tent under the flyover, right under the ZULUS graffiti and the water dripping from the bridge.

Music thumped from inside the house, voices were talking all at once. He threw the pile of Job Club leaflets he'd been given down on the kitchen table, put the kettle on and walked into the front room. Jason Banks was dancing around to the music on the radio, ill-fitting grey suit trousers riding up his ankles. He had a can of beer in his hand. Jason's mates, Dekker and Carl, sat laughing with Anna on the settee. His mother and one of Anna's friends, Katie, stood at the back of the room, eating McDonald's from a bag.

Community service. Community fuckin service, Jason kept saying and laughing. Cutting the grass up the churchyard. Bit o painting over the bungalows. Nice one. He took a swig from his can of beer. Nice one. Had a bit of a result this morning, Risley.

Arr, I con see.

Help yerself, mate. Jason waved his arm expansively at the McDonald's bags and unopened beer cans lying around the room.

Risley picked a cold cheeseburger from one of the bags. Cheers, he said and stood there watching his sister giggling and Banksy carrying on with his dance.

He walked over to his mother. She was smartly dressed in a black blouse and grey skirt. Did yow goo an all? he asked, looking at the clear liquid sloshing around in her glass.

I went for Anna, she said defensively.

Well, her wor up for nuthin, was her? he hissed at her through clenched teeth.

I went for Anna, David. To give her a bit o support. Her voice was firmer this time. The two lads munching on burgers looked furtively at Risley and then back at Jason's celebrations.

Yow could support her by tryin to mek her goo back to school this year, cos I doh think iss gonna happen. Yow could support her by tellin her to pull herself together, yow could support her by pullin yerself together.

He was shaking. She bit her lip, looked down at her glass and then the floor. He saw her face crumple, fall apart; he sensed the bottle of vodka sitting on the cabinet, the glue that would fit it all back together.

He turned and walked back through the kitchen, not raising his eyes to look at anyone. Over the sound of the radio he heard his sister complain, Woss up wi him now? As he fiddled with his key in the back door he heard Banksy say, Leave him, Maggie, the miserable sod, he ay wuth it, to his mother. His own mother. He closed the door behind him, stood for a while listening to the laughter, then turned and walked away.

The back door at Luke's house slid open.

All right, David. Thass a surprise. I thought it was our Mick.

All right, Mary. Is Luke back from work?

No, he ay comin straight back tonight, mate. He's seein that new girl. Has he said anythin to yer abaht her?

Nah, not really.

Yow all right? Dyer wanna come in for a cup o tay?

No, no. Yome OK, Mary. He shifted his weight from foot to foot.

Is it anythin important, Dave? I'll tell him yer called. Me potatoes am nearly boilin over. She glanced back into the kitchen.

Nah, nah. I jus called rahnd on the off chance really. Arr, tell him I called. I'll see yer Tuesday, tomorra.

OK, mate, I'll see yer. Ta-ra.

*

Risley walked past the debris of yesterday, the *Express & Star* and a copy of *Shoot!* tucked under his arm, through the chips mashed into the carpet, and upstairs. When the bedroom door was shut behind him he put the newspaper and magazine down on his bedside table. He went to the cupboard and took out a new scrapbook from the top of a pile of old, battered ones. He placed the scrapbook on the table, took glue and scissors from his bedside drawer and sat down.

For a while he sat and stared out the window. He looked down at the fat, healthy roses growing in next-door's garden. Larry, their neighbour, walked through the beads that hung across his back door, bent down and poked at a pot of freesias with a lollipop stick, then stood up and went inside. Risley looked at the matted grass of their own garden, the broken-down fence, the skeleton of the freezer that had overheated and nearly burned the house down last year and was now covered in slugs. He could just imagine what Larry and Brenda said, sitting in their garden in the sunshine, looking across at that. Or when music came booming from Anna's room in the middle of the night. Or when Jason Banks and his mates slammed car doors out there in the street or just sat staring at everybody with their headlights switched off. I've got to get organized, he thought. Cut the lawn, move the freezer.

He turned the newspaper over and sized up the West Brom team photo on the back page. He clipped it out carefully and laid it in the space in the scrapbook where he wanted it to go. Then he turned his attention to the magazine. Humming softly to himself, he read slowly through it, then cut out the articles and pictures he wanted until he had half a dozen arranged next to the team photo. Satisfied, he flicked back a couple of pages to the start of the book, a fixture list cut from the pink pages of the

Sports Argus, glanced at the pile of scrapbooks sitting in the top of his cupboard, then turned back to today's work. He traced a finger over the shiny magazine print, the neat edge he'd cut. It was in place, in order. Everything was under control.

A gravel path sloped away from the road, between empty warehouses, to a falling-down fence. Behind the fence was a long, brick factory with a chimney at one end, all its windows and doors barred with shutters, but with a caged ladder running up the outside of the chimney to the top. The chimney was brown and red brick at the base and blackened nearer the top. Something had once been painted down its side in white paint but all that remained now were the letters E and F about halfway down. Risley's heart swelled when he gripped the bottom of the ladder, shook it, and it remained in place.

The view was amazing. He gripped the rusty guardrail of the ladder as tightly as he could as the wind blasted past his ears and ruffled his hair.

Beneath him and all around was a sprawl of houses and high-rises, empty factory sites, criss-crossing roads and canals. To his left was a row of cooling towers, further on were red-brick buildings and a gas holder. He could see the tall buildings in Birmingham, pick out the Post Office Tower. The sky was a milky colour as the sun tried to break through the clouds. Across Birmingham, a haze of exhaust fumes blurred the horizon, like smudged mascara. If he looked down beneath his feet he could see the slender rungs of the ladder, one after the other, and the tarmac a hundred feet below. His stomach churned and he gripped the guardrail more tightly and looked into the distance.

He'd spotted this place a while ago. There was nothing to stop you getting in, just a few signs with pictures of Alsatians. Most of the fence around the factory had fallen down. Risley had thought the two works either side were empty as well, but now he could see a fork-lift truck driving in the alley between two buildings and someone in yellow overalls walking behind it.

The wind dropped and everything became still, just the sound of distant traffic and the clanging of metal somewhere. He looked closely at the rivets that held the ladder to the side of the chimney, where the cement between the brickwork crumbled slightly, hoped he could get down OK, his legs feeling like jelly and then like steel rods. Higher than he'd ever been. When he was up here he felt free and, what was the word? Articulate.

There were two small plastic tables next to the window. He sat down at the one nearest the door, a foil ashtray and packets of ketchup on its surface. He put his cue case next to them, to make it obvious that he was going for a game of snooker, that he wasn't some loner sitting in the window of the chip shop because he'd nowhere else to go. He'd never seen anyone sit down to eat in here before, even on a Saturday night when the pubs finished. He didn't feel like eating, kept running his fingers over the crack in the edge of the plate. The older woman walked over with his mug of tea. Some of it sloshed over the sides of the mug when she put it down. She lifted it again and wiped the plastic with a cloth.

There seemed to be a thousand chips on the plate. He took a sip of tea, but it was too hot and burned his lips. He sat there blowing on it, knowing he was going to have to force them all down. It'd look bad otherwise.

She came out from behind the plastic curtain. She had her hair tied up, smaller earrings on. He'd timed his visit for her break. She took her cigarettes and lighter from the shelf and opened the hatch in the counter. When she saw him she smiled.

Hello, all right am yer?
All right, arr.

She walked to the open door, lit a cigarette and blew a stream of smoke out into the street, leaning against the doorframe. He took a mouthful of chips, had to chew them for ages before he could swallow, watching her in the big mirror behind the counter. When she took a drag of her cigarette she squinted and tapped the ash off onto the pavement away from her, holding her arm right out, like the cigarette was something she'd rather not be holding.

On yer break, am yer?

Arr, if yer con call it that. Time for a fag an to run to the toilet an he wants yer back servin or cookin the chips. Tay as if wim gonna be rushed off we feet tonight, is it?

Woh it get busy?

No, not really. She'd turned so that she was looking at him but still holding the cigarette outside.

Yow've bin in here a lot, lately.

Nice chips, I spose.

Yer missus ay turfed yer aht, then? She grinned at him. He forced a laugh.

No, nuthin like tha. I ay, er, seein nobody at the minute.

Just as well. I doh blaeme yer.

She stubbed her cigarette out and stepped back inside. She sat down in the seat opposite him, all of a sudden, making a shivering motion and putting her fingers on the back of his hand.

I'm froze. Yer think I'd be warm workin in here. I get really hot but me fingers stay code.

Code onds, warm heart, he said, blushing.

She leaned back in the seat, taking her hand back but not too quickly. He picked up the mug, but his hand was shaking and he put it down again. More tea spilled over the sides. Careful, she said, I'm the one thass gorra clayn up in a minute.

Sorry.
I thought yow'd a needed a steadier ond than that for snooker.
I spose so, arr. He caught her gaze and held it. She smiled and looked away, out of the window, then she turned back and he was still looking at her.
What is it, then? Dyer come in here every time yow goo to the snooker club?
Arr, summat like tha.
What, dyer meet yer mates dahn theer?
Sometimes, arr.
I've never played snooker. I like pool, though. I've played down the pub wi me brothers.
Wheer's that then?
Dahn the Bramford.
I know it.
Wheer yow from?
Cromwell Green.
I thought yer was.
Why dyer say tha?
Yow con jus tell.
All this time, looking straight at him. She glanced at the clock, moved to get up.
Look at me, sitting here talkin to yer, I doh even know yer naeme.
David.
Mine's Louise. She got up. Well, iss bin very nice to talk to yer, David. I'll see yer soon, she said stiffly, like she didn't know how to end the conversation. Neither did he. The soles of her plastic sandals slapped on the floor as she walked across the tiles and went through to the back of the shop. He pushed cold chips around his plate for a while and looked to say goodbye properly, but then just got up and left. He could've flown home, though.

*

There was smoke everywhere. It stung his eyes as he hurried down the stairs, caught in the back of his throat. Flames were leaping out the chip pan when he reached the kitchen, his mother standing staring at it and screaming. He stopped, put his hand over his mouth, narrowed his watery eyes. He'd seen a programme about this on television. Grabbing a towel from the radiator, he pushed his mother to one side, threw the towel into the sink, turned on the cold tap, splashed water everywhere as he wet the towel. He turned the gas off on the oven and threw the wet towel over the chip pan. There was a hissing sound, steam and smoke everywhere. Flames licked out from under the grill. He pulled the grill pan from the oven and rattled it into the sink under the stream of cold water.

Four black sausages rolled off the pan and into the sink. His mother was bent over coughing, hard. He was coughing now, too, so he pushed the window open and the smoke began to clear.

He sat on the back step, his eyes streaming. I put a fire out, he thought, shaking, feeling a warmth spreading through him. Relief and elation. Like the feeling when he'd finally got back to the bottom of the ladder on the chimney. He sat for a while and realized he couldn't hear anything inside and turned to go back in.

The smoke had almost cleared and a breeze was blowing through the house. His mother had put the plates on the table and was arranging two burnt wet sausages on each plate next to the piles of charred chips. It was the first thing she'd tried to cook in a week. She looked up and smiled at him, her eyes glazed. Here yow goo, son, she said.

Ris looked at the black mess on the plate in front of him and started to laugh. He couldn't stop, was shaking uncontrollably. He put his hands on the back of the chair and bent double. He laughed and laughed, but his insides felt cold.

*

He knew that Louise finished at eight, but still walked too quickly and now he was standing on the corner watching the hands on the clocks move slowly in the jeweller's window, looking down the street, then looking at his reflection in the window, running his hand up and over his hair. At least he'd had it cut. The orange sign above the chip shop glowed. Eight o'clock came, and he shifted from foot to foot. He pushed his hand into his pocket; all day he'd bitten at the skin around his thumb and now it was sore. Nearly five past.

There was some movement at the door. It was her. She stepped out onto the pavement. She had a skirt on tonight and her hair was down; he noticed her brown calves as she turned to walk down the street. She swayed as she walked and her ankle chain glinted before she moved into the shadow. Risley took a breath and began to walk after her, fifty, sixty yards behind her. She slowed down just before she reached the corner where the bus stop was and waved across the road to a tall man in a baseball cap. She turned towards him. As he stepped up the kerb she held her arms open. This shouldn't be happening. Risley stopped. Maybe it was one of her brothers. She was smiling and they started kissing, shuffled with their feet together towards the wall of the boarded-up pub. They were still kissing when Risley turned and began to walk home. He threw the flowers in a bin as he cut through the bus station.

That Friday afternoon, the view from the sloping roof wasn't as good as last time he'd been up there. It'd been raining and the wind blew the first leaves from the trees. Slowly he edged his way along the brick ledge, bringing more of the main road into view, the back of the Wren's Nest. He could see kids fishing in the Donkey Pool and the traffic lights at Roseville, a green and yellow bus pulling into the stop on its way to Wolverhampton, beyond that a crest in the road and just greyness, the sky feeling close to the ground.

He shuffled along the wet brick to the opposite end of the long factory building. There were puddles in the yard below, a rainbow of oil in them. He looked back to the tree he'd climbed to get onto the roof. It wasn't that high, to tell the truth. As high as a house, he guessed, maybe a bit higher. He pressed his face to the sloping glass skylight below him, making out blurred, brownish outlines of equipment still sitting on the factory floor. The place hadn't been closed long. He looked across the skylight to the apex of the roof, wondered if there was any way to get up there, ten feet or so higher. Not today, he decided, leaning back, looking at the grey sky. It began to rain again.

A dog barking and a rattle of keys: security guard. He heard the man's footsteps turn the corner of the building. The dog barked again. Risley pulled himself up, began to move back along the ledge.

Hey!

He glanced down and saw the peaked cap and white shirt of the guard, looking up, saw the dog trotting alongside him growling. He turned and began to walk along the brick ledge. If he could get to the other end of the building and along the tree branch he'd be over the wall and away before the guard and the dog could get round to the gate.

Hey! What yer doin?

The dog barked.

The ledge, already slick with moss, was becoming more slippery with the rain. Shit! He had his shoes on, not trainers. They would have made things easier.

The guard was keeping pace with him. The dog was going mad now, off the lead, leaping up the factory wall twenty-five feet below him as if it was snapping at his heels.

Risley slipped, felt his left foot shoot out over the ledge into mid-air, righted himself, thought, That was close, then stepped across onto the glass of a skylight to correct his mistake. The glass shattered. He threw his arms out to break the fall as he went through the glass. Everything slowed down. The air in the factory was musty. He saw the clock hanging at the far end of the building, upside down. He was upside down. He saw the rough texture of the yellow cement floor and the brown rusty machinery as it got closer and closer. His feet were still working in mid-air, trying to find his step, but he was falling, falling.

Kerry

It was the morning of Risley's funeral and they were arguing.

I've just never heard anything so stupid. What if I run out of petrol? What will I do? I can hardly make me mom run to the garage with a can, can I?

You won't run out.

Tim, I've got to go from here to Ruth's to drop Alice off, then up to me mom and dad's, then back to the Crem, then back again and there's bound to be somebody that needs a lift somewhere. The needle's almost on the red now.

I've had enough o this. No. Yome using much too much as it is. I'm not filling it up all the time just so you can go and run your family around.

What do yer mean, run me family around? It's a funeral, for Christ sake! What am I meant to do, tell em all to get the bus?

They hissed at each other in the kitchen, trying to keep their voices low because of Alice sitting in her high chair and playing with toast soldiers.

Please, Tim.

He was bending over on the stool at the breakfast bar, tying his shoelaces and taking his time, his face thin and his mouth tight shut.

I promise not to go anywhere tomorrow and Friday so I can save on petrol then. Please, Tim. I promise. Please.

She never pleaded, but she *had* to use the car today. He knew it. Her chest felt tight. She could feel tears welling up in her eyes and she swallowed to blink them back, her makeup done.

Come on, she said with more resolution. You'd have bin to the garage and back by now if we hadn't been arguing. You know I've got to use it today. Please, Tim.

That ay the point. What's up with yer old man's car this wik? You've used a full tank since I filled it up last wik. It's all the time. Constant. I wouldn't mind but it ay even yower family. Yer brother's mate! I mean, they've got no money supposedly and then they volunteer to do all this. I bet there'll be a right party on. Yer brother's mate. How many other hangers-on have I got to goo and work for?

They're not hangers-on. Her voice cracked. He stared at her and she looked away at the floor. A tear dropped onto the tiles in front of her. You're just being horrible. Why am you being so horrible to me?

They do nothing. They sit around all day on their fat arses and take the piss. It teks em all their time to talk to me but they're quite happy for me to go an slave away so they can get chauffeured everywhere.

Don't, just don't. That's so unfair. Just stop it.

Yow cor even see it. I just get so angry with em.

They haven't done nuthin to you. It's me anyway. I'm asking yer. I want the car. I need the car today.

Mommy, Mommy, Alice shouted from the high chair.

Iss all right, darling. Mummy's coming. Kerry blew her nose on a piece of kitchen roll.

You're just a selfish bitch, he hissed as she squeezed past to get to Alice.

Tim took both sets of car keys noisily from the fruit bowl by the door and left, banging the front door on his way out. As Kerry cleaned Alice up, she could hear him moving the cars around on the drive so he could get hers out.

Risley had still been alive when the security guard opened the padlock to the steel doors at the entrance to the factory and went rushing in and then went rushing out again to throw up and telephone for an ambulance. He was alive when the ambulance arrived and alive for the slow crawl to the hospital as the paramedics tried not to jolt his mangled neck and skull. He'd been alive as they wheeled him through casualty strapped forlornly to a trolley, but only just. He was conscious for some of it. Just before he'd hit the ground his head crashed against the corner of a rusting nail-counting machine. If not for that he might have survived, the doctors said.

After the funeral, people were going back to Kerry's parents' house. Her mum had volunteered, considering the state of Risley's mother. There wouldn't be many anyway. She'd cut the sandwiches neatly and pulled cling film tightly over the plates of ham and cheese and sausage rolls.

Mommy, Mommy, Mommy.

Mommy's coming, darling. She inhaled from her asthma pump. Thank God she'd be able to drop Alice at Ruth's soon, she'd been annoying her all morning. Kerry thought that maybe, as long as Tim had filled the car up, she'd be able to call in to the Merry Hill when everything had finished that afternoon. She felt guilty thinking about shopping, maybe she was just being selfish, should've been worried about arguing with Tim or about poor Risley dying like that. Funerals reminded her of Adam. His funeral was the first time she'd ever felt grown up, standing with the adults, staring at the little coffin, thinking about her brother shut inside it.

She hadn't really known Risley. He was just one of Luke's dead-loss mates who used to come round for tea on Tuesdays. There was only Jamie next door you could have a proper conversation with. The others – the others were just hopeless. It was terrible he was dead, though. Just horrible, the whole thing. She worried about the poor man who'd found Risley and her dad in his new security job. He must feel terrible, she thought, shuddering, wiping the work surfaces with a cloth and dropping onionskin from the sandwiches into the waste disposal unit. She heard Tim reverse a car against the garage door. He was back, but he wouldn't come in. He'd just drive off in the van, they were shop-fitting in Wolverhampton today. She looked out of the window across the lawn at the blue and orange slide sitting in the middle of it, waiting for Alice to grow a bit bigger. Once, she'd been standing there and a squirrel had appeared from by the fence, hopped up the steps of the slide and slid down, twisting around on its back and then leapt – with apparent joy – away into the bushes on the far side.

There were more people in the small crematorium chapel than she'd expected. Risley's mother leaned against her daughter, Anna. There was no sign of his father but then there never had been, Kerry thought. Behind them was a group of men in cheap and badly fitting suits, tattooed hands wrapped around the hymn books. Kerry looked across at her dad and smiled weakly. Luke was standing next to him, to attention, as if he was in the army or something. Next to him was Jamie from next door, standing with his eyes closed. The long coffin sat there as the vicar made a speech about Risley's life. What was there to say?

Her mind wandered as she stared at the coffin. There was a wreath in the design of a dartboard and one with a throstle and blue and white stripes as the background which Luke and Jamie had organized. It must have cost a bit. The vicar droned on and she waited to see how he'd deal with Risley's accident. She wondered what he'd been trying to steal. Everyone else said that there was something wrong about what happened, that it wasn't like him, that he wasn't a thief. Perhaps he just wasn't a very good one, she thought.

Tim had worked at a coffin-makers for a couple of months after he left school. He told her about it once when she'd been telling him something about Adam. He said it was the best laugh he'd ever had in a job, a young kid making the tea while these old craftsmen measured and bevelled the wood and polished the brasswork and teased each other. The best laugh, he said, until they had to make a child's coffin and the men would bend double over their work, and a sense of quiet would come over the workshop and they'd stand and look at the small box when it was finished, the wood literally cut short, and be quiet with their own thoughts.

Cut short. That was what the vicar said about Risley's life. Obvious, she supposed. She thought about Adam again, the three of them sitting out the back at Granny's, playing schools. Kerry, the teacher, reciting times tables and ticking the little books she'd made for her brothers, getting them to answer the register before they crawled off to a different game. She remembered how in the months after she had Alice, she would wake with a jolt even between feeds and rush to the cot to check she was still breathing, that she was OK, her little heart fluttering under pale, luminous skin, all those lives and deaths becoming one thing.

Organ music started up and the coffin began to slide behind the screen. The whole thing was pathetic, she thought suddenly, violently. The coffin, the football and darts wreaths, the plastic flowers either side of the room, the piped music. It sounded like something played on the end of Blackpool Pier. Kerry got the urge to giggle. She shook, snorted, and bit the inside of her cheek to stop herself. Her mother rested her hand on her arm, her own eyes wet. Kerry could taste blood in her mouth.

When they turned to leave Kerry noticed a pale, frightened-looking man in an open-necked shirt at the back of the chapel. Later, someone said it was the security guard who had chased Risley. One of the darts players said he was glad he hadn't known that or he didn't know what. Her dad told him not to be so bloody stupid.

It was awful back at the house. People took sandwiches from the kitchen table and moved to the front room with drinks. There was a crate of beer on top of the spin-dryer and a bottle of whisky shoved back against the tiles behind the sink. Her mum made cups of tea in the china set Kerry had fetched from Granny's. Kerry talked to one of the few women there, Risley's Auntie Rose. Rose kept her hat on and rattled the cup in her saucer as she talked.

Alice, thass a lovely naeme, ay it tha. A lot o the young uns am gooin for the more ode-fashioned naemes nowadays, ay they. And wheer'd yow say yow left her? Oh, at yer mate's, wor it. Thass nice. Iss nice to have a break from em sometimes, ay it. Our poor mother had nine a we. I doh know how her coped, I doh. Like yower great-granny, I suppose. Dun yer see much on her? Coupla times a wik? Ooh, thass lovely. Her's marvellous, ay her, for her age. I doh see many o my nieces an nephews at all, like, now. We day a no children weselves, me an Jack. Shaeme, really. He passed away in 1984, used to work at GKN. Things am different now, ay they? Dun yer goo up the Merry Hill much? Dun yer? I love it, I do. Course yower daddy worked theer, day he, afower it was the Merry Hill, when it was the Round Oak. I love it, I do. I book up the ring-an-ride bus, yer know, an goo up on tha.

Every time Rose extended her tobacco-stained fingers towards Kerry, she pulled back, hoping her face didn't give too much away.

Her mum sat with Risley's mother on the settee. The men

were all standing up in front of the window. As Kerry listened to Rose's monologue she could see through the half-open kitchen door. Luke and Anna were talking to each other. He was holding a glass of whisky, swilling it around in the bottom of the glass the way their dad did with a cup of tea. There were dark makeup smudges under Anna's half-closed eyes.

People drifted away. Jamie asked where Luke was and then said he liked her hair. She helped her mum clear up, made another cup of tea for Risley's mum, Maggie. When Kerry got close to her, passing her the tea and when she'd helped her get out the car outside the house, she noticed the broken veins under her skin. She smelled of alcohol and sweat. Maggie and Kerry's mum sat talking, or not talking, just silent for a long time, in the kitchen. Her dad changed into his uniform and came to kiss her on the cheek and told her she'd been a good girl to have helped out so much.

The shiny escalator slid up through the shopping centre to the sound of piped music, making her think of the organ music at the funeral that morning. Window displays came into view. It was quieter here where the shops were smaller and more expensive. The clamour from the chain stores downstairs rose into the light, airy upper tier like the sound of a distant seashore. Kerry felt warmth on the back of her neck as the sun shone through the skylights. The sky felt close here.

She stood outside the window of a small clothes shop. Three mannequins wore clothes for the new winter season and she gazed at the long, flowing browns, the russets and ambers. Scattered around the models' feet were teardrop-shaped petals and pine cones, a few pebbles. Ferns and feathers stood in tall vases.

Kerry looked at the display and at her own reflection in the glass, her hair tied back neatly, the smart black funeral suit and silver jewellery, then back at the display. She moved slowly into the golden light of the shop. The assistant looked her over, checked she was worthy.

She browsed along a row of skirts, felt their newness, their crimsons and ivories. She felt a million miles away from the funeral. The skirts were beautiful.

His head split open. Adam, Risley. These images falling from her, gathering like petals around her feet.

Watch what yer like.

I am.

How am yer if yer keep flickin channels?

I'm watchin both.

They were sitting at opposite ends of the settee.

Dyer wanna chocolate?

No, they're yours. You eat them.

They sat watching television. He'd arrived back that night with a box of chocolates, late but not moaning any more, half smiling, the box there in his hand.

Belgian, mind you, she thought as she pushed a truffle into her mouth.

I would've bin all right for petrol in the end anyway, she'd said and turned away from him.

He changed channels again, from a cooking programme to a police chase documentary. She sighed. He looked pained.

I've told yer, I'm watchin both.

Having said that, he left it on the police chase for a while. The monochrome picture showed a white Toyota hurtling around the streets of an estate. The Toyota slowed, clipped a parked car, almost hit a young girl standing on the pavement – she jumped backwards into a garden hedge – and sped on.

Ooh, Kerry and Tim said together.

Cromwell Green, look, Tim said.

Kerry looked sharply at him.

Sorry, I meant the car being nicked, not the other thing.

Sometimes she'd play on the upset. When she was little, if people asked her if she had any brothers or sisters she'd always answer, Yes, two, but one died. That she didn't want to talk about it. Which was true of course, up to a point.

You mean Adam, not the *other thing*, she said, hammering it home. Tim always preferred allusion. Laugh if it was Cromwell Green, she said.

The screen changed to show the view from the police helicopter, flying above the chase. It was grainy, the flashing lights of the police car weaving through the static glow of streetlights and houses. Then the Toyota left the estate and joined a main road, slicing across lanes of traffic: a lorry screeched to a halt, the police cars followed. The pictures flicked back to ground level.

Kerry looked at Tim as he watched, his face working, his expression transparent, changing with the car moving across the screen. She pulled her legs underneath her into the soft cushion and ate another chocolate.

They'd been married over four years. The time went so quickly, especially now they had Alice. Things weren't so good. She told herself it was all to do with the money. Tim went out to work. He'd taken on his dad's shop-fitting business now that his parents had retired to Spain and did – be fair to him, she thought – work all hours. She didn't work. She'd wanted to, but Tim said no and then kept track of all her spending. They argued about it all the time. It should have got easier, having Alice, but it hadn't. But sometimes it was OK.

Got him, Tim said cheerfully, as a gangly boy in a baseball cap raced across the screen from the crashed Toyota and was rugby-tackled by a policeman. There were muffled shouts. Another figure was in the car, not moving. The policemen approached and the screen turned to static.

*

Her nan showed her the shopping on the kitchen table at Granny's house.

Dun yer like these teacakes, Kerry?

I don't know as we've tried em, Nan.

They'm ever so good value. Forty-nine at the Kwik Saeve, look.

Oh, yeah.

Here, have these uns. Tim might like one with a cup o tay when he comes in from work.

Iss all right, Nan. Yow've bought em for yerself. You keep em. Her accent would waver, get broader as she got dragged into conversations or felt uncomfortable. She felt uncomfortable now, about the box of teacakes.

Her nan carried on. I day. I bought em for yow. Or for yer mom to tek. They'm buy two get the third free at the minute.

Oh, right.

Iss allus that, these days. Never two for one. Allus three for two. Iss just to get yer to buy more, I think.

Kerry picked up the box and crinkled the cellophane wrapper under her fingers.

Goo on then, put em in yer bag.

Thanks, Nan, she said and leaned over to kiss her. She felt like a little girl. Her mum came back into the room. She'd been feeding Granny. Kerry had watched her earlier as she mashed potatoes into a bowl, poured in a bit of milk and mixed a few scraps of lamb chop and onion, like how Kerry prepared food for Alice. Her mum reached across her to pick up her cup of tea.

Her ay very bright again today, is her? She nodded back towards Granny, talking quietly.

Her's bin the saeme all wik. Iss them new tablets. Her was much better on the ode uns. Her doh know wheer her is half the time.

I'll have a word wi the nurse when her comes.

Kerry looked at her mum and her nan sitting opposite her in the dark kitchen, the curtains pulled across against the sun. Their likeness struck her; something she usually took for granted. Her mum sat on the edge of her chair, ready to get back to work, her sleeves rolled up; but both of them had that broad-shouldered, strong-jawed look. Determination maybe. Sometimes it was a look that said, Don't mess with me. Kerry realized that people sometimes worried about speaking to her because she too seemed so severe. That could be a good thing, though. She was even more like her mum since she'd had Alice. They were all dark skinned and sat like squaws with their hair tied back, Kerry thought. She'd been called a Red Indian by the boys at primary school for a few weeks after their class had seen a film about them. And now here they were, sitting in their wigwam waiting for the medicine man.

Yer dad all right wi Alice? her nan asked.

He's fine. He's tekkin her up the swings, I think.

What time's he at work?

Two till ten this wik.

Tis better now he's workin again, ay it? Gonna have me a walk up the butcher's after to get some o that ham thass on offer for me trip on Friday.

Kerry ull gi yer a lift, Mom. Her mum got up to go back to Granny.

Arr, I'll gi yer a lift, Nan. Wheer's yer trip to?

Llangollen. Llangollen. She said it the English way, then the Welsh way with a *th*.

Lovely.

They sat and waited for the nurse to come.

Why did yer tell me I killed Adam? Luke asked her a couple of days later, his hands shaking.

What?

Why did yer tell me I killed Adam?

What dyer mean, when?

When we was kids. When things was really bad. I was nine or so. Yow said I killed him, said it a few times.

Oh, Luke. I doh know.

She had as well. She wouldn't have thought of it now if he hadn't mentioned it. She'd said all sorts of things at that time, been really horrible, told her dad he wasn't her real dad, told her mum she wasn't as nice as other mums, told Luke he'd killed their brother. It was a stage she went through. She'd had a tough time growing up. Before Adam died she'd do everything with her mum, then afterwards there was a barrier between them, like her mum was too busy cutting flowers or looking at pictures of Adam to spend proper time with Kerry.

I doh know, Luke, really. Kids say horrible things to one another, doh they. Woss med yer think o that? I was always sayin nasty things to yer. Then yow ud thump me.

She tried to smile, but he just kept looking at the kitchen table.

I know, arr, but why did yer say that?

I doh know. People say things to hurt one another, thass all. I must've thought I'd upset yer.

Well, yer did.

God, Luke, I'm sorry. Iss a long time ago now.

There was a reason she'd said it, though. She'd heard them playing under her bedroom window. Luke got angry with Adam because he wouldn't do what he wanted, so he tried to find ways of getting rid of him, like telling him their mum was calling him. Kerry nearly went down to get him, but she was brushing her hair and didn't want to stop. Eventually, Adam started babbling on about the shops. Luke said, Yes, why don't you just go to the shop? That was when he'd toddled through the house to the front door. They'd never talked about it, nobody ever talked about it.

Ken walked in. What yow two on abaht? he asked, cheerful in his uniform.

Nuthin much.

Alice looked like Adam. There was no getting away from it. Her nan had mentioned it one Sunday night and nobody replied so she started to say it louder, but then got the message and shut up.

And now the resemblance was becoming more obvious. She looked more and more like him as she neared the age that he was in the photos up on the wall. That was why Kerry was trying to grow her hair. Of course she looked like him. When Luke had kids or if she had any more they'd look like Adam too. Kerry and Luke had looked like him once. Kerry wondered if the visual reminder was a good thing for her mum and dad, a way of Adam living on, or whether it just became another excuse for not burying the past.

Alice, come on, darling, it's time to put your shoes on.

No. Want Daddy do it.

Alice lay on the bottom two stairs, wiggling her feet around. Kerry was crouched in front of her holding a blue sandal, waiting for an opportunity to get the shoe on.

Come on, Alice. If you don't let me put your shoe on we can't go to Granny's. You want to see everybody at Granny's, don't you?

No, Daddy do it.

Alice's legs thrashed around on the stairs. Kerry gripped her ankle more tightly and bent over her, trying to force the shoe on. This time Alice's leg kicked backwards and caught Kerry on her cheek. She dropped the shoe. Alice's legs kept kicking. Kerry slapped her, harder than she meant to, and felt bad immediately. A red mark appeared on Alice's leg and the little girl screamed. She stopped kicking her legs, but kept hitting the top of a stair with the flat of her hand, bawling.

Tim appeared at the top of the stairs, splashing after-shave on inside his unbuttoned shirt.

What's the matter?

You won't put your shoes on, will yer? Kerry slumped and sat with her back against the wall. You'll look well now, she said tiredly, your face all red from crying.

Come on, what's the matter? Tim came downstairs slowly, coaxing Alice. Daddy's here. What's the matter?

Tim took a sandal from the floor and put his hand out to take the other from Kerry. His face was open, calm, but all Kerry could read in it was a look of triumph. She passed him the shoe.

Come on then, come on, let's get your shoes on. He talked to Alice in a soft voice, which Kerry thought sounded like he was calling a dog and she nearly said as much. Let's dry your tears. Slowly Alice sat up, and stuck her feet out towards him. She let him wipe her face with a tissue.

Kerry got up unsteadily and walked down the hallway.

That's it, that's it, Tim said gently to Alice. Then we'll be ready to go. That's it, ready to go. Good girl.

They argued on that Saturday afternoon, returning from shopping at Merry Hill. Autumn was coming. It was windy, rubbish was blowing everywhere, and it seemed to set their moods on edge. Tim was angry because he'd cleaned the cars that morning when it'd been dry. He'd asked her if she thought it would rain and she'd said no, then it poured.

That's my fault now, as well, she said.

Alice got some grit blown in her eye and started screaming. It took ages to find a parking space and then it was miles away from the entrance.

When they got back they opened a bottle of wine. Tim

put Alice to bed while Kerry made toasted sandwiches. They sat on the kitchen stools to eat their sandwiches and drink the wine, and talked about buying a new wardrobe for the spare bedroom and maybe booking up a week in October to visit Tim's parents.

Everything was OK. Maybe it was the wine that did it, she thought. Tim rarely drank because he always needed to get up early to drive off to that week's job. Kerry could drink more than him. Given half a chance, she thought.

A few people had been invited to Tammy's tomorrow but he said they couldn't go.

Why not?

I doh wanna goo.

Iss onny a couple of drinks at Tammy's. It'll be nice.

No way.

Miserable sod.

Look, it wouldn't be so bad if we hadn't gotta goo up to yer granny's after tha but yer woh give that up.

Wiv gorra goo. Yer know tha. Anyway, why should I wanna giv it up? Yow doh have to go all the time anyway.

It's pathetic.

I doh know what yer problem is.

Fine. I'll go to yer granny's. I've said I will. Iss just I have to spend time around folks I can't stand all the while.

And what's that meant to mean?

Do I have to spell it out?

Look, I doh know what yer problems with my family have got to do with gooin to Tammy's tomorra. Iss just a few drinks. Everyone else'll have their husbands or their boyfriends with them. I get sick of having to say you're working or making up some excuse.

Don't say anything then. Doh goo.

Why won't yer come?

Just give it a rest, will yer?

His face was a mixture of hurt and anger, like a little

boy's. She thought there were tears close to the surface and searched around inside herself for some clue to his strength of feeling. What was the matter with him? It was only some stupid Sunday-afternoon drink.

Come on, Tim. It's not fair. There'll be other blokes there. Rob'll be there. I thought you got on with him, last time.

Just give it a rest.

All right, doh cry abaht it.

She turned to go into the kitchen, catching the reflection of her blouse in the window at the bottom of the stairs. He got up and walked heavily across the room. Going to storm out. They arrived at the doorway together. She wouldn't move. He put his arm out in front of him to push her away from the door and grabbed at the tight flesh beneath the neck of her blouse. Hard enough to leave finger-shaped bruises afterwards. She gasped and slapped his arm away. He crashed through to the garage and started banging things around in there.

She put her coat on to go out. Then she decided she couldn't go to her parents' house again, so came back in, drank some more wine and watched television.

Later, she curled up on the edge of the bed, pulled the duvet over to her side; it was patterned with screwed-up blue and pink tissues. The bedside lamp was on. He came to bed and lay motionless for a while looking at her freckled back before turning the lamp out.

When they'd first met, Tim's parents had been in Spain for the summer and he had the house to himself. It was similar to the one they lived in now, not far away. It had a gravel drive with stone lions on either side, French windows and a swimming pool out the back. Kerry and her friend Alison would get the bus from Dudley to Kingswinford, their towels and swimming costumes in their bags – or Tim would pick them up in his Volkswagen at the Merry Hill

McDonald's – and laze around all day with Tim and his friend Dave. Then Alison and Dave fell away and it was just the two of them. She'd loved the swimming pool. They were going to get one at this house. Maybe next year, maybe the year after. It would be lovely for Alice. Kerry remembered the hum of the pool filter and the blueness of the water; cold, bottled beer clearing the chlorine tightness of her throat, the shape of Tim's outdoors-body as he dived from the side of the pool, the smell of the coconut suntan lotion sliding off her wet skin in the evening sun.

She'd fallen in love with all that. Sometimes it annoyed her when she thought about it, like the music at the funeral had, or the whole pathetic Risley episode, or the obsessing about Adam, or her old granny sitting there and living for ever, or the fact that some people watched car chases on television for entertainment, while others spent their whole lives trying to get away from places where you could lean out of your bedroom window and watch them for real.

The money was good, though. A balm against cheap tea bags and nicking from factory roofs and joy-riders whizzing around your estate. That was about it, though. She'd rather sit in a house like this, burglar-alarmed, double-glazed, centrally heated, looking at a husband she wasn't that bothered about, than do the same on Cromwell Green estate, but only just.

She shifted, wriggled more to the middle of the bed. He turned and put his face against her back and his arm around her.

Kerry spotted Alison in the queue outside the post office and pulled into the kerb. She felt conscious of people in the queue looking at the car and quickly leaned across the passenger seat and wound the window down. Ali. Ali.

Alison looked hazily into the middle distance. She'd always needed glasses. All right, Kerry.

All right. How am yer?

Oh, yer know. Yome lookin really well. Is this yower car? How's Alice?

Fine yeah. Alice is good. Yer look well yerself. Look how tanned yow am. And slim.

I doh know. I doh feel it. I bin sittin out a lot. What yer doin? Gooin to yer mom's?

Yeah, her's got Alice.

Oh yeah. Me mom's lookin after Brandon this mornin while I come dahn here, like. She nodded at the post office queue.

How yer doin with him, all right?

Iss OK. Iss difficult sometimes, y'know, but me mom and dad help at least. Like yowers, I suppose. He starts school after Christmas. I doh know wheer the time guz.

What yer gonna do when he does?

Ooh, put me feet up, I think. Alison laughed. Maybe I'll try an getta job. I doh know. I doh know what I could do.

Yow could do loads o things. Thad have yer back at the shop, wudn't they?

I doh know. Will yow goo to work when Alice is bigger?

I doh know. I doh know if I need to or nothin. I mean, not like, I doh know what Tim ud say. Kerry enjoyed bragging to some people about what she'd got, but not to her mates. Not when she hadn't seen Alison for ages and not given the things Alison had been through. Alison was still smiling.

Well, thass what happens when yer marry money. Is Tim all right?

He's fine, yer know. Kerry grinned, happy not to have caused offence.

Aaagh. Still in love look, Ali said. Hey, guess who I sid the other day?

Who?

Wayne Pearce.

Did yer? Wheer?

Oh, they had karaoke on dahn the Shakespeare an he was in theer.

Wayne Pearce had been the cock of the school. He'd grown a moustache when he was fourteen and punched the headmaster on the day he left. He ended up in Winson Green not long after that; bitten a man's ear off in a fight along the road from her mum and dad's house, spat it back into his garden rockery, the blood glistening on his lips and bare torso (he always took his shirt off to fight). It had been in the paper.

Is he still . . . ?

Alison leaned into the car and touched Kerry's arm with the tips of her fingers. He's still a fuckin great shag, I tell yer.

They laughed and everyone in the queue turned around.

I'll atta get back over theer. I'll be here all day otherwise. I'll see yer soon, yeah. Gi me a ring. Say hello to yer mom and dad.

Yeah, I will. Seeya, Ali. Tek care. Love to everybody.

As she drove away she could see Alison waving in her mirror. She drove towards the flats where Wayne Pearce used to live; still did, maybe. She remembered a party there one summer night, not long before she met Tim. They'd launched pint glasses off the balcony and into the street at midnight. She stopped the car and sat for a while outside the flats. Net curtain flapped out of a window in the top left-hand corner of the block. She reversed the car and turned it round, drove back to the post office, but when she got there Ali had gone. She must have sat for longer than she thought.

As Kerry turned the car into the alley she had to swerve to avoid hitting Jamie's van and almost hit the house wall instead. Jamie came darting around from the side of the van holding a chamois leather, and for a moment she thought he was going to start shouting at her for going too quickly.

All right, Kerry, he said, smiling. Sorry I've got it parked so near the corner, I day think anybody ud be driving up here. Yer dad's car's dahn the garage.

She wanted to shout at him, her hands shaking from the near-miss. Iss all right, Jamie. Tim's always havin a go at me for taking corners too quick.

I bet he wants yer to look after it, doh he?

Kerry rolled her eyes. He's always moaning about something.

Iss a lovely car, though.

Yeah, iss nice. Bit dirty, though. Yow can do this next if you want.

He smiled again. If yer want me to, like.

No, don't be silly. She got out the car, wishing she could look more ladylike but having to take a huge step because it was so high off the ground. Tim said they made them like that so you could look down on everybody as you drove. As she headed towards the back gate, she tried to think of something more to say, stopped with her hand on the splintered wood of the fence.

They'm nice jeans just to be washing the van in. She nodded down at his Armani's. Jamie always dressed nicely.

Doh be fooled. I got em cheap on holiday last year. They was all right for a bit but they've gone really baggy now wi washin.

He was funny, the way he always took such care. She imagined everything about him, his clothes, the van, the gel in his hair, was all sparkling and new.

No, they still look good.

Yer pickin Alice up?

Yeah, give me mom a break.

Her's gerrin bigger now. I cor believe wheer the time guz. Her's a lovely little girl.

Thanks, Jay. Takes after her mother, eh?

Yeah, probably, why not?

She looked away, opened the gate. I'll go and see how tham gerrin on. Seeya, Jay.

Seeya, Kerry.

As she walked down the path she could feel him looking at her. Like he used to when they were kids and he was round playing with Luke. In a sweet way, nothing bad. That was true enough about the time going. It was funny now to remember the door on Luke's room opening and Jamie looking out across the landing, her walking back from the bathroom with a towel wrapped around her, getting ready for a night out, spraying dewberry perfume everywhere, and with Jamie looking; knowing he was looking, and swaying a bit with the towel as she walked.

When she got to the back door she turned and looked at him. He was looking straight at her, didn't turn away embarrassed, just smiled and put his hand up to wave.

Yow look like a bloody battered wife wi them glasses on this weather.

Kerry and Mary sat peeling potatoes into a plastic bowl. She pulled the glasses halfway down her nose and looked across the kitchen table at her mum.

They'm all right. They'm Police. Iss a good make. I wanna get me wear out of em.

Oh, is that it?

Back at home, she put on her best telephone voice and said that of course she could come for an interview at eleven forty-five and that the computer test would be no problem.

The Wayne Pearce memory was playing on her mind after seeing Alison. She should give her a call – it wouldn't do any harm just to ring her up.

On the last day of school she'd sat with Wayne on the

bench on the top field, before he went and punched Mr Allcroft. Just the two of them, the way they'd worked it. Her legs were covered with the eggs and flour they'd been hurling at each other from first-floor windows. His face. She remembered his face as he turned to look at her.

I've had enough, Kerry, you know. Fightin all the while. I've gorra grow aht on it. Iss jus tha. Iss jus. Well, folks expect yer to, doh they? Iss this place ay it, really.

The expression on his face, tired and bewildered; like the faces of her parents, she thought. He shook his head and looked across the field, took a swig from one of the plastic bottles of whisky and Coke they'd brought to school. It was melodramatic and adolescent, she knew now. Whatever it was, it worked, that sadness in the way he shook his head. She'd touched his arm, then his cheek; him still shaking his head and staring into the distance before they'd disappeared into the trees behind.

And then the drama of the swimming pool. After Adam, her whole life had turned on that. Not the pool itself but the idea of it, having things that other people couldn't have.

The phone went three times early the next morning, but each time she picked it up there was no one there. When it first rang she'd assumed it was a work call for Tim, but he was leaving at six that week in order to get a job finished. She could've sworn she heard a sigh at the other end of the line as she said, Hello, hello, who's this? into the silence. That was all she needed, pest phone calls.

The third time it rang a woman asked for Tim, in a young, nervy voice. Then she put the phone down as Kerry was halfway through answering her. It put Kerry on edge for the rest of the morning. Next time, she'd give someone a mouthful.

She was trying to feed Alice her spaghetti hoops, but the little girl was having none of it. There was tomato sauce across her face and bib and all over the high chair and up Kerry's blouse. Kerry tried to poke the plastic spoon into Alice's mouth but she twisted her head away, threw her arms up in the air and almost knocked the spoon away.

Come on, darlin, please. Kerry felt the bowl. It was cold. Alice blew an orange, tomato-sauce bubble at her. Kerry walked away, around the breakfast bar, and bit her tongue.

No like, no like, Alice moaned, playing with the spaghetti with her fingers. Kerry turned the radio on and paced up and down the kitchen.

When she first had Alice she was determined to give her everything she wanted. If she didn't like spaghetti hoops then she could have something else. She was going to spoil her child; the intention had been there right from when she first knew she was pregnant.

But now it was the most important thing in the world that Alice ate her spaghetti. Kerry took the bowl away from her before it really did go everywhere. She'd warm it up in the microwave in a minute.

She still wanted to spoil her, but not in that way. It was a funny word really, made her think of something gone off, ruined. She'd got so nervous during the pregnancy and in the weeks after giving birth that she'd cry – desperate for her baby to be perfect. For nothing bad to happen. She got like it now, sometimes, but not so often – had calmed down a bit.

What happened to Adam made me a different person, she'd think. She was warier, jumpier than the mothers at playschool – even the other first-time mums, neurotic as they all were. Terrible things happened and they happened to you, not just other people. She knew that. She could remember everything about the night Adam died, every detail. She was nine years old, in her bedroom, the window wide open over the back garden. It was June, one of the longest days of the year. She'd just washed her hair and was brushing it and singing ABBA songs into the hairbrush, listening to Luke and Adam outside. She should have gone and got him when Luke didn't want to play with him, that's what she thought. She loved playing with Adam, mothering him. She'd dress him up or play hospitals or schools or post offices and wrap a bandage round him or make him listen to her lessons or put stamps on pretend letters. Luke was always a bit too close to her age, unwilling to be bossed around. He'd push her away, call her names when their mum wasn't looking.

Kerry hated the way the family skirted around Adam's death. Not one conversation about it, and all that guilt for everyone. There was that picture in the living room, bigger than either hers or Luke's, and the flowers always being cut and prepared on the kitchen table. A procession of flowers. Kerry had done everything with her mum, but that had stopped when the flowers started. The memorials, his birthday. There was all that rigmarole, but when it came to talking about it there was nothing. He'd never grow up, make mistakes, get into trouble, marry, work, *live*. All that. They adored Alice now and always would, she knew, but imagine if she was dead, never made her own mistakes. Maybe she could understand it. She could see how people got into that way of thinking, that worship.

Kerry put the bowl of hoops into the microwave.

You can stop that screaming, Alice. There's no tears there. You're just playing up. You're not moving from that chair until you've eaten your spaghetti.

That was the way, she supposed, just caring for her, doing her best.

After the phone call, the interview, then the job. It was four mornings a week in a call centre for a debt collectors on the fifth floor of a new office block at the Waterfront. Alice stayed at Ruth's or her mum's. She hadn't told Tim. She had to talk into a headset to desperate people trying to keep up with interest payments and penalty charges on loans they should never have been given. It was OK. The girls she worked with seemed nice enough, although there wasn't much time to get to know them in the ten-minute break they had when most of the women rushed down-stairs to have a cigarette on the canal bank. Her boss said she'd made an excellent start.

Yome gonna atta tell him, her mum said when she collected Alice at the end of her first week.

I know, Mom, I know. Not just yet, though, eh?

I doh know how much longer yow can goo on. Doh expect me to lie for yer. Alice will be able to tell him soon.

It'll be fine. Just for a bit longer. I'll get meself settled and then talk to him.

I doh know. Iss no way to carry on, yer know. A man an wife keepin secrets from one another. If Alice doh say nuthin soon he'll notice the money, woh he?

He won't – this is my money. Iss going into a separate account. That was the problem in the first place.

I doh know. Her mum was shaking her head. Iss no good y'know. Yow'll atta get yerselves sorted out. Imagine if me an yer dad had carried on like that when yow was little?

Kerry giggled. I know. Things am different now, though, today. Me and Tim am hardly yow and Dad, am we? We never will be. I wudn't even wanna be the same.

An woss that supposed to mean?

Nuthin. Nuthin bad. Just, you know. Things am different now, that's all. We couldn't be like you and Dad. We couldn't live like you and Dad.

Look, a lot o the time wiv had no choice on how we lived. Yow never wanted for anythin, you know.

I know. Kerry didn't believe that. She'd grown up wanting things she couldn't have. She sighed and tried to explain. I'm not on about that, Mom. I don't mean like that. God, Mom. Doh goo all funny about it.

I doh know what yome on abaht. I doh. All I know is a couple shudn't have secrets from one another.

All right. I'll sort it out. I promise. Onny not just yet.

She wished she could put things more clearly. Her mum looked tired. Kerry wondered if it was too much for her, always looking after Alice. She told herself it would be OK. Perhaps she could buy her something nice when she got paid, take her to the Merry Hill. But then she'd already spent the money she was earning several times in her head. Her mum was wrapping up a tin of biscuits for Kerry to take round to Auntie Eileen's for her birthday.

Lerrus do that, Mom. She leaned across the kitchen table.

Goo on. Iss all right. I'm all right.

He provides for yer, though, looks after yer. He's great with Alice.

She'd been moaning. Luke hated Tim, which was why she was asking herself if he was genuine. Was this a plea for her to see the good things she had, or an automatic reaction? Masking that secret desire to see everything fall down, destroyed, like in the last days of the Round Oak when they'd creep guiltily to the edge of their parents' room to listen to panicked conversations.

Yeah, I suppose you're right, she said.

She sat at the kitchen table. He was sprawled in the chair by the door. Their mother stood with Alice in the garden. They'd sat in these positions many times, not saying much. They never really spoke to each other, not properly. Luke came over as the protective brother when it came to Tim and he loved Alice. He looked awful today, though. She could probably help him, if she knew what to say. She wanted to ask him about breaking up with Sarah, how he felt about Risley, the conversation about Adam the other day. She didn't have the words, though. Not for it to come out as she meant it.

That was what you did – skirted around emotions and events. Everybody did. Perhaps nobody could say what they really meant, but it'd be a relief to talk to someone properly sometimes. When Luke mentioned Adam the other day, it was only the second time she could remember that they'd ever talked about him. The first time was after she'd been allowed to go to the funeral and Luke had stayed at Solomon and Iris's.

What was it like?

There were lots of flowers and the church was packed and lots of people cried, but Mom didn't until the end and Dad didn't at all.

Does that mean he ay sad?

No, stupid. He was just trying to be brave.

The moment she said she'd do it she regretted it. A Saturday-morning shift was available, did she want it? She was so pleased to be asked – first out of all the new starters, that she had just blurted out yes. It was time and a half on a Saturday, too. It was a one-off, that was the way she justified it to herself. The woman who usually did it was going to a wedding.

But she still hadn't told Tim. He was going out that morning, to check a job in Telford.

She padded downstairs in her dressing gown. Alice was sleeping, curled right up in a corner of the bed with her hair plastered halfway over her face. While she made breakfast she thought how it was right what Luke had said, she was lucky, the deception over this job had made her think that. She didn't want to lie to him.

She had to be at work by half nine. He wasn't even up yet. Usually he was off early. Typical. She'd tell him they were going to Merry Hill, then to her mum and dad's, and she promised herself she'd tell him all about it at Sunday dinner. She wanted to contribute, she'd say. Perhaps they could put the money towards the cars or save for the swimming pool. If he said to stop then that'd be fine.

Upstairs, Tim was still sleepy when she balanced the tray on the bed. He'd worked late all week at a big job in Oxford. She worried about him driving up and down the motorway, on his own and dead tired. He'd fallen asleep at the wheel once on his way to a job in East Anglia somewhere. He was driving along into the morning sun when the next thing he knew he was rattling along the grass verge and half in a hedge. He'd been shy when he told her about it, probably half in mind of her worries about cars and accidents. She'd shouted at him, told him to be more careful, that he'd been so, so lucky and that she didn't want his dad or the police banging on the door with bad news. She needed him. Partly it was put on, copied behaviour, she knew it was how he wanted her to respond. In a way she was secretly thrilled by the story, as he was when he told it, his coy eyes bright with a sort of wonder at suddenly finding himself bumping to a halt across the grass. Even with what happened to Adam, at eighteen you think you're going to live for ever.

God, this is nice. Woss brought this on?

Sshh, nothing. Just that Alice is still asleep and you've bin working hard. Tim pulled himself up the bed and she put the tray of tea and croissants down.

They kissed and she got into bed.

Come on, it'll get cold, she said.

With the breakfast and Alice sleeping in, she went from having plenty of time to having none at all. She wasn't used to having to be anywhere on time. The odd hospital appointment she ran her nan to and Alice's check-ups at the clinic. Even the playgroup had no definite start time; you could drift in and have a coffee between nine and ten.

It was no big deal if you were late, whereas now she could have money stopped or lose her good reputation. She rushed back and forth between the bathroom and Alice's room. There was no time to wash Alice because Tim was in the shower. She just pushed her into her clothes. Of all the mornings to sleep late, it had to be this one. Kerry kissed the top of Alice's head as she started to cry.

Don't put that shirt on, Tim. Iss one o yer best. Wear it for Sunday dinner tomorrow. I doh want you ruining it in some dusty building.

I'm only going up there to have a look at the place.

I know, yeah, but you won't be able to resist having a crawl around, will yer?

Tim began to unbutton the shirt. Kerry kissed him on the cheek.

Right, we'll see yer later, she said.

Bye, darling, Tim said to Alice and kissed her. Her face was wet and red with tears.

Alice was still crying in the car as Kerry made a mess of reversing off the drive. Tim would have laughed at her if he'd been watching. They had to stop at every set of lights along Brierley Hill High Street, Alice still grizzling.

Come on, darling, it's OK, Kerry said. Look at the bus, look. Wave to the people on the bus.

It was the fifth time that week she'd dropped Alice off with her mum. Too many. When she'd asked her about Saturday morning, her mum had just nodded, said nothing.

The wheels on the bus go round and round . . .

She'd be late for sure.

That's it, darlin. Kerry started singing again. She thought of Tim putting on a good shirt to go and crawl around some dirty unit. He needed her. She pulled over in front of a bus stop and took out her phone.

Shall we just go home, Alice? Yeah, let's just go home.

Yeah, Nigel. Hello, yes, it's Kerry Jones. Yes, well I was.

Something's come up with my daughter and I can't make it in. I know, yes. If I could make it I would. I'm sorry – I'm not sure a Saturday shift was such a good idea. Yes, yeah. I'll see you on Monday. Bye.

It was easy. She thought that perhaps Nigel fancied her. Well, he was only human.

Let's go and get you in the bath, darlin.

A bus pulled into the stop behind her. She was blocking its way. Only a little bit, she thought. The driver mouthed something, some of the people in the bus queue tut-tutted at her. She smiled and waved, then tried to call her mum on the mobile.

The driver on the bus goes shout, shout, shout, she sang as she swung the car into the opposite lane.

When they got back Tim's car was still on the drive. He must have been really tired, she thought. She'd tell him about the job stuff tomorrow. He was standing in the living room talking on his mobile.

Not now, no, right, I'll speak to you later, he said, sighing as he came off the phone.

Hello, she shouted.

What you doin? he asked.

Ooh, don't ask. She had it planned. Look at us. I'm all done up and her's not even had a wash this morning. I've come back to bath her. I doh know what I was thinking of.

I thought she was gonna have a bath at yer mom's.

Yeah, but her looks well. Especially me being dressed up. She felt herself going red and moved across the room. I thought I told yer to take that shirt off?

I'll wear what I like.

God, yome in a good mood all of a sudden.

I don't know why you've got to go out and then come rushing back. Why am yer all med-up for like that anyway?

Well, I was off to see my fancy man but he stood me up.

Iss Saturday, I want to look nice. I thought you was going to Telford.

Yeah, I, er, might not be now.

Who was that on the phone?

The bloke up there. I gorra ring him in a bit.

Well, if yer do go up there, please change yer shirt. Come on Alice, let's start yer bath.

It was only upstairs that she started to think about it. He was even jumpier than her. And she had something to be guilty about. Tim was on the phone again, outside in the garden. She could hear him talking but not what he was saying. She put a towel on the side of the bath and let Alice hide her eyes in it while she shampooed her hair.

Her mum eased Granny from the chair towards the edge of the bath. Granny groaned.

Iss OK, Granny, yome OK. Mary spoke to her in a gentle voice, much gentler than she did even to Alice, and held the old woman's shoulders and back firmly. Kerry copied her and said the same things, although with less certainty. Things looked far from OK to her.

Slowly, her mum undressed Granny, perched with her on the side of the bath.

If yow con just ode her here, Kerry. Kerry, standing above the two of them, held Granny's left arm. Towels were draped around the small bathroom. The room smelled of bleach, of chlorine, like a memory of the swimming pool, and underneath was the smell of damp from the carpets and the wallpaper.

Thass it, Granny. Kerry's got yer an all. Yome OK.

Granny's head was on one side, her chin down on her left shoulder. Kerry looked down over her; wispy, white hairs covering her scalp, her face screwed up and her eyes tiny and bright but distant. As Mary slowly removed Granny's clothes, Kerry couldn't help but marvel at her body. Every bit of skin was wrinkled, her flesh was waxy and sagging, like a melted candle.

She'd soiled herself just earlier, started crying silently, wouldn't look at them at all; ashamed. When Mary removed her tights the smell became awful. Kerry looked away. Her mum was squeezing the sponge into the water to wipe her down. Kerry thought she was going to be sick. A shower would've been more useful, although even the power of the water might bruise her. Perhaps one of those plastic things you plugged onto the taps, Kerry thought.

We'll soon be clayn, Mary said in a cheerful voice. Soon have yer nice.

Kerry was trying not to breathe because of the smell. The water was slowly changing colour. She concentrated on keeping a tight grip on Granny's arm as her mum worked. She was more scared of dropping her than of being sick, listening to her mum's encouraging words and the water dripping from Granny's body, half into the bath, half onto the towels. The wallpaper pattern was making her eyes go funny, she'd been staring at it for too long.

Kerry wondered if she'd ever have to do this to her own mum. Of course she could do it – she'd had Alice, cleaned her, looked after her, but it was different with Granny, not fresh and new. The smell was of something ancient. Kerry thought that maybe she smelled like death, but then felt terrible, as though she'd jinxed her. Granny ull live for ever, everybody always said.

The way to do it was to watch and learn. You couldn't just know how to get this sorted out, she thought. All the towels down and this arrangement on the edge of the bath and the plastic chair. That was how you did it. I'll just have to concentrate, Kerry thought, in case I have to do it one day. She looked at her mum's face, coaxing Granny gently.

Iss OK, iss OK, she said, sponging her down, her strong arm holding her safe.

You learn what people expect you to do and then do it. Everything: love, grief, anger, happiness, all these things you learn. She helped dab Granny dry with the clean towels, opened the dressing gown to swaddle her.

It was late and the light was beginning to fade. Kerry was aware of the sky turning a darker blue over the estate as she watched Alice run up and down the back garden path. The little girl waved her arms in the air and skipped between them and the gate. She was shouting something she'd heard on television that morning. Kerry couldn't work out what it was, even when she asked her to say it more slowly. Kerry and Luke stood side by side, waiting for Tim to come by on his way back down from Telford, or wherever he was.

This ull tire her out. Luke smiled.

Some hopes.

Her's really gerrin bigger.

Yeah, I know. I doh know where the time goes.

They stood watching her, letting her run, her arms flailing above her head. She did strange things sometimes, Kerry thought, went off into a world of her own, shouting *awawawa* like a mantra, running around and laughing. She was happy, just being a kid. Every time she turned, her face was caught half in shadow, framed there, and Kerry knew they were watching something magical. It was the quality of the light, all shadows and fuzzy outlines. But they could see how like theirs her face was, like their parents', like their dead brother's.

Go to shop, Mommy? Alice was tiring, running more slowly.

No, darlin, what shop? Daddy'll be here in a minute.

She stood in front of them and rubbed her eyes with the back of her hand. Kerry had bought some ice cream from the newsagent's earlier. Alice wanted to go back.

I go to shop, Mommy. I go.

And they were back in that night again. To what Adam had been babbling on about – To the shop, to the shop – when Luke had told him to go, to get out of his way. Kerry heard it all from the bedroom window.

Yow killed him, she'd said, so angry, wanting to put the blame somewhere. Now she just wanted it all to end. The recriminations went on for too long, went on for ever.

She felt her brother's body stiffen and turned her head to look at him. He was staring at Alice in bewilderment, panic, his face draining. She felt her own legs going rubbery. Luke looked away, over the fence, then back again.

Oh God, he said.

Alice shouted again about the shop.

Nobody's going to the shop, Alice. Daddy'll be here in a minute. Quiet now, darlin.

She even sounds like him, Kerry thought, wanting to shake her, to shut her up, to force the childish games, the innocent running around, back down her throat. Instead, she picked her up and hugged her.

They stood there, Luke shaking his head.

Shit, I can remember it, he said.

What, Luke?

Thass what he said to me, abaht the shop, an I said yeah, goo on then.

Alice was wriggling in Kerry's arms but she managed to reach out towards Luke.

Thass how it happened. I said, Yeah, goo on then, goo to the shop, cos I day, I day want him playin if he cudn't play right.

He shook his head; bewildered, like someone lost then suddenly found. He grabbed her and Alice, hugged them tightly.

Iss OK, Luke, come on. Didn't you know this bit?

He was shaking his head and crying against her shoulder.

No, I could onny remember playing with him an then sitting next door after it ud happened. I've thought all sorts.

Come on, iss OK.

He pulled his head back, his eyes wide. Oh my God, an we all went runnin aht an saw him.

We did, Luke, yeah.

An he was there on the side of the road.

I know.

I couldn't remember, just couldn't remember.

Kerry couldn't forget. She could hear the sound of the truck now, too loud through the open front door, and her mum's panicked shouts as she realized something was wrong. Kerry's stomach had flipped over as she jumped down the last half-dozen stairs following her mum and dad as they ran down the front path. Along the street her little brother's body was lying in the gutter, the front wheel of the truck at an odd angle next to him. In the wailing and the panic she'd turned to see Luke behind her and she'd grabbed him, the overwhelming urge in those few seconds to protect him, to stop him seeing. Chaos; everyone out of the houses. Iris from next door had put her arms around them both and tried to pull them away. Luke trying to run but being picked up by Iris, his legs running in mid-air like in a cartoon. Kerry struggled loose, wanted to know what was going on.

She remembered it all: the strange angle of the body until someone draped a blue coat over him, the driver of the van, unable to move, sat in his cab, staring straight ahead. Screaming. She used to force herself to remember it all. As a teenager, after shouting at everybody, her eyes closed at night, she'd run through every detail.

What colour was the driver's shirt? Yellow with tea stains on it.

What colour were Adam's shoes? Blue sandals, good ones from Beatties.

What were her dad's first words on seeing what had happened? No, oh God, oh God, oh God, Adam.

Her mum's? What? Oh, oh. Adam. Ken. Adam. A variation on a theme.

Alice was *awawaw*ing again. Kerry kissed her cheek and stroked her hair.

Nobody's going to the shop, Alice. You have to have Mommy or Daddy or Uncle Luke or Nanny or Grandad with you. She looked at Luke. You OK?

He was pale, had stopped crying. He nodded his head, looked away again.

Iss OK, Luke, y'know. Iss OK.

Not really. His chest was heaving up and down.

Oh Luke, I'm sorry. It felt unreal, talking about what had always been there, now, in this narrow time and place.

He shook his head.

Luke, we all, we all could've stopped it, you know. Her voice faltered. It was an accident.

He was looking at her and at Alice, wrestling in Kerry's arms, trying to get down.

You OK? She didn't know why she kept asking that.

All right, yeah. Shook up. He was wiping his eyes with the back of his hand. Need to be on me own a bit.

Give Uncle Luke a nice kiss, Alice. Daddy'll be here in a minute. Then we'll go inside and say bye-bye to Nanny and Grandad.

Alice held out her arms to Luke, and he hugged her.

Try not to worry, Luke.

He pulled a face.

It wasn't your fault. It was nobody's. It was an accident. Nothing's changed. We just need to talk properly about it.

She heard the sound of the front door. Tim had arrived.

You OK? she said again. What do you want me to do? Shall I stay?

No.

You want to be on yer own?

He nodded.

Phone me if you need to. Whatever time, just phone. Try not to worry tonight.

He didn't call that night and she lay in bed biting the flesh around her fingernails, worrying and waiting for the phone to ring. She kept thinking of him in his room, in the house they'd grown up in, in the room he used to share with the brother he thought he'd killed. You poor boy, she thought, waking up from a shallow, nasty sleep.

She phoned early next morning. She shouldn't have left him. What if he'd done something stupid? But no. It was fine. Is Luke OK, Mom?

Arr, he's all right. He looks terrible, though, like he's coming dahn wi summat. Iss all a bit much for him I think, wi Sarah an then what happened to David.

Tim's phone was charging in the kitchen. The last six calls were all the same number. It wasn't a Telford code. She let it ring, holding the phone awkwardly against her ear, still plugged in at the wall.

Tim?

The woman's voice from the other day.

Tim never usually walked anywhere. He'd arrived home early from work, or wherever, and they went for a walk with Alice, swinging her between them in a game. Alice kicked her legs out, wearing her new frog-eye Wellington boots.

Nobody ever walked around where they lived. It wasn't the sort of place where you nipped out for a bottle of milk or strolled to get the paper. There were no pavements on a couple of streets and they had to walk uncomfortably along the edge of the road. Kerry was anxious they were going the wrong way. Imagine not knowing the way round your own area, she thought. She didn't even know the name of the road they were on. When she was little, she'd known every blade of grass on the mushroom field, the hollows in the uneven pavement on Cromwell Green, the paths through the allotments, the broken glass and weeds and graffiti in the alleys behind the house. Expensive cars, four-by-fours and BMWs, sometimes a Volkswagen or a Fiat playing dance music, eased past. They came to a narrow bit of road and a bright blue Jeep squeezed past them.

This is why I never walk, Tim said.

No, you never walk because you're lazy.

They found a bench on the green next to the canal. A group of teenagers with bikes were messing around on the low wall, pretending to try to push each other in. They all had caps on, seven or eight of them, boys and girls. A uniform of tracksuits. They passed a large brown plastic bottle between them. Tim looked warily at them and shook his head.

Scruffs. I don't think they'm from round here.

Kerry laughed. Children am children, wherever you are.

I wouldn't let Alice out like that when her's their age.

What? In a tracksuit on her bike? They're not doing any harm.

Smoking as well, look.

You sound about a hundred.

So do you trying to sound all laid back. Sound like you've been having a smoke of summat yerself.

Shut up. It was rare he made a joke.

A middle-aged couple walked slowly past. The woman smiled at Alice, looked up and said hello to them.

Bet we look like the perfect family, Kerry said when they'd passed.

We are, Tim replied.

You working in Telford next week?

No, some of the lads are gonna finish it off. We've got a

regular lined up next week. Finch's in Wolverhampton, you know. All back to normal.

I don't know whether to believe you.

Tim said nothing.

Shall we go back?

How am yer? She stood at the door to Luke's bedroom.

All right.

Really?

Still just, yer know.

I do, I spose, yeah. You've got nothing to feel bad about.

No. Iss different now.

Luke, you was a little boy. You didn't know what you was saying. You were just playing with him.

He tried to say something, but she carried on.

How do yer think Mom feels? Not noticing as he walked past her? How do yer think Dad feels, he left the door on the latch? Probably the onny night it was like it in twenty years. How about the driver? A little boy running out in the road in front of him like that. I doh think he ever worked again after. We've all gorra live with our part.

No, stop, stop it, yer doh understand. I thought I'd killed him.

How much can you understand at six years old? I mean, really. Really.

No, I mean I really thought I'd killed him. Done summat to him. Like took him out there meself or pushed him in front o the lorry. I thought that was why I cudn't remember properly. I thought that was why yow used to say I'd killed him.

Oh, she said. Why did yer think that? The question just sounded ridiculous, her voice seemed small.

I doh know, cos yow said it to me, it just got stuck in me head. I mean, iss bad enough, but I thought I'd actually killed him.

Oh, she said. We can do terrible things without even noticing, she thought.

He was grinning and then he started to cry.

Come on, she said and put her arms around him, rocking him gently. Come on. Iss OK. I'm sorry. I'm sorry. Iss OK.

The nurse said tham gonna replace that cheer her's in.

Thass a good thing. I doh know as her con get comfy in it any more.

Thass good, Kerry said. She was trying to look at Luke, finishing a bowl of soup at Nan's table, but Uncle Mick kept walking across her view.

They tode her it ull be an early birthday present.

I know arr. Ninety-nine. It woh be a bad age, ull it?

It ull be early, it ay for three months yet, Luke muttered into the soup.

Yow doh know what the council's like, Luke, be more likely her hundredth birthday.

Woh be a bad age though, ull it? Touch wood.

No, it's amazing really.

Ninety-nine. I wonder if her'll get to hundred, with the way her's bin. Her mum touched wood again.

I con hear yer talkin abaht me in theer, her gran's voice came through the open kitchen door. They smiled.

Yow ay lost yer bloody hearin then, an yer?

He's lookin better, the fresh air might do him good, her mum said quietly as Luke waited on the path.

Saturday morning, and they'd walked up to the top of Cawney Bank. The last time she'd been up here was when it snowed when they were kids and everyone came up with trays or bin bags or plastic sledges. Things looked different from up here. Netherton Church, tall and spider-brown, a hill looking down on a hill. Brierley Hill flats shadowing each other, next to the valley that was sprawling Merry

Hill, the buildings indistinct, glints of sunlight bouncing off some of the cars. She tried to spot the building where she worked but couldn't.

You could see for miles. The Malverns, like a fuzzy blue whale lolling in shallows, the shape of Wren's Nest behind the castle and beyond that the hazy outline of western hills.

How dyer feel now?

OK.

Really?

Iss funny.

Not really.

Listen. I thought I'd killed him, got to thinking I'd done summat terrible.

Yer didn't though, did yer. Yow've done nothing wrong, Luke. Yow've just gotta let the past go, she said.

I know. Easier said than done.

You can make it go away.

Luke sighed. I spose. People do it, though, yer know; live in the past as much as now.

You can't live like that. Thass no life. Yer atta get on with things the best you can.

He went to say something else, then stopped, picked at his jeans. Thanks, he said.

Iss OK. Everything's gonna be all right.

The light changed; shadows moved. The hills in the distance shifted. Hills or clouds? The more she stared the less clear it was.

A few days later and Luke was still off work. The doctor had signed him off for another week. Kerry didn't know how much he'd told him. You couldn't read the certificate because of the handwriting. It'd be good if he'd talked to somebody else. Perhaps he would with Jamie. Perhaps she could say something to him.

She drove slowly along the main road, a queue of traffic

alongside the pavement barriers. They'd put them up all around the estate after Adam's death, replaced them every so often when a stolen car went off track. A seventeen-year-old lad had been killed a few months before, down near the Birmingham Road. Hundreds of flowers had been tied to the railings.

There were a couple of football magazines and a packet of tobacco on the passenger seat, which he'd asked her to get. She thought maybe he was looking a bit better, some more colour to his face.

Thinking he'd killed his brother. He said the fear had always been somewhere inside him, then he'd worked himself into really believing it. He needed to speak to someone. She needed to speak to her mum and dad. How could she have been so cruel, telling him he'd killed his brother?

That morning she'd woken from a dream that everyone in the world was blind but that she could see. People blundered, crashed around, put their arms out to try and reach each other, but in their eagerness groped and pushed and scratched clumsily, doing more harm than good and there was nothing she could do about it.

Daddy's always at work, Alice, isn't he? Working all hours again, she said bitterly. *Work, work, work*. He will be tired.

She was third in a line of cars waiting at the crossing. She saw her dad walk across in his uniform and waved to get his attention, suddenly feeling everything was going to be all right.

There's Grandad. Look, Alice.

Halfway over the crossing he stopped, looked back and turned round. A car started to go but he put his arm up to stop it. He looked official in his uniform. Iris from next door tottered to the edge of the kerb. Ken took her arm and they walked slowly across. Her dad said something and Iris laughed. A horn sounded impatiently. On the other side of the crossing Jamie's van pulled out into the road and drove away. She saw his face as the van turned; his tanned arm half out of the open window. It was a shame she'd missed him. Maybe she could time her arrival a bit better in future. Her dad helped Iris onto the pavement. Somebody behind Kerry began shouting for her to get a move on. She started to drive, blinking back tears.

Mary

The pain came again that morning, even before the alarm had sent Ken rolling from the bed for an early turn.

It was funny, she thought, how when he was out of work he'd struggle to get out of bed, lying still, a dead weight, his head stuck to the pillow, but now – working shifts like he hadn't worked for thirty years – he'd be out of bed on the first note of the alarm, moving vigorously around the room getting his uniform together. But maybe not that funny at all.

She'd shifted against the mattress with the pain as it moved from her side to the small of her back, the bottom sheet creased uncomfortably beneath her. The pain merged with the sound of Ken moving around the room and she felt annoyed with him. The hollow in the bed where he'd been was warm. When he leaned across with a *Bye, love* and a kiss, she pretended to be asleep.

She thought of those other days of shift work, years before. They'd lived in a flat on Wolverhampton Street when they'd first been married. She'd wake with him on earlies and send him off after a bacon sandwich and two cups of tea. On nights she'd stay up as late as she could and sleep some of the day with him. She'd had the first miscarriage there. Afterwards, they'd thought she couldn't have children and then she'd become pregnant with Kerry.

Now, standing in the bathroom in Cromwell Green, her legs buckling with dread, she felt the same fear and loneliness of that miscarriage, years ago.

That morning Kerry banged on the back door just before nine as usual, but when Mary opened it there stood Kerry and Alice and a hurriedly packed bag of clothes; Kerry all but keeling over the back step, Alice hanging from under one arm.

Thass it, thass it, I've left him, she said and shook her head so violently that tears hit the wall. Kerry dropped the bag as she stepped inside and Mary took her and Alice into her arms. Mary felt Alice's chubby little fingers tangled in her hair. In turn, she stroked Kerry's hair, saying, Come on, come on, iss all right, as Kerry sobbed. Mary felt the tears soaking and spreading through her blouse. They stood there for a while; Kerry crying, Mary holding them, Alice saying, Nanny, Nanny, and then beginning to cry too.

Nanny's here, darlin. Alice screamed and wriggled to be put down. She kicked at Mary as she struggled. All right, *shshsh*. Iss OK, Mary soothed.

She spent the morning moving boxes in Kerry's old room, washing bedclothes, up and down the stairs a dozen times, the pain now a hot ache around her side and back, the feeling of something come loose.

Kerry was curled up on the settee and said, Leave it, Mom, I'll do it in a bit, every time she walked past, crumpled tissues scattered across the cushions, drinking sugary cups of tea. A *Postman Pat* video played over and over while Alice tottered in front of it.

If it wasn't one thing. Ken had finally got a job and then David died and Luke got ill. One day they'd have some peace. It was Luke's first day back at work. He looked no better, grey and drained still. Mary tried to talk to him a few times, tried to get him to talk about David and how he felt. It was strange, he only seemed to be talking to Kerry lately, and they'd never had much to say to each other. Mary hoped Kerry wasn't burdening him with talk about her and Tim. That was all they needed, Luke giving out advice, the state he was in. She hoped he hadn't told Kerry to walk out.

Luke had been to the doctor's a couple of times, got signed off work. His hand was OK now, but he said this was a virus. Mary thought it was just all the upset after David's death. That and the thing with Sarah. He'd been like it a couple of months ago when they broke off the engagement; moody, unresponsive. And when he dropped out of college. What he needed to do was get back to work, take his mind off things. It was strange because they'd never had it with him while he was growing up, never had the big teenage thing, not like with Kerry. She was still in hers, the way she was acting.

Mary pressed her face to the mattress in a corner nearest to the wall. Twenty years old; it was musty with sweat and perfume, smelled faintly of too many memories. It would have to do. As she stood up, suddenly, in order to pull a crisp bottom sheet over the mattress, she got lights in front of her eyes and had to put her hand on the wall to steady herself. The worry clenched in her chest and she felt her breathing go tight.

She wanted to put the bedroom straight to keep herself out of Kerry's way. There was hardly any work to do at all, making the bed and moving a few boxes. Ken could've done that when he got in. No, she was staying out of the way, keeping busy, trying to work out what to say.

Your husband was your husband was your husband, no matter what, that's what she'd been brought up to believe. You had to work at marriage. Mary knew she'd been lucky. Ken had his faults but nothing she couldn't put up with. She loved him, after all. There'd been difficult times, awful times really. They hardly spoke to each other for years after Adam died, after the recriminations began to set in. He'd left the front door on the latch. She didn't know what he'd been playing at. She hadn't noticed what was going on, Adam wandering past her like he did. Guilt and blame. They never talked about it, but sometimes she'd catch him looking at her or, worse, she'd see him notice the way she looked at him. They kept it together, though, made it OK for Luke and Kerry, and slowly it got better. Neither of them was going anywhere. You find your own ways of coping.

Mary knew Tim wasn't right for Kerry, not really, but wanted to tell her to go back and try. Kerry was unhappy with more than they ever had. That was how it seemed to be these days, fewer troubles and more unhappiness. Perhaps she was just getting old. She had to stay away from her for a while, though, for fear of telling Kerry truths she didn't want to hear. You never knew; tonight, or in a few days, things might all piece themselves back together.

Mary had never really been able to say it, that Tim wasn't right for Kerry. She didn't know why. She'd gone on enough at Luke about Sarah. She'd always held back from criticizing Tim and it became more difficult to even try as time went on. They'd turn up and announce, We're going to Marbella for a week or, Look at these new watches we've bought, and Mary wondered how she could say, He's not right for you, love.

Deep down, she wondered if it was just jealousy. After all, she'd made her choice and where was she? Living on the Cromwell Green estate and still scrabbling around for money like her parents fifty years ago. They'd pushed their children to try for a better life and it seemed stupid to resent them for it now. Kerry had made her bed, Mary thought, smoothing down the undersheet, so she'd better lie in it.

Was it all her fault? Mary asked herself that all the time. After Adam died they wanted to make everything perfect for the other two and they'd give them everything they could. Kerry would just point to something she wanted and get it. They'd all been at it. Mary, Ken, her mum and dad, Granny – just the relief of having the two of them still there. Until she started demanding things they couldn't afford. They'd spoiled Kerry, maybe. Luke as well, but in a different way. Then later, when the children grew up and couldn't compete with the ghosts any more, she wondered if she'd pushed them away. Kerry's selfishness; Luke's laziness. All these things – half thought, seething, nagging away under the surface.

She went downstairs. Kerry was sitting up now but still crying gently.

Thass that done. Come and have a look in a minute. Yow con put it how yer want it later. Come on, love. Iss all right. I'm gonna ring yer dad in a bit, let him know woss happened. He ull have a shock when he walks in otherwise, woh he?

Kerry smiled and wiped her nose with a scrap of tissue. I don't know. I'm always here anyway.

Thass better. We'll have a good talk in a bit, love. Just rest theer. I'll put the kettle on, have we another cup o tay.

The ghosts were always there. The first one would've been a little boy, was a little boy. She'd turned the radio on that day, trying to feel that she wasn't alone in the world, listening to Ken move around in the flat, and heard that Bobby Kennedy had been shot. When she closed her eyes she could see the little boy's body, pink and unformed, his veins and organs and rubbery bones enclosed in transparent skin.

Kennedy would've have been president, they knew that. Some visiting American Democrats had come to the

Labour Club on an exchange visit. They were from Chicago. She liked Americans and in her head she called the baby who would've been a boy Robert. Every year she celebrated his birthday in her head silently.

Then she got a real son to grieve for.

Why was she always telling people bad news? she thought. The neighbours might not realize for a few days because Kerry was always there anyway, but after a while they'd notice the car or Tim not calling in at tea time and then the questions would come. Everythin all right, Mary? Well, no, not really, for a change. She'd talk to her mum. Maybe they could get away with not telling Granny; it might all blow over after all.

It ull be very cosy in here. Ken sat down on the edge of the bed and looked around the bedroom. Wi the two on em in here, like.

I know. We doh know how long iss gonna be fower yet.

Kerry was on the phone to Tim now, while they sat up here in the bedroom and Luke played with Alice downstairs.

Well, her con stop here if her wants to.

I think her is, Ken. Mary half laughed.

Yow know worra mean.

Her's gonna have to try an sort summat aht wi him.

I know, arr. Ken rubbed his face. There were shadows under his eyes. For all his jumping out of bed, it was a lot to start working shifts again at his age.

I chased these kids off today. They was tryin to get into one o the outside sheds, yer know. Whacking the padlock off wi a half-ender. There was a girl wi fower or five lads. Should of heered the language they was usin. They had aerosol cans wi em, yer know. I doh know if they was gonna graffiti wi em or sniff em. God knows what they was up to. They cudn't a bin above thirteen, fowerteen, I tell yer.

She sat on the bed next to him and touched his arm. Watch what yome doin. I doh want nuthin happenin to yer.

I'll be all right. They was onny young kids.

I know. An yow've jus said yerself the language on em an them high from sniffin I doh know what. Jus be careful, eh?

Luke came upstairs, banging his feet down on each step. Hers still on the phone, he said from outside the open bedroom door.

Is Alice all right, love?

Tired I think. Her's sittin in the cheer. I put the video back on for her.

Luke leaned against the doorframe, his shadow sloped into the bedroom across Ken and Mary's slippered feet.

All right, I'll goo an see to her now. Her ull have sin that bloody video half a dozen times today. Yow come up here for a bit now?

Luke nodded, then looked around the room. Looks all right in here now. They'll be all right in here.

Arr. Yow all right, love? It ay took too much out on yer today, has it?

He shrugged. Nah, I'm all right like, feeling a bit better.

Doh worry love, eh.

I cor understond it. He was allus such a nice chap, I thought. Allus called me Nan.

He was bloody seein another woman, Mother.

A wife should stick by their husband, yer know, even when theer's problems. We cudn't a gone runnin off at the drap of an hat like some on em dun nowadays. Yow atta work on it.

They am gonna work on it. But her ay the one in the wrong.

It teks two to mek a marriage or mess it up, yer know. I doh know as anybody's got divorced afower in this family.

They ay gerrin divorced yet. Her's just stoppin wi us for a bit. Her'll probably be back theer in a few wiks. Her's gorra think abaht Alice an all, any road.

Arr, I know. Plaece for a child's wi its mother and faether.

Anyway, nobody divorced? What abaht Auntie Esther?

That was different. He just upped and left. One day he was theer, the next he was gone. Her cudn't a done nuthin abaht that. They never got divorced any road. Theer wor nuthin for her to divorce, he'd just vanished.

When Mary was about four, her mum's sister's husband, Frank, had disappeared from their house on Nightingale Lane. He'd always been a rogue, a bit of a spiv during the war, apparently, on the run from the Red Caps for a while. The story was that he owed some people a lot of money. Strange men would call on Esther at the house for months after he'd gone, even though they knew she didn't know anything. Rumours started that Frank had run off to America or Australia, that he was dead and lying in the cut. It'd been a local scandal, especially when Esther moved in with Harry Long, the landlord of the Cannon. He'd been a character as well. He had a false eye and would take it out and drop it in a glass for the children peeking through the off-sales serving hatch. Mary had loved her Auntie Esther. She had blue hair with a tobacco-yellow streak at the front and would always have a packet of crisps or a bottle of dandelion and burdock for her and Mick.

Mary's mum smiled. Her ay like Esther any road, nor would her want to be. We had some good nights over theer in the Cannon, ode year's nights and that, all yow children upstairs in the living bit, but I doh think her teks after Esther. It ull sort isself out, I spose.

Well, it will. Either her ull decide to goo back to him or he'll persuade her to goo back or her ull leave him an her'll atta sort summat out. Iss as simple as that.

True.

*

Luke was off work again. He'd only been back a couple of days. He was sitting in the front room, messing with the Lego bricks he'd been putting together for Alice.

How yer feelin?

All right, a bit better.

Am yer gonna give the doctor's a ring?

I doh need to.

What they gonna say at work? Iss a lot o time the past few weeks.

I know, I ay very well, though, am I?

Well enough to argue. I doh know woss the matter wi yer.

Yer know woss the matter wi me. I've gorra virus, like the doctor said.

Am yer sure it ay summat else? Iss bin upsettin for yer Luke, the business wi Sarah an then what happened to David. Iss all right to be upset, you know.

I know, just doh goo on abaht me missin work.

Work might tek yer mind off things.

Iss hardly a great job, is it?

Yow said that, not me. Yow could still do whatever yow liked, yer know.

I know. He got up from the settee and went upstairs.

On Thursdays she'd go to the churchyard. First she'd see to Adam's grave, clean the headstone and put new flowers on and then do her dad's and grandad's. If the weather was fine then her mother would walk over in the afternoon, to see the flowers and report back to Granny. She always said that they were lovely and that Mary was a good girl.

Mary rolled on some rubber gloves and wet a cloth at the tap fixed to the back wall of the church. Adam's grave was a small marble slab, hard to clean because of the colour. In the summer, tree sap made it sticky and if it rained the stone became streaked with dirt. She wished they'd not chosen marble. It stood out too much. The darker graves seemed to weather back into the ground, whereas all she seemed to do every Thursday was make Adam's grave shiny and new again. But this was all she had, this scrubbing at the tree sap, this turning over of the dark soil with a trowel, this scouring of dirt from the grooved letters of his name, as if they were likely to forget it.

When it was done she'd move a few yards down the hill to her grandad's slate headstone. She remembered him bed-ridden downstairs, the sound of his coughing seething and bubbling from behind a closed door. One morning the men in the black car came, a ragged band of curious children in procession behind it, and everyone was crying. Granny's eyes were red for weeks. Mary and Mick had tea at Auntie Esther's, in the upstairs rooms of the pub, that jutted out over the estate like a ship ploughing through giant waves.

With Grandad's clean, she'd move onto her dad's grave.

This was where she remembered, here in the churchyard. Talking to Adam or to her dad in her head, out loud if no one else was there, her voice sounding separate from herself.

She remembered school holidays as a girl, walking across the fields to the corner of Cromwell Green and Birmingham Road, before they put the new lanes in, before all the traffic. She'd walk there with her brother and play a game of following Dad, like secret agents, or else he'd pick them up, one in each arm and carry them back to the kitchen door. He'd wash in the sink with the door open, stripped to the waist, the smell of his soap and of the allotments, his work clothes on the floor full of steel shavings like glitter. He'd pause at the birdcage and let their blue budgie out to fly around the room, as if daring it to make the break through the open window or door. It never did. Proof, in the way that he'd sink into the chair with the paper and a cigarette and cup of tea was proof, that no one in their right mind would ever leave. Proof that you could never leave here. Then her mum or granny would come in and put their foot down – that was what you had to do – close the door on the chimneys and blue hills and tell Dad to put his shirt on and quieten the bird so they could start the tea.

When she was done with washing the stones and organizing the flowers she'd stand (knees aching these days; she needed some sort of mat), and look further down the slope. A dirt path ran through the brambles under the spreading arms of a sycamore tree and the graves became hidden by undergrowth. There were rectangular patches cut in the low forest of weeds where people still tended the graves. The ground tumbled roughly after that, down the hill until the grass became shorter again and ran into a field where children played.

Under the sycamore tree she'd stop and leave the off-cut flowers pruned from the three arrangements. Flowers for the lost babies. They had no graves, of course. Elizabeth and Robert, she'd named them. She'd read somewhere that Elizabeth would have been no bigger than a thumbnail when she lost her. A brother and sister for Adam to play with; she couldn't stand the thought of him alone. No; no graves. Things were darker here, in the shadow of the tree – a pair of wood pigeons *wu-wu-wu*ing in the branches above – and she hugged her arms around herself. She never told anyone about this time with her lost children, her ghosts. Some weeks she'd be disturbed by lads on community service cutting back some of the jungle, or young Asian boys, shouting to each other in Black Country and Urdu, jumping the wall as a short cut on their way to the mosque – and then she'd feel cheated, pine for the following week.

The roots of the sycamore spread wide in humps and bumps through the churchyard. She imagined them writhing through the dark graves and shuddered. The first few leaves were falling and lay flat and wet, still green some of them, against the ground.

She'd walk back to the other side of the church and meet her mother from the bus and they'd walk back again to inspect the graves together.

Then there was David Risley, without a grave as far as she could make out. Just his name in a leather-bound book in the office at the crematorium. It wasn't the same. Maggie would never have been able to look after it, she supposed. She had enough trouble with everything else.

She'd grown up with Maggie. The Shays had lived at the end of their street, a big chaotic family. Mary was two years older than Maggie, the same age as her brother Ted. He'd been sent to Borstal, lived in a caravan in Scotland now and worked on the oil rigs. She'd kissed him once, on one of the paths that ran out of the allotments to the fields, just briefly, leaning against a trellis of runner beans, a scarecrow of an old overcoat and tin cans knocking in the breeze above them.

There were five boys and then Maggie. Her mother just kept trying until she got a girl. Not that Maggie had been ladylike. She and Mary became friends when they both joined the anarchic games of football that surged up and down the street and the fields beyond, returning home with scuffed shoes and scabby knees.

Mary used to be thrilled by the chaos of the Shay house: clothes strewn across the floor, nobody ever certain who was in the house or out. It was the same feeling of being around Auntie Esther; the opposite of the organization at home – her mother and granny whipping everybody into shape. Maggie was always the first to do new things: smoking cigarettes stolen from her brothers, drinking half a bottle of rum from out the pocket of her dad's coat one Christmas Eve while he was passed out on the living-room floor. They didn't have Christmas dinner until Boxing Day that year, but sometimes they never had it at all. She understood about men, too. It wasn't that Maggie was beautiful or anything, Mary thought, but she knew how to talk to men, growing up with all those brothers fighting and getting into trouble. There was no helping her now, though.

They'd drifted apart. While Ken was courting Mary on Saturday nights at the Plaza, Maggie was seeing a married man from the sales department at the Babcock works. She'd go off with him at weekends, come back talking about Brighton or Blackpool, about cocktails in big hotels, days at the races; her head turned. It got a bit embarrassing and Mary stopped seeing her. Then she turned up on the estate again a few years later, pregnant at the same time as Mary with Luke, just married to John Risley, a boy from Fairfax Road, a carbon copy of her brothers, always fighting and taking off, never in any regular work, a disaster waiting to happen.

But when Adam died, Maggie had been good to her. She'd come round to the house a lot on quiet mornings when it got really bad. Times when you'd keep going over it in your head if there was no one to talk to, someone who didn't feel as bad as you. She wasn't drinking then. She always liked a drink, but not like now. Now she had a reason for drinking, Mary supposed.

She'd tried to talk to her on the day of David's funeral, but she couldn't find a way of reaching her. She tried to explain to her how she'd feel, tried to tell her how to feel.

Iss allus with yer, all the time. Yow'll keep gooin over it in yer head, over an over. Yer keep lookin for somebody else to blaeme, keep tryin to blaeme other folks but it just comes back to yow. Yow cor never leave it. Yow just atta work round it.

It was different for her, maybe. People did things in different ways. David was older. It was his own fault he was on the roof in the first place. Although he'd been dragged up, having to come round to their house to get a decent meal, frayed collars on his school shirts, never made to go out and look for work. Still, dead sons. You needed people around you, your family.

Kerry only went out to empty the rubbish and now there she was, twenty minutes later, still leaning on the fence talking to Jamie. Leaning all the way over towards him from what Mary could see. He had his hands resting on the top of the fence, close to hers. She'd been laughing for most of the time but now she'd leaned even closer and they seemed to be talking about something very serious. She was looking straight at him. If their hands touch, I'll bang the window, Mary thought.

Mommy? Mommy? Alice said, playing with her bricks on the floor.

Mommy ull be in in a minute, darlin, Mary replied. In a minute. And then added in a quieter voice, And this is all wim gonna need now, ay it.

Later, she called the doctor's. The telephone rang a few times then cut to a recorded message about surgery opening times and only calling the doctor out in a real emergency. She rang back again and the receptionist answered but Mary couldn't say anything, just held the phone for a while and listened to a voice go, *Hello? Hello?* and then she put the telephone down.

I just cor gerrit aht o me head, Mom.

Finally, he was going to say something about how he was feeling. Luke was sitting on the settee, he'd turned the television off. Mary stood at the ironing board.

What?

I cor gerrit aht o me head, how he died.

Iss all right, son. What dyer mean?

I con remember. Not like how I was befower. I con really remember it.

David?

Adam. We never talk abaht Adam.

Doh, Luke. Yow'll work yerself up. Iss just all the upset lately got yer to thinkin abaht it.

Yer want me to talk abaht Risley but yow never wanna say nuthin abaht Adam.

That ay true.

It is. Listen, I con remember what we was doin.

Doh, Luke.

No, listen. We was playin aht the back an Adam kept gooin on abaht gooin to the shop an I told him to goo, like in the gaeme, an so I spose thass why he went to the front door. In the game he was gooin to the shop.

Yer wha?

He said, I'm gonna goo to the shop, in the gaeme, like, thass why he went to the front door. Iss why he went runnin into the road.

She gripped the ironing board. Luke, doh keep gooin over it. We know yer was playin.

No, dyer see what I'm sayin? I tode him to goo aht theer.

I doh know what yome sayin, no. Yow was six years old. Yow con goo over an over it, Luke, it was an accident.

I keep thinkin abaht it.

Oh, Luke. Yer doh have to. Come on, yow've gorra get over it. She tried to think of something to make it OK, that was her job, after all. I doh care what yer said in a gaeme wi him in the back garden. I doh care wharrever yow did. I doh care, yer dad doh care. I doh want us talkin abaht it or thinkin abaht what might have happened or what we could o done any more. I want yer to concentrate on yerself. Nobody's gonna get brought back. Iss all right to be upset but wiv gorra get on wi things. It was fifteen years agoo, for God's sake.

Thass easy to say, though, ay it.

Mary laughed. No, Luke, it ay easy to say at all. It ay easy to do either. She walked round the ironing board, sat down on the settee, put her arm round him.

I think abaht it all the while an iss done me no good. Thass it. I doh want yer dwellin on it. Yow just atta do things the best yer con. Please, yow'll hurt me more if yer doh mek yerself happy. She held his hand.

I thought it was my fault.

Her voice got harder. Doh be so saft. There ay one of us that ay thought that. Think abaht how yer poor dad feels, leavin the door open. Adam walked straight past me, his mother, an I day even notice. Iss just selfish, Luke, to keep feelin sorry for weselves abaht it. Iss gonna stop. I doh wanna see yer in this staete.

All right.

Serious.

All right, I'm sorry, Mom.

Yow ay gorra be sorry abaht anythin. Some things am better left, Luke, but if yer wanna talk abaht it I'll try an do it.

Rain tapped against the window. A crack in the window frame meant that water came in at certain angles. It pooled across the window ledge and began to drip onto the carpet.

Come on, now. Thass enough. I'll goo an get me a cloth an clear this mess up. She kissed the top of his head. Goo an have yerself a shower in a bit an then come an play with Alice. Come on.

Jamie said the police was at an house up by Granny's last night.

No change theer then. Yow seem to have bin talkin to Jamie a lot lately.

Well, yeah, yer know. He's a nice bloke.

Watch yer doh get too friendly, eh.

What dyer mean?
He's gorra girlfriend, yer know. A lovely girl. And more to the point yow've gorra husband.
They're not going out any more, Jamie and Julie.
My God, I cor keep up wi yer all.
I'm onny talkin to him across the back fence, anyway.
Theer's talkin an theer's talkin, ay theer.
I don't know what you mean. The onny reason he was talkin yesterday was that he's thinkin of lookin for his dad again and he wanted me advice.
What does he want yower advice fower? And God knows what his mother ud say abaht such saftness. He's bin tode to leave well alone by his grandad when he was here an by his own mother. Iss nuthin to do with us, wi yow, any road.
I'm onny talkin to him. Maybe he likes talkin to me because I can talk properly about things. I don't know what the big deal is.
Look, I doh know nuthin abaht his dad. All I know is that his mother tode me he wor a very nice mon an he's better off aht o the picture. Thass it. It ay wuth rakin up the past. Some things am better left alone.
Thass ironic.
Whass that meant to mean?
Nuthin, but I'm onny talkin to him.
Arr, well, theer's talkin an theer's talkin, ay theer.

That was what it was like; a feeling of something coming loose, hot, uncomfortable, scary.
She fainted in the kitchen and nearly cracked her head on the table but instead landed across one of the chairs, her arms and legs sprawled. Kerry was there first and Mary was already coming round when Ken came rushing in. He kept asking if she was all right and, once she was sitting up, she kept nodding. Kerry gave her a glass of water.

After a while, her head feeling fuzzy, she said she wanted to lie down. Ken helped her upstairs slowly. She shrugged his arm off a couple of times.

I'm fine.

Thass jus normal, ay it, fainting in the kitchen like tha?

I'm all right now. I'll have me a lie down an I'll be fine.

Yome gonna have to goo to the doctor's. I doh know why yow ay bin already if yer ay very well.

I'm all right. Probably just me age. I'm fine.

Yome fond enough o sortin the doctor aht for everybody else. Yer wanna think o yerself.

All right, doh start gooin on. I'm all right, yer doh atta ode me up. I'm just feelin a bit off.

I'm gonna ring em meself, mek yer an appointment. Yow cor keep feelin bad an ignorin it.

Jus leave off. I'm fine. I'm all right, look. She walked the last bit into the bedroom on her own, feeling better, just a bit shaky, and lay down on the bed. Just gimme a call in a bit when I've had a rest.

She could feel Ken standing in the doorway looking at her as she tried to get comfortable.

Her Uncle Ted had called round with a bag of pears that a mate of his at the ex-serviceman's club had brought back from his caravan in Stourport.

She searched through them, here in Granny's kitchen. They'd been bruised and battered in the bag, despite the pages of the *Sports Argus* insulating them from each other, and a couple had turned to mush. They had rough, uneven skin and were blotchy and soft in places. Mary had been annoyed at first at having to search through them. Most were windfall fruit, bruised and squashy on one side, and a few had worms in. She cut one open every now and then to check.

After a while, though, it became quite satisfying as she

made a pile of fruit on the draining board, the rejects going back into the bag. It was unusually quiet. Granny was asleep in her new chair. Kerry had taken her nan to the chiropodist. Alice played on the kitchen floor while Mary worked. Alice wasn't interested in the new doll Tim had bought her. Instead she searched through the shoebox full of Luke's old model cars, the paint on them chipped and flaking. She was lining up all the red ones in a big traffic jam, winding in and out of the table legs, and singing tunelessly to herself.

Once the pears were sorted, Mary filled the sink to wash and peel them. The trail of peel grew on the work surface; the oven made a low booming sound as its insides expanded, she could feel the heat against her legs. Mary checked Alice was well away from the oven, then reached for the bag of flour and threw some out onto the surface. It hung lazily in the air and settled slowly. A draught coming through the back window blew some of it onto the floor.

Yer ready to come an help me with the rolling, Alice? Mary asked.

Alice carried on arranging her traffic jam.

Con yer do summat wi these? they ask, Alice. Iss pear pies tonight, flower. I doh know wharriss gonna taeste like, mind yer. I doh know. *Con yer do summat wi these?* We ull atta tek a piece round for yer Uncle Ted when iss done. Come on up then, come an help Nanny wi the rolling.

Luke seems a bit better.

I hope so.

No, he does.

I spose. I cor believe he's still gooin over everythin abaht Adam. Try an have a word wi him Saturday, see what he's gonna do abaht his job. Mention college stuff again.

All right. Yer know wharriss like.

I know. Try to, though. Mention it.

That new girl phoned for him again. Lisa her naeme is. Asked how he was.

Again?

Arr.

Might do him a bit o good.

How abaht Kerry?

Her's seein Tim tonight. I think he's tekkin her aht for a meal.

Is her gonna goo back or not?

I doh know, Ken. Her keeps tellin me her ay gonna rush things. It ull onny be on her terms, if her does.

Fair enough. Yow med a lovely job o these pies, yer know.

There was a whole pile of photographs on the settee. The problem was none of them were big enough. She'd got the negatives for some so she could go to the chemist and get one enlarged but she had to do it now before she lost her nerve, while nobody else was there. She could've just taken it down but that would leave a big square on the wall where the wallpaper hadn't faded, and that would be even worse.

There were photographs upstairs as well, in the top of Kerry's wardrobe, so she went up even though she knew it'd be more of the same. They were in a mess. Somebody had been looking through them. There were piles at Granny's, too, up in the loft. Really old ones. Christmas ones with her dad in, party hats all askew. Demob suits and her mother with Vera Lynn hair. Maybe she could get Kerry to go through them with her. They could buy some albums and get them done properly.

She took the picture from the wall again. Perhaps they could just redecorate, she thought, looking at the dark square on the faded wall. She dusted the frame again, then slowly took the photo out. She had one of Alice that they'd done at playschool. She found it in the kitchen cupboard.

Kerry noticed straight away when she came in later.

Oh, that looks great, Mom. Much better. Look, Alice, it's you at playschool. Look at the funny face you're pulling. We'll have to get another one done of you, won't we?

Yer sure yer doh mind. I know yer wor that keen on that photo.

Iss great, Mom. Iss a great idea. Yow all right doing it?

Mary nodded. Kerry kissed her on the cheek.

Right, I ay movin from here until yow've phoned the doctor's. It ay right. Everybody else gets sorted aht an yow just want to ignore things when iss yerself. Ken was stood at the living-room door and wouldn't let Mary pass.

I'm all right. I doh want to. Mary felt she might cry.

I know yome all right, but yer woh be if yer doh goo to the doctor when yer ay very well. Iss common sense.

She twisted the coil of the phone wire in her hands.

I mean it.

She dialled the number and spoke quietly when the receptionist answered. Her hand was shaking.

Thass it. Ken smiled, relieved, when she put the phone down with an appointment booked. I doh know what yome worried abaht any road, all the women in yower family live for bloody ever. Yow'll be the saeme. He kissed her and she tried to smile, said she was going upstairs for a lie down.

She dreamed she was running through the paths of the allotments behind the house and down to the fields. She was a little girl again but Kerry was there, and Luke and Adam. Lots of children all running along the paths. They were too small to see over the grass banks or fences that divided the allotments, but they were all looking for something. She ran and ran, becoming panicky. They were looking for something, but she didn't know what. Every turn in the path filled her with dread. She got hotter and hotter as she ran. Suddenly there was a beating of wings. One of the other children had taken off. They were flying, swooping and soaring above the others. Adam ran across one of the paths in front of her, then Maggie went in another direction. Wings brushed the top of her head. It was Kerry. Mary knew she had to run faster to take off, the sky was filled with flying children, but she was getting more and more tired. Spikes of grass shadowed across her path. Then suddenly she was up, flying, the houses on the estate stretched out below her. Everyone was in the sky, shouting and screaming. She did a somersault and her stomach turned over, and she swooped down and brushed a hand against a string of tin cans and old net curtain protecting a wigwam of beans. Up into the air again, flying faster and faster, all the children shouting.

The morning of her doctor's appointment she threw up everywhere in the bathroom, trying to be quiet so nobody could hear. In the surgery, when they called her name she started shaking, couldn't stop.

But on the way home, there was a clear blue Indian summer sky. She climbed up the slope of the footbridge, over the traffic streaming below. She didn't trust the pedestrian crossing and liked the view from here anyway. The shopping bags pulled on her arms; they were fat with treats, crisps and cakes for Alice. Well, Alice was her excuse for buying them. Kerry had said she'd drive her when she got back from work but Mary had said no, she hadn't walked for ages, she wanted some air. She looked out for Kerry's car in the traffic. Probably already at home.

It was funny how the doctor had come right out with things like he had. It's nothing serious, Mary, you can stop worrying about cancer or anything like that. Just like that he'd said it. Then he'd drawn a little diagram of her insides on a pad of paper and talked her gently through what he was going to do. Some tablets, a referral to the specialist, a small operational procedure maybe, just as a day patient, routine stuff. She didn't take it all in really, just felt relieved at his calm tone of voice and at the sense of being looked after. Everything was going to be all right. And when was the last time she'd felt like that?

Mary paused and blew out her cheeks. She was out of shape with having lifts from Kerry and not feeling well. The castle looked wet and grey, the colour would lighten as the stone dried. Below it the zoo was green and brown; colours of autumn making the hill seem like one of the pears Ted had brought round. She adjusted her grip on the carrier bags, thinking about how many times she must have looked at the castle without really seeing anything, just looking at it, other things on her mind, taking it all for granted. The sun shone. A flag fluttered on the castle flagpole.

As she walked, she looked forwards up at Kate's Hill. It was still in shadow, the tortoiseshell back of the church, the green field below it, and the houses, strange and unfamiliar from this angle. Then the view shifted and she saw the shops on Cromwell Green looking all pushed together on the rise of the hill.

It was uphill all the way now. She was hot and worried quickly that she was going to feel bad again, but realized it was the sun coming out and the exertion. Thursday and no flowers, and she got that feeling of being set free again, exciting and scary. She still had a chance to get some, there was the florist at the top of the precinct, but she wasn't going back. That was another reason for using the bridge. When she'd been a girl there'd been a faggot shop just here, it had been their boundary marker, the end of their world. They could wander down and get a dip of crusty bread in the gravy with a few coppers her grandad had given them.

Big boards were up about the new road. There was always something changing. The outside wall of the works wobbled towards the pavement, plants growing in it. An abandoned placard advertised a car boot sale on Sundays. Mary didn't know what people saw in them. Luke had done one with Jamie once and come back with a couple of pounds from a five o'clock start and a morning's work. Mind you, Jamie had probably done OK.

Past the Salvation Army building and the ex-serviceman's club and the clinic, and she thought again about how little attention you could pay to the places around you, like they were going to be there for ever so you never noticed them. It was only when things changed that you thought about the difference. It was strange to have felt how she had recently: weak, vulnerable and – strangest of all, she thought – alone. Most of all, she hated feeling alone.

Thursday and no flowers, just these shopping bags pulling on her arms. She swayed as the wind picked up, pools of leaves whipped around, a shower of them falling from the tree outside the Methodist church. Little rainbows in the puddles. She walked up the hill, pretending she was as strong as she used to be, across the top of Cawney Bank, the wrong way, not the church way, the wind blowing harder here.

They were all outside when she got there. She waited to cross the road, thought one of the bags was splitting. Kerry walked down the front path to help her. Her hair looked nice now she'd had it cut. Ken was sitting in a garden chair, his uniform half on for a late turn. He'd done the lawn before the showers. Alice was running around with clumps of cut grass, throwing them when the wind blew. Green shards were in her hair and stuck to her face. Her little body turned like a top as she danced, young and growing, her face lifted so that she looked like Kerry, and Luke, and

Adam, and Granny when she was a girl for all Mary knew. Luke stood on the front step. Everyone was laughing. Mary crossed the road between the barriers, didn't think she'd make it down to the crossing with the bags.

Come on, Mom, you'll wear yerself out carryin all that.

I'm all right, I'm OK, she said. Kerry took a couple of bags from her and she stumbled as she adjusted the weight of the others. Ken and Luke came down the path as well and she smiled at Kerry and down at Alice and then at all of them, at her family, at the little victories of life over death.

Luke

I swear to God. If yow mess me sister abaht I'll fuckin kill yer.

What dyer mean? Jamie was trying to look innocent but Luke knew him too well.

Yer know exactly what I mean.

All right, Jesus, wim onny gooin aht for a drink.

Her's got an husband an a kid, mate, an woss more her's me sister so yer better mek sure yer doh mess her abaht. Luke was banging his hand on the arm of the chair as he spoke. It was no way to be talking to Jamie, really. Not after he'd given him the holiday he'd booked to Majorca with Julie, told him and Lisa to go. He was enjoying it, watching his tanned arm bang up and down on the chair arm to emphasize his point. It ay just gooin aht for a drink, yow cor afford not to be serious. Am yer listenin?

Arr, I'm listenin.

Kerry walked in. Is he givin yer the concerned brother talk, Jay? she asked. He did it to Tim when he was about fourteen. She pulled a face and did a voice that was meant to be Luke's: *Yow mess me sister abaht, I'll fuckin kill yer*. I'd promised Tim Cromwell Green wasn't as bad as everyone said an that's the first thing he hears. Honestly, I thought you were trying to be a bit more relaxed.

All right. I'm serious, though.

Luke pretended to be annoyed, but he was glad that

Kerry was enjoying herself. She'd gone out with Jamie a couple of times while him and Lisa were in Spain. Luke guessed that was why Jamie had given him the holiday. He could've just asked him. Majorca had been great, though, everything he'd imagined: the sun and the sky, walking along the beach with Lisa.

That night his mum went to bed as soon as Alice went to sleep. Which left Luke and his dad in the front room with the television on low, tidying up the Lego bricks. They ended up building things with them, like they had the first night they got them out.

What yer mekkin?

A house for these people. How abaht yow?

I was trying to mek this into a cone shape, it looks like a furnace.

Remember when yer used to tell me abaht it when I was a kid. Yer used to tell me yow was a dragon-keeper.

Arr. Ken smiled. He picked up a figure in uniform and put it in front of the Lego building. Me, look.

Luke grabbed a few people and put them outside his house. All o we.

Arr, nice house. They looked at the Lego. Wim a tidy pair, look, playin wi kid's toys. Come on, less clear up an a wi a drink.

He'd been back at work a week, and as they were clocking off, Alf asked him if he'd hang on for five minutes. Mario was last out, pulling a vat of pigs' heads through the plastic doors, shouting goodnight. It was eerie standing next to the empty lines, like the place had been abandoned, the hooks swinging above their heads like alien harpoons. People were still working elsewhere and the noise they made came echoing through the freezer area.

Listen, I wanted five minutes like this so as it was private.

I doh want nobody else knowing yet. I'm fifty-eight in November, Luke, an I'm gonna finish. I'm retiring. Wim off to live at the caravan. The thing is, I've bin talkin to Peter abaht it an we wanted to know if yow was interested in tekkin my job when I leave?

Oh, right. Well, arr, I spose.

Yer doh atta say now, have a think abaht it but I think he'd like yer to do it an I think yow'd do a good job.

Cheers, Alf. Congratulations wi yer retirement an that.

Yer doh need congratulations for that, iss just a question of endurance. Alf looked around the empty room, like it was already his last day, then started to say something about the job but shrugged and said, Well, yer know what the job's like. They shook hands, which made it seem formal, then Alf winked and made towards the doors.

Seeya, lightnin.

Luke supposed he shouldn't have been that bothered. It was only a supervisor's job at Paradise Meatpacking for God's sake, and he'd talked to Lisa about handing his notice in; but still, they'd wanted to ask him. It was a step in the right direction.

He walked to the bus stop in a good mood, daydreaming about ordering Banksy around.

Jamie had an invitation the same as his.

What dyer mek o this, then? Luke asked, turning the bit of card over in his hands.

I doh know. Iss genuine, ay it? *Sarah Foley invites you for a few drinks at the Three Crowns to celebrate her leaving for Southampton University*. I doh know, mate. Maybe her wants to burn a few bridges, or maybe iss an ambush an her's gonna get yer back for the business wi the ring.

Doh joke.

I think we should goo.

*

Luke ran down the alleyway, this last bit really taking it out of him, sprinting and taking big, noisy breaths now that he wasn't on the road. He clattered against the back gate, gasping, then took a couple of strides away from the fence and bent double and spat into the gutter. It was getting better. When he'd first gone out he couldn't believe how difficult it'd been, even with the season started, the tightness in his chest, and his legs not doing what he told them to, but it was definitely getting better. Lisa had told him it would. He was dying for a cigarette, though.

When he came through the back door everyone was in the kitchen. He went to the fridge and took out a carton of juice. He drank some straight from the carton, tipping his head back like he'd seen people in Spain do with a wine bag. He missed his mouth and some sloshed onto the lino. Sweat dripped from his hair and ran down his back.

What yer doin, yer saft sod? His mum was washing dishes in the sink.

Luke sighed when he'd finished drinking and grinned.

If yome gonna drink tha then con yer get a glass an stop throwin it everywheer? I doh know. Have yer got no sense? Mary looked annoyed.

Sall right, Mom, here yam, I'll do it. Kerry stood up from the kitchen table and grabbed the floor cloth. She tapped Luke with it to get him out of the way. He put the juice carton down on the work surface.

Is there any water on?

No. Yow con put the immersion heater on if yow want a shower.

I'd a thought yow'd a wanted code showers as part o yower new regime, his dad said, talking to the newspaper.

I doh know what good gerrin in that staete is gonna do yer, yome drippin sweat everywheer. Leave it, our Kerry, I'll do it all in a minute.

Sall right, Mom. Less do it. Kerry wiped around Luke's

feet, tapped them to move him again. Yer could do this yerself, yer know.

Alice called from the front room. She was lining her cars up again. Ken got up to see to her. Dyer want the immersion on, yer say?

Thanks, Dad, Luke replied, and reached over to the pack of cigarettes Ken had left unattended on the kitchen table. He helped himself to one and moved to the open back door to smoke it.

I thought yow'd given up?

I have mom but yer gorra do it gradually. Yow cor go gooin mad-headed at things.

Oh, right. I see. Perhaps yow con sweat a bit more gradually then, instead of all over the kitchen.

When Ken came back, Luke held his arm outside the back door so his dad couldn't see the cigarette.

If yome havin a shower yow'll atta hurry up an have it cos yer tay ull be ready in a minute.

They were already eating when he came down from the shower. He'd sprayed himself with the aftershave he got in duty free and spent ages trying to gel his hair in the bathroom mirror. It had always been the same: no matter what he did he couldn't get it to go like Jamie's.

His dad sniffed when he sat next to him and tried to wolf-whistle through his teeth. He couldn't get the whistle right, though, tried it again and then gave up, cutting into his lamb chop.

These potatoes am great, love, Ken said, his mouth full.

Kerry did em. Her does the butter different to me. I'll atta start doin em like this.

Lovely, our Kerry.

Thanks, Dad.

Iss nice, Nan! Alice shouted and banged her spoon on the table. Everyone laughed.

Is it, darlin? Thass lovely, you eat it all up. Mary stretched her hand out and touched Alice's cheek. It ull be strange having the house to weselves again tonight.

Kerry and Alice were seeing Tim. There was no sign of them moving back yet but there was plenty of time. Luke didn't really want them to go back, he liked having them in the house, playing with Alice, talking to Kerry. It might be for the best, though, he supposed. Jamie was doing OK, too, playing with Alice, being nice to Kerry.

An wheer yow gooin tonight, Luke?

Up the Three Crowns wi Jay for a coupla pints.

I thought yow wor drinkin? Kerry asked.

Ken snorted. I've bloody heard it all now. When did this start?

I ay not drinkin. Jus cuttin dahn, like.

Yer doh need it to have a good time anyway, Kerry said, cutting up some of Alice's meat. Luke and his dad smiled at each other.

Does help things along a bit, though.

Eh. Luke touched his dad's arm. Did I tell yer abaht me goal on Sunday?

I was bloody theer, yer fool.

His dad had been driving them to games on Sunday mornings since the season started. He was enjoying it; Luke wondered if he might end up managing the team.

Am yer gonna get Lisa to come to yer gran's on Sunday?

I doh know yet, Mom. We'll atta see. I doh know if her's workin or not.

Yer said that last time I asked yer an yow've had chance to speak to her since then.

All right, I'll talk to her tonight.

Mek sure yer do. It ull be nice for yer gran to meet her, especially after her ay bin very well.

Granny had been in hospital while he and Lisa had been away. By the time they came back she was out, back in her chair, the same as ever, but it'd been touch and go for a couple of days. Luke was relieved he'd missed it. They'd brought Granny a shawl back from one of the market stalls in the old town, away from the English pubs and the karaoke. Everyone said it was a good present.

If it ay one thing iss another, his mum had said, telling him about Granny and about how she'd gone to see Risley's mum. Iss jus one thing after another.

She'd taken some old photos round to Maggie's after sorting through them with Kerry. Her's in a bad way, his mum said, but then added that Maggie had smiled at the photos of them in mini-dresses and boots, laughing together about where the time went to.

I day think yow'd come.

Well, yer know. I'm surprised yer wanted me to.

I'm glad yome here.

They stood at the bar in the Three Crowns. Sarah's mates were all sitting round a couple of tables in the corner, the rest of the pub was quiet. Jamie was talking to Michelle.

Yow've been away, ant yer? Was that wi the money you got back off the ring?

He couldn't look at her. I was hopin yer thought yer'd just lost that. I gid the money to me dad. It was his. The holiday was free. Iss a long story. I bet yer could o done wi it to goo to university, cudn't yer?

Couple of hundred quid woh mek any difference.

Southampton's a long way, yer know.

Thass the idea.

His hand was resting on the wooden bar next to hers. He rubbed his fingers in the grooves where people had scraped coins or keys. His name was there somewhere. With hers probably. He nearly slid his hand across to hers, still just looking at the bar. There was a burst of laughter from the corner.

She looked over and smiled, picked her drink up, but then spoke quietly. I'm really sorry abaht Risley, Luke. I woulda come to the funeral but I never knew how yow'd be, especially wi it at yer house, an yer mom an dad an tha.

Yow coulda come. It doh matter.

How yer feelin?

I'm all right. Course I am. His mother's in a bad way. Bound to be, I spose.

She laughed suddenly. Dyer remember that night his mother vouched for us in the offie?

Fuckin hell, arr. I'd forgot abaht tha.

They'd been buying drink in the off-licence on Dixon's Green Road and the woman wouldn't serve them. Risley's mother was in there, said she knew them, they were all right. They'd bought all sorts, rum, vermouth, God knows what, and all gone back to Sarah's. Loads of them. Her mum and dad came back early. Luke and Jamie had hidden on the garage's flat roof, half naked, giggling, as her old man turfed everyone out. He and Jamie staggered home with each other's shirts on, throwing up by the old cottage, then telling Risley about it the next day.

Yer nervous abaht gooin away?

No. Yeah, course I am. She smiled and they stood in silence for a while, listening to the chat from the tables.

Andrew doh fancy seein yer off then?

Andrew's tryin to get back with his wife. I onny did it to mek yer jealous, yer know.

No yer day.

No, I spose there was more to it than tha.

One of her college mates had got up to put some change in the jukebox. Luke searched for the right thing to say. Listen, I said I was onny gonna stop for one.

Yer can stay.

No, I'm gooin. He kissed her on the cheek and pulled away quickly.

Bye. Listen, I hope everything guz all right. Good luck, yer know.

Bye, Luke. I'm glad yer come up.

He put his hand to his cheek where he'd felt her lips, then walked towards the door.

Yow off, Luke? Jamie called to him. Michelle was almost sitting on his lap.

Yeah, I'll seeya tomorra, he said at the door.

Luke crossed the street. He'd said he'd meet Lisa in the Lamp Tavern for a quiet drink. He was glad he'd gone, though; his head felt clear, like he'd made some sort of breakthrough. Jamie came running behind him.

Hang on, I'm comin wi yer.

I thought yer might a wanted to stop wi Michelle.

No, mate. I'm seeing somebody.

Never stopped yer befower.

Arr well, things change.

He got back late that night but Mary was still in the kitchen, making a cup of drinking chocolate to take to bed.

Yer dad's just gone up, she said as Luke sprawled out in the chair. Dun yer want one o these?

No thanks, Mom.

Dyer have a nice night?

Arr, it was all right.

Iss nice to see yer back in and sober, I must say.

He grinned. Work tomorra.

She paused at the door, wanting to say something else. Have yer thought what yer wanna do abaht that supervisor's job?

I'm gonna tek it. It doh mean I'm stayin theer for ever, though. I'm gonna tek it as summat a bit different an see how it guz. Iss more money any road – I can pay more keep. It was good, this feeling of life opening up a bit, having a few choices. He could do anything he wanted.

Doh worry abaht that. Just sort yerself out. Decide what yer wanna do. An all that frettin abaht Adam, has that stopped?

Iss like yer said, ay it, yer just atta gerron wi things.

Well arr, an not worry. Night, son.

As she turned to leave he called her. Abaht yow, am yow all right, Mom?

I am yeah. She smiled. Course I am.

He lay on his bed staring at the ceiling. The problem with not drinking was that he'd had about a gallon of Coke and felt wide awake. Jamie and Bella were out, underneath his window. She was snuffling around for something and Jamie was complaining. Luke nearly pushed the window open and leaned out to have a talk, like they'd done when they were kids. He didn't, though, and the downstairs window opened and he heard Kerry's voice. He didn't know what he thought about those two. Lisa told him not to worry about it, everything would work out for the best.

He could hear Jamie talking softly and he tried not to listen to what he was saying. They chatted for a while and then there was silence, then they were saying goodnight and the window closed. Luke lay back on his bed, thinking about how lucky he'd been, how lucky he was, with all that had happened and the state he'd got himself in, no one really having a clue, even though people tried so hard to search each other out. He stretched, closed his eyes, leaned across the bed, switched out the light.

Also available from Tindal Street Press

KISS ME SOFTLY, AMY TURTLE

Paul McDonald

'Funny, moreish, and puts Walsall on the map in the way that Dante's *Inferno* did with hell'

Mil Millington

The will-sapping tedium of life as a *Walsall Reflector* hack has given Dave 'Ichabod' McVane a serious thirst for the devil's juice. Now, after years of debauchery, the booze has bitten back. Cathetered, bed-bound – and with what feels like a rhinoceros buffeting its way through his stomach – Dave wakes among 'regulars' in a hospital notorious for its high mortality rate. And if his darkest hour wasn't dark enough, a sinister figure from his student days at the Walsall Academy of New Knowledge reappears . . . to leave Dave reeling with pain and paranoia as he faces a scalpel-happy surgeon.

'The most fun I've had all year – fast-paced, witty and surprisingly moving. A distinctive Midlands voice – Paul McDonald has done the impossible: he's made Walsall funny' *Patrick Thompson*

'One of the funniest writers in Britain today. Ignore him at your peril' *Malcolm Boyden*

ISBN: 0 9541303 7 5

Also available from Tindal Street Press

GOING THE DISTANCE

edited by Alan Beard

'Triumphant proof that the short story is alive and kicking in the UK'
Peter Ho Davies

All the way from Birmingham to Trinidad, Colombia and Canada, by way of Wales, Essex, Liverpool and London, *Going the Distance* offers 20 'honed and accomplished' short stories to enjoy. Be enticed by a heartbreaking tale of an illiterate couple told as a raw and insistent letter from a prison cell; a spot-on portrait of a girl on the verge of losing her virginity; a beautiful, poetical allegory about a man's love affair with the bottle; plus 17 other deft, vigorous stories.

'Annie Murray's "The Tonsil Machine" is written with a delicate but edgy lyricism that evokes the flowering of revulsion in a child's mind'
Birmingham Post

'"Homing Instinct" by Maria Morris is outstanding. Every word carries the perfect weight, each image is as vivid as if it were your own memory' *Time Out*

'Always powerful, original, perfectly understated, each voice strong and enticing' *Laura Hird*

ISBN: 0 9541303 5 9

Excellent contemporary fiction from Tindal Street Press

WIST by Jackie Gay
ISBN: 0 9541303 4 0 * £7.99

WHAT GOES ROUND by Maeve Clarke
ISBN: 0 9541303 3 2 * £7.99

ASTONISHING SPLASHES OF COLOUR
by Clare Morrall
Shortlisted for the Man Booker Prize 2003
ISBN: 0 9541303 2 4 * £7.99

BIRMINGHAM NOUVEAU edited by Alan Mahar
ISBN: 0 9541303 0 8 * £7.99

BIRMINGHAM NOIR
edited by Joel Lane and Steve Bishop
ISBN: 0 9535895 9 5 * £7.99

A LONE WALK by Gul Y. Davis
Winner of the J.B. Priestley Fiction Award 2001
ISBN: 0 9535895 3 6 * £6.99

SCAPEGRACE by Jackie Gay
ISBN: 0 9535895 1 X * £6.99

THE PIG BIN by Michael Richardson
Winner of the Sagittarius Prize 2001
ISBN: 0 9535895 2 8 * £6.99

All Tindal Street Press titles are available from good bookshops, online booksellers and direct from www.tindalstreet.co.uk